BAD INFLUENCE

CHARLEIGH ROSE

Bad Influence
Cover Designer: Letitia Hasser, RBA Designs
Cover Model: Nick Keller
Photographer: Gavin Grace
Interior Formatting: Stacey Blake, Champagne Book Design

"Nothing gold can stay."
—Robert Frost

CHAPTER ONE

Allie

MY DAD ALWAYS SAID THAT BOTH THE BEST AND worst things in life are unexpected. They're the moments that change your life indefinitely, and even if you see them coming, you're never prepared for the impact. It's what you do in the aftermath that matters. It's how you deal with the crisis—or good fortune—that defines you.

It's safe to say I failed miserably in that department.

The needle pricks my finger and I let out a hiss, dropping my jacket onto the bed before sucking my finger into my mouth. I peer down at my dad's old jean jacket, every surface full of colorful patches from his favorite bands. Social D. Pennywise. Rancid. NOFX. The list goes on. I cut the too-long sleeves off on a whim, deciding to sew on my sleeves and hood from an old sweatshirt so I can wear it. I bring it to my nose and inhale, trying desperately to catch a whiff of his scent. I haven't worn it or washed it, afraid I would lose the smell forever, but I think now—more than half a year after his death—it's finally gone.

Most days, I'm fine. Other days, the grief is so potent it feels like it was yesterday.

"Allison!" my mother shouts, her voice child-like even when she's yelling.

I pull one of the headphones away from my ear, looking up at her expectantly from my bed.

"I know it's your birthday and I'm supposed to let you call the shots, but are you sure you don't want to do anything? I have a sushi date tonight. You could join us?"

I roll my eyes. Yes, I'd love to spend my eighteenth birthday with my mom and her flavor of the week eating food I hate.

"I'm good."

I see the relief flash in her eyes, but she conceals it quickly. She doesn't really want me to go to dinner, but how would that look if she didn't at least invite me on my birthday of all days? Pushing off the doorframe, she walks toward me. I flip my journal shut, stashing it under my pillow.

"You should go out. Call Courtney and Maddison." *She reaches a slender hand out to twirl a strand of my hair between her fingers.*

I laugh bitterly. I haven't been friends with those girls since freshman year when they grew tits and decided nothing else mattered but boys and parties. "Okay, Mom," *I say just to pacify her.*

"Good. I'm going to meditate before my date," *she informs me, standing. If Snow White and Willie Nelson had a love child, it would result in my mom. She's tragically beautiful, soft-spoken, and charismatic. Her smile is infectious, and everyone loves her. She's also the biggest pothead I know. Flighty. Self-absorbed, yet somehow painfully insecure. She's a walking contradiction.*

I pull my headphones back over my ears, effectively ending the conversation. Once she leaves, I flip my phone over to see a voicemail from my dad. Shit, I must not have heard him over my music. *I take my headphones off once more, bringing the phone to my ear.*

"Allllliisonnnnn," he greets in the tune of Elvis Costello's famous song. The one he serenades me with every time I see him. "Don't worry. I won't sing the whole song this time. I just wanted to wish you a happy birthday. This is also your daily reminder to try to be nice to your mother. It's not her fault the weed has started to turn her brain."

I crack a smile. My parents met when my dad was touring with his band in the late nineties. They fell hard and fast, and after a few months, she traded her cushy life in for a tour bus. She got knocked up almost immediately. My dad quit the band, bought a house, and tried to put down roots. That's when the trouble started. My mom resented my dad for getting her pregnant. My dad resented my mom for having to leave the band. Long story short, they split when I was born.

When my mom deemed me old enough, summers were spent in River's Edge with my dad, and the rest of the year with my mom here in Southern California. They don't get along, always throwing jabs at each other's expense, but my mom has never truly moved on—even though she's had more boyfriends than Cher and Taylor Swift combined.

"Anyway, I wish I could be there, but we both know it's best that your mother and I don't occupy the same zip code. I've got a birthday slash graduation present waiting for you here. I'll give you a hint—it has four wheels and it's sitting in my garage."

A car!? I flop backwards onto my bed, barely containing my excitement.

"Can't wait to have you here permanently. Happy birthday, kid. You're the best thing I ever did. I love you."

I smile, wishing he was here, but in just a few short weeks,

I'll be staying with him and starting college in River's Edge. The line goes silent for a second and I think he's hung up, but then I hear him again.

"Oh, I almost forgot." He clears his throat, and I groan, knowing what's coming next. "Haaaaappy birthday to you," he sings, his raspy voice obnoxious and loud. "Happy birthday to you. Happy birthday, dear Allie. Happ—"

His singing stops abruptly, followed by a curse, and my heart nosedives into the pit of my stomach. It all happens in a split second—the sound of tires skidding, metal colliding with metal, glass shattering, my dad's anguished scream. Then, I hear nothing at all other than my heart pounding in my ears.

"Dad!"

I shake the memory from my mind, focusing on the sleeve I'm stitching. It's been eight months since the accident. For the first couple of months, I holed up in my room, doing a whole lot of nothing. I missed my start date at Kerrigan University, and the few friends I did have dropped me when I wasn't fun anymore. My mom was too lost in her own grief to give a shit about me—even though they had been divorced for years—and quickly jumped headfirst into a new relationship.

When my mom informed me that she was moving to Hawaii with her latest victim, another one of those fun little unexpected moments, I knew it was time to move on—as if I had a choice in the matter.

I tie off the thread before holding up the jacket to inspect my handiwork. I slide my arms inside the sleeves, pulling it over me. Grabbing onto the handle of my suitcase, I take one last look at my childhood room, at the posters, drawings, and lyrics plastered on every surface of my black-painted walls. This feels like one of those defining moments my dad spoke of. The only question is, will I sink, or will I swim?

CHAPTER TWO

Jess

"**L**ATE NIGHT?" MY SISTER, LO, ASKS, ARCHING A BROW at me from the other side of the bar from where I'm sitting. It felt like I had only just passed out when she barged into the room she keeps for me at her place, demanding I come have breakfast at Blackbear—the bar slash restaurant where she works—so we could hang out before I leave. Still half-drunk, I grabbed my bag and followed her out to the car.

Lo dumps a bucket of ice into the ice bin, and the sound has me clenching my eyes shut. She chuckles, shaking her head.

"No more than any other night." It was Sully's birthday and my last weekend in River's Edge for a while. Come Monday morning, Coach is going to ride my ass and it's back to school with little-to-no booze, no fights, no parties, and no drugs. In a nutshell, *no fun*.

"Where's your friend?"

I smirk, remembering last night's festivities. Last time I checked, he was sandwiched between two naked coeds.

"Judging by the look on your face, I don't even want to know." Lo laughs, sliding a glass of ice water toward me.

"He's...occupied." I'd be surprised if he was able to peel himself out of bed this early after last night.

"You gonna see Henry before you take off?"

My jaw tenses. "Probably not." It's not exactly a priority to see the man we thought was our father up until recently. He took off when I was a kid, leaving Lo and me with an unfit mother and a whole host of daddy issues. When shit hit the fan back in Oakland, Lo moved us out here to stay with him, only to find out he wasn't our real dad after all.

Good times.

"He's trying, you know."

"So am I." *Trying to change the fucking subject.*

Lo gives me her big puppy dog eyes and reaches under my hood, mussing up my hair like I'm a kid. When you grow up like we did, it's hard not to resent the adults who did a shit job protecting you. And blood or not, Henry walked out on us instead of taking us with him.

"Shit, the food truck is here," Lo says, already heading toward the back of the restaurant. "Be right back. And don't leave without saying goodbye."

I nod, giving her a thumbs-up, and the door chimes, drawing my attention toward a girl with headphones over her ears. A Nirvana shirt peeks out from under her denim jacket with a fuck-ton of patches sewn on. Elbows propped on the bar top, I study her. She's in her own world, bobbing her head to the music only she can hear as she approaches. She stops about a foot away from me, fishing around in the bowl of Dum-Dums on the bar, oblivious of my presence before settling on one. *Butterscotch.* She peels the wrapper off and stuffs it into her jeans pocket before wrapping her lips around the sucker, making my dick twitch at the sight.

Sensing my gaze on her, she lifts her eyes to mine, and I do nothing to hide the fact that I've been staring.

Gray-blue eyes widen for a fraction of a second before narrowing into slits. Then she walks away, heading for the dining area.

The fuck was that about?

The door chimes again, but this time, it's Sierra Hayes. And she's on a mission if the furious expression on her face is anything to go by.

Probably has something to do with the fact that I unknowingly hooked up with her older sister.

Sully came down for one of my games a few weeks back. We ended up partying with some senior sorority chicks, and it wasn't long before they dragged us upstairs. We'd barely stepped foot into their room when the one with red hair had my pants around my ankles and my dick in her mouth. I arched a brow, shooting my eyes over to Sully who covered his mouth to smother his laugh. Her two girlfriends just giggled, pushing Sully toward one of the two queen-sized beds while the redhead kept sucking away, uncaring of the fact that we had an audience. I, on the other hand, didn't necessarily feel like busting a nut in front of another dude.

I cupped my hands around her face, prepared to pull her suction cup of a mouth away when Sully interrupted with his stream of angry expletives. "Fuck, Shep, *tell me* you have a condom," he called out.

The girl on her knees in front of me froze before pulling back and releasing my dick with a pop. "Shep? As in *Shepherd*?" she asked warily. I nodded. "As in *Jesse Shepherd*?"

"The one and only." I smirked. It's funny. Being a Shepherd in Oakland was synonymous to white trash. Here, it carries a whole new meaning.

She fell back onto her ass, wiping her mouth with the back of her hand. "Oh my God, I just had my sister's ex-boyfriend's penis in my mouth." I mentally went through the short list of girls who could have ever been considered my girlfriend. I dated, sure. Hooked up, definitely. But girlfriend? That was a title reserved for…well, none.

"Sierra Hayes?" she prompted upon seeing my confused expression. I groaned. Just hearing that name is enough to make my dick shrivel up and run away. Not because she isn't fuck hot, but because the girl is certifiable.

"She was never my girlfriend," I corrected, pulling my jeans back up and zipping my fly. That's the truth. Sierra liked to call herself my girlfriend, and I let her, mostly because I didn't give a shit. She could label it all she wanted. Didn't mean I was going to play the part of a doting boyfriend. She knew the deal. When I left town for school, I cut it off.

"Doesn't change the fact that you just…just…double-dipped!" I heard Sully snort out a laugh half a second before I broke, my lips stretching into an unintentionally amused smile. How the hell was I supposed to know this was her sister? I didn't bother arguing. Before making a hasty exit, I simply told Sully to hit me up when he was done.

Without thinking twice, I jump off the barstool before she has a chance to say anything and catch up to Dum-Dum Girl. I'm not equipped to go head to head with Sierra in my current state. As casually as I can manage with someone I've never met who seems to somehow already despise me, I circle an arm around her hip as I fall into step with her. Her body stiffens, and she jerks back, looking at me like I'm a lunatic.

I pull the headphones off one ear, leaning in close. She doesn't shiver or give me that dreamy stare I've become accustomed to, and I start to second-guess my half-assed plan. "You're my girlfriend," I say quietly. From the outside, it would seem like I'm whispering sweet nothings into her ear as opposed to accosting a complete stranger.

Her eyebrows pull together, the end of her sucker sticking out from her pursed lips, and I can tell she's not thrilled at the prospect of playing along.

"Okay, pretend you're my *friend*," I amend, growing desperate as Sierra gets closer. Dum-Dum Girl pulls her headphones off with a huff, stuffing them into her bag, and that's when I realize they're attached to a CD player. A fucking portable CD player. I have to stop myself from asking her if she's also got a pager in her bag of tricks. Maybe a floppy disk.

She slides into the closest booth and I scoot in behind her, sealing my side to hers. Her spine is ramrod straight, big gray eyes side-eyeing me as I sling an arm around her shoulders. "Relax," I whisper into her ear right as Sierra makes it to our table. *Still no shivers.*

"You're a prick," Sierra accuses, pointing a finger at me. I lean back in the booth, bringing my leg up to rest my ankle on my other knee as Sutton, one of the servers and my sister's friend, maneuvers around Sierra to drop off a couple of glasses of water.

"I'll just…give you a minute?" she asks with a knowing grin. I nod.

"Nice to see you, too, Sierra." I rub my thumb along Dum-Dum's collarbone and Sierra's eyes zero in on the movement before narrowing. No doubt feeling awkward, the girl next to me avoids eye contact, ditching her sucker in a napkin before reaching for the ice water in front of her.

"Can we talk?" Sierra clips out as she sizes up the girl I've got my arm around, trying to deduce whether she's a threat or not. She's not my typical type, but there's no denying she's hot. The kind of hot she couldn't hide even if she tried, which I think she might be. Trying to hide, that is. Her clothes aren't necessarily baggy, but they're definitely not formfitting. She doesn't appear to be wearing much makeup and her light brown hair is slightly wavy, coming to rest on top of two perfect tits. Sex hair. That's what it looks like.

"Now's not a good time. I'm trying to have lunch with my girlfriend."

The girl next to me chokes at the word *girlfriend* and sets the glass back down on the table. "Sorry." She pats her chest. "Went down the wrong pipe."

A smile tugs at the corner of my mouth, but I flatten my lips to hide it.

"*You* have a girlfriend?" Sierra asks, arching a disbelieving brow.

"Yup." I smirk.

Sierra crosses her arms, eyes darting back and forth between the two of us, and *dammit*. This chick's uptight body language is a dead giveaway. "There's no way. Not buying it."

"I don't really give a shit what you believe, but if you'll excuse me, my *girlfriend* and I are trying to spend some time together before I have to leave."

"Since when?" she presses, ignoring my blatant dismissal.

"It's new."

"Does your girlfriend know where you were a couple weeks ago?"

Well, fuck. I didn't think she'd start an interrogation. But I'm nothing if not a quick thinker. "Like I said, it's new. Really new."

"So, you met her *after* hooking up with my sister, and now she's your girlfriend? Is that right?"

"When you know, you know." I shrug, and to my surprise, the girl next to me snorts out a laugh, and I catch a quick flash of her dimples before she schools her features.

"What's her name?" Sierra asks, clearly losing patience.

Good question. I look over to my *girlfriend* for help, but she only stares back with an innocent, expecting expression, batting her eyelashes, waiting to see how I'll answer that one. I send her a look in return that says *I'm so glad this amuses you.*

"Don't be rude, Sierra. If you want to know her name, ask *her.*"

Sierra huffs, crossing her arms as she focuses her attention on the girl next to me. "Do you have a name?" she speaks slowly, enunciating each word as if she's talking to a toddler or someone who doesn't speak English. "Or did you guys not get that far? Usually the exchanging names part comes after the sex with this one."

"It's Allison," she replies, rolling her eyes. "And he knows my name. Trust me." She leans forward on her elbows for dramatic effect—her fingers toying with the tip of her straw—and lowers her voice. "He was yelling it. All. Night. Long."

Holy fuck, I just got an instant semi.

Sierra's nostrils flare and her gaze snaps back to me, but I'm still stuck staring at the girl next to me, suddenly seeing her in a whole new light, thanks to that comment. "I don't know what the hell you're trying to pull, but you wanna know what I *do* know?"

"Not really, but I feel like you're about to tell us anyway," I say, sounding bored as I twirl a lock of Allison's hair between my fingers.

"Hooking up with my sister was a clear message, Jesse. You wanted to hurt me."

Christ. This chick is delusional.

"And you know what that tells me?" she asks knowingly.

"Enlighten me."

"It tells me that deep down, you still care. You still want me. So you can stop pretending with White Trash Barbie now."

I'm speechless. Literally fucking speechless because she's so far off base that I have no words. What kind of fucked-up girl logic is that? I didn't even know she *had* a sister.

"Or maybe," Allison chimes in, lowering her voice to a conspiratorial whisper, "*just maybe* it means that he doesn't care about you enough to consider your feelings on the matter."

Sierra's eyes narrow, but she doesn't have a rebuttal to that.

"Or maybe I have no idea what I'm talking about," she tacks on when no one else speaks. Sierra spins on her heels without a word, and then she's gone.

"You know you just made her want you more, right?" Allison asks, putting some space between us. At my confused expression, she laughs. "Girls always want what they can't have. Flaunting me in front of her was practically a challenge in her eyes."

"She knows better."

"Not if she thinks I'm actually your girlfriend. Now she thinks she has a chance to fill that role."

Good thing I'm not sticking around to find out.

"Was it true? What she said about her sister?" she asks.

"Technically speaking?"

Allison's lip quirks up at the corner, but before she gets a chance to answer, a gruff voice shouts out her name, causing her head to whip around to see where it came from. Her eyes light up when she sees some guy with a lip ring in black jeans, black boots, and a black zip-up. It doesn't escape me that he's the complete opposite of me in my hoodie with my Lobos lacrosse logo on the front, gray sweats, and backwards hat.

"Excuse me," she says impatiently, gesturing for me to let her out of the booth, all but forgetting about me.

"Who's that?" I ask, standing.

"My boyfriend," she deadpans, and I can't tell if she's fucking with me, given the circumstances, or if he really is her boyfriend. I don't have to wonder long, because she runs to him and he wraps his arms around her tiny form, lifting her off her feet. Now the lack of shivers makes sense. She's into the broody, emo type. Not college lacrosse players who just rolled out of bed and still reek of liquor.

CHAPTER THREE

Allie

"**F**UCK, IT'S BEEN TOO LONG." DYLAN CHEWS ON his lip ring, peering down at me. I press my nose into his hoodie as I hug him, inhaling his familiar scent, something I've never been able to pin down, but belongs to him and only him.

"I'm sorry," I say, looking up at him, trying to read his reaction.

I haven't so much as returned a text, let alone stepped foot in this town since the funeral. Also known as the night we lost our goddamn minds. I was so lost with grief that I tried to make myself feel something—*anything*— other than the overwhelming sadness threatening to swallow me whole, and when Dylan leaned in to kiss me, I let him. It shouldn't have happened. We don't even like each other in that way. But if he's not going to acknowledge the elephant in the room, I'm happy to pretend like it never happened.

I met Dylan a couple of years ago, after I started spending summers with my dad in River's Edge. I was sure he hated me the entire first year I knew him. Slowly, his icy demeanor started to melt, and after he stole my journal and discovered my hormone-induced, mediocre at best lyrics, we became friends. It made sense. The aspiring rock star and the daughter of a musician.

"I should kick your ass for staying away that long," he informs me, taking a seat at our table. The same table we always sat at with my dad and the rest of Dylan's band. Blackbear was our "spot".

"I know. I just…couldn't." I don't elaborate, but Dylan nods, knowing exactly what I mean. "But," I say, straightening my shoulders and perking up my voice, "you don't have to worry about that anymore."

He looks at me with a questioning expression.

"I'm staying."

"For good?" he asks.

I pull my worn composition book out of my bag, setting it on the table while I rummage for the complimentary pennant I got at orientation. "You're looking at the newest Wildcat," I say, waving the felt red and white flag with the Wildcats logo.

"No shit?" He chuckles, a deep sound that I swear vibrates the tabletop. I was supposed to start at Kerrigan University in the fall, but I never showed. Luckily, once I explained that I had a death in the family, they gave me the okay to start during the spring semester. Never mind the fact that the accident was months earlier. The only downside? They filled my spot at the dorms. Thank God for Halston.

"Yep. I'm rooming with Halston at Manzanita Hall." *Illegally*. But that's neither here nor there.

Halston is my only other friend in the world. My dad used to teach guitar at the high school, and on the seldom occasion that I'd visit during the school year, I'd go with him, disappearing underneath the bleachers to listen to music and write in my journal. Imagine my surprise when a tall brunette in designer shoes showed up, asking if she could hide out with me between classes. I reluctantly obliged, and this girl who looked like she had just walked off the set of a CW show would light up a cigarette and give me all the latest gossip on River's Edge. At first, I ignored her presence. But Halston is nothing if not persistent.

"If you ever need a place to crash…" he trails off.

"Thanks, but I'm good." Dylan rents a house with his bandmates where every surface is covered with beer bottles and flakes of weed. Calling it a bachelor pad would be the understatement of the century.

He shrugs. "Suit yourself. Got anything for me?" he asks, brown eyes eying my journal expectantly. It's creased in the middle from rolling it up and carrying it everywhere I go.

Dylan reaches for the notebook, but I slap his hand away.

Out of the corner of my eye, I see Jesse walk past our table. As if he senses my stare, he turns his head to look at me and tosses a wink in my direction before turning back around. I roll my eyes. I don't know why I told him Dylan was my boyfriend. I guess I just wanted him to know that I wasn't lusting after him like the rest of the females in a two-hundred-mile radius.

That's not entirely true, though, is it? He's a fine specimen, I won't deny that. But he's exactly the type of guy I should avoid.

"Who's that?" Dylan asks, looking him up and down, seemingly unimpressed.

"*That* is Jesse Shepherd." I recognized him right away. He looks older than I remember. Taller and more muscular, with cheekbones sharper than razorblades. I used to see him around town before he went away for college. We've even spoken before, but clearly, I didn't make much of an impression on him.

There was a brief moment that I thought he might be different from the rest of the jocks he hung around. Something about him didn't seem to fit. He acted the part. He definitely *looked* the part with his lacrosse jacket over broad shoulders and a tapered waist. Cocky smile firmly in place. But he had an edge to him. His eyes held a hardness that made me wonder if there was more lurking beneath that pretty exterior. But then he opened his mouth, ripping that theory to shreds.

"Friend of yours?" Dylan asks, watching him with an unreadable expression.

"God, no," I say, peeling my gaze from him. "So, what's new with you?"

"The Attic shut down a few months back, so we've been trying to find another place to play."

"No way." Dylan and his band played there every single week. The Attic was their home. It was the place locals and tourists alike went to drink and listen to live music. "How the hell did that happen?" That place was always packed.

"Not sure. We showed up to play one night and the parking lot was empty. All the lights were off and the doors were locked."

"That's messed up."

"We'll find something."

I nod, knowing they will. Dylan is the real deal.

"For now, it's pizza joints and random events." He leans back in his chair, bringing his hands behind his head, taking a deep breath. "What's next in the life of Albert?"

Albert. I roll my eyes at the nickname. He used to call me Al for short, and as if that wasn't bad enough, it somehow morphed into Albert. Never mind the fact that it has the same number of syllables as *Allie*.

I look over to the *help wanted* sign hanging on the wall, biting on my lower lip. "A job, for starters."

CHAPTER FOUR

Allie

"**W**E DON'T HAVE TO STAY LONG IF YOU'RE not into it," Halston promises as she leads us through a crowded living room. It smells like sweat, Victoria's Secret body spray, and desperation in here.

"I'm fine." College parties aren't my scene, but Halston loves this shit, and since she's one of the two real friends I have in River's Edge, I'll try my best to conceal my resting bitch face and enjoy it.

"Maybe tonight you'll find the perfect candidate." She wiggles her brows. She's made it her mission in life to get me laid. At eighteen years old, I'm the only virgin I know. I'm not saving myself for the perfect guy, but one I could actually stand to be around would be nice.

I roll my eyes. "Doubtful. If I were going to hook up, it wouldn't be with anyone who'd hang out here."

"That's exactly why this is the perfect place to find a one-night stand to practice on," she argues. "You won't fall for any of these boys."

Well, there is that.

Reaching back for my hand, Halston pulls me through the room where the main party seems to be taking place.

I catch myself bobbing my head to some catchy pop song—"Youngblood," I think—and roll my eyes at myself. Dad would never let me live this down if he were here. While I get my impeccable taste in music from him, I've also been known to enjoy a top forty song or two. So sue me.

I shake off the sadness that tries to creep in at the thought of my dad. He wouldn't want that. He was always after me to get some friends my age. He wanted me to have the college experience, which brings me to another reason I'm here, going against my loner tendencies.

"So. Many. Boys!" Halston gives an excited squeal and I laugh, shaking my head. If *boy crazy* were in the dictionary, a picture of Halston would sit next to the definition. She's the complete opposite of me, with her lean body and legs for days. Dark hair curled to perfection, a creamy complexion with a perfectly-placed beauty mark on her cheek. She could have any guy in here, and she knows it.

We scan the crowd of drunken frat boys until she sets her sights on a guy with too-tight khakis and no shirt standing next to the keg with a circle of admiring females around him.

"I'm parched," she states with a gleam in her eyes, and then she's tugging at my wrist once again.

"For the boy or the beer?" I yell over the noise.

"Both. Definitely both."

We make our way to the keg through the sea of people, and with all the confidence in the world, Halston casually cuts through the circle of girls surrounding her newest victim.

"Hey," she says simply.

Frat Boy looks her up and down, obviously liking what he sees before he tips his chin at her. "Hey back. Thirsty?"

She nods, and he fills a cup for her, all but ignoring the other girls. I laugh softly. It's that easy for her. I hang back while the girls pout, but their despair doesn't last for long because suddenly, the energy in the room shifts, and their gazes are fixed on someone else. I look over my shoulder to see none other than Jesse Shepherd walking through the door. A couple of guys high-five him, and girls throw themselves in his path for a hug.

"Shep!" the guy with Halston calls out. Jesse gives him the *bro nod*, acknowledging him, and makes his way toward us. I quickly spin back around, hoping he doesn't notice me standing here.

"What's up, Sully?" Jesse asks.

Halston wrinkles her nose. "Sully?"

"Last name's Sullivan," he informs her. "But you can call me Daddy." He tosses a wink at her.

I roll my eyes. *That's embarrassing.*

I take a step backwards, trying to slip away without being seen, and accidentally back up into the girl behind me.

"Shit, sorry—" I start, but when I see who it is, the apology dies on my lips.

"Watch it," Sierra snaps, shooting me a dirty look right before she tips her beer to slosh all over my Doc Martens. She doesn't deem me worthy of any further attention, her focus quickly shifting back toward Jesse…who is now looking right at me, thanks to my clumsiness. Amusement gleams in his eyes, and I know he's about to put on a show.

"That's no way to talk to my girlfriend," he admonishes, curling an arm around my hip, bringing my side flush with his. Halston's eyes widen comically, shooting silent accusations my way. I didn't tell her about what happened at Blackbear.

"I'm going back to the dorm to change shoes," I tell Halston, lifting a foot to shake off the excess beer that's now starting to seep into my socks.

"Do you want me to come?" she asks, torn between wanting details and staying to jump on her chance with Sullivan.

"It's fine. I'll be right back."

She shakes her head, setting her cup down on the table. "It's late. I'm not letting you walk back to Manzanita alone."

"I'll walk her," Jesse says, and I whip my head around, shooting him a glare.

Halston smiles triumphantly. "Deal."

"What…" I start, confused, but Jesse takes my hand, locking his fingers with mine. Like we're a real couple. All eyes are on us, the odd pair, as we make our way toward the door. Me with my black, ripped skinny jeans, my dad's jean jacket tied around my waist, and Doc Martens. Him with his backwards hat, fitted jeans, and a maroon shirt with his school's name emblazoned across the front of his wide chest.

Once we're outside, I drop his hand. "Thanks…for that," I say, heading toward the girls' dorms.

"Whoa, whoa, whoa," he says, falling into step next to me. "Trying to ditch your boyfriend already?"

I stop short, cocking my head to the side as I study him, trying to figure out his angle. "What are you doing?"

"Walking you to your dorm," he drawls out slowly, like the answer should be obvious.

"Why?"

"It's late. Manzanita is across campus." He ticks off the reasons.

"I'm not going to fuck you." I narrow my eyes at him, crossing my arms over my chest.

Jesse's lips tug upward into a grin and he chuckles as he looks me up and down. *Jesus, he's hot.* "Okay."

"*Okay*?" I ask, lifting a brow.

"Okay," he repeats, sweeping an arm in front of him. "Lead the way."

I eye him skeptically for a beat before turning back toward Halston's dorm. Jesse hooks an arm around my shoulder, smirking down at me when I shoot him a glare, even though my stomach flips at his nearness.

"So, where's your real boyfriend?"

It takes me a minute to realize who he's referring to. "Who, Dylan? We're just friends."

"Friends who see each other naked?" he asks casually, as if asking about the weather.

"And that's any of your business, how?"

"I'm just making conversation," he says innocently.

"I already told you I'm not having sex with you," I remind him.

"You think about having sex with me often? You sure bring it up a lot."

My cheeks heat and I stare ahead. Jesse's not exactly hard up for female attention, but if he's not trying to hook up, then what *is* he doing?

Once at the entrance of Manzanita Hall, I pull away, leaning my back against the brick building, one hand on the door handle. "Thanks for walking me."

Jess snorts out a laugh. "You're not going back to the party, are you?"

"Probably not," I admit. "Halston won't miss me. Trust me."

Jesse nods, giving me one last once-over before turning to leave, but then I hear a rustling in the bushes that has my hand jerking out to snatch his wrist of its own volition. Jesse's eyes are amused, giving a pointed look at where my fingers clutch his arm.

"Did you hear that?" I ask.

Moving in slowly, he cages me in, bracing his right arm on the wall above my head, his left hand by my hip. He brings his lips close to my ear, and I fight the shiver that rolls through me. "It's probably Sierra," he says, his voice hushed and husky. I swallow hard, looking over his shoulder as he nuzzles closer. We both know it's not Sierra. My pulse pounds in my ears as his mouth skims across my cheek, stopping at my parted lips. I don't even know him. I should push him away. I should stop the charade. But instead, I find myself waiting for his next move.

"Is this convincing?" he asks. He's so close that I can feel his breath on my lips, and I realize that I want him to close the distance. I *want* him to kiss me.

I give a slight shake of my head in response.

"No?" He smirks. His left hand leaves the wall to curl around my hip and presses his chest to mine. "How about this?"

"Almost," I whisper. I wet my lips, and the tip of my tongue grazes his bottom lip. His expression goes from playful to heated in an instant, and then he closes the final distance. It's soft at first, just a brush of his lips against mine, but then he's cupping my face with both hands, tilting my head back as his tongue sweeps into my mouth.

My hands find his shirt, pulling him closer as his mouth fucks mine. Because that's exactly what this is. This isn't kissing. Or maybe it is, and I've been kissing the wrong boys.

Jesse groans, fitting a firm thigh between my legs, and the need bubbling inside me threatens to boil over at the sensation. All too soon, he pulls back, leaving me breathless.

"Convincing enough?" His words are playful, but the glazed look in his eyes tells me he's just as affected as I am.

I try to find words, but before I do, we hear it again. The rustling. Both of our heads snap in the direction of the bush just in time to see a racoon dart out and run behind the building.

"Jesus!" I jump, before laughing, my forehead falling against Jesse's chest as I calm my racing heart. Except, it's not calming. It's beating hard and fast for an entirely different reason. Slowly, I lift my gaze to Jesse's. His jaw is set hard as he stares down at me, and I feel the thick ridge beneath his jeans. I bite down on my lip as my hips shift into his, seeking the friction. *What the hell am I doing?*

With that move, Jesse snaps, bending to grab the back of my thighs as he kisses me again. He moves toward the door, and I fumble, one-handed, to push it open behind me. He carries me past the empty common area toward the dorms, clearly knowing his way around.

"Room number."

"One-oh-eight," I say, barely getting the words out before his mouth is on mine again. When we reach the door, I slide down his body, digging into my jeans pocket for the spare key Halston gave me. I work fast, not wanting to give myself time to second-guess my very questionable decision to hook up with a guy I barely know in a room that isn't even technically mine. But maybe Halston was right. Jesse Shepherd is a playboy. I won't be in any danger of falling for him. Even in the highly unlikely event I did catch feelings, he'll be two hours away at school by Monday.

Once I get the door open, Jesse grabs me by the ass, my legs automatically wrapping around his waist as he lifts me. Crossing my ankles behind his back, I toe off my sopping boots.

I sense him hesitating for a beat, staring at the two beds, trying to decide which one is mine. The answer is *neither*, but he chooses the one I'm using for the time being, probably guessing that pretty, pink princess-style bedding isn't me. I don't know why that thought appeases me. As if him knowing this small detail somehow justifies my willingness to sleep with a near stranger.

Jesse tosses me on top of the twin bed with my black comforter, fitting himself between my legs. I hook my calves behind the backs of his thighs, pulling him closer.

"Fuck," he rasps, pushing his hips into me. I curl my fingers into the bottom of his shirt and pull upward. Jesse sits back to rip it off, his hat falling to the floor with it. Jesus, he's beautiful. Muscular but lean. Still soft. Messy hair falling into his eyes.

"I'm not having sex with you," I say again, just to be clear.

"You said that," he mumbles. Leaning down, his hands slip under my shirt, and I freeze when his lips meet my stomach. He looks up at me, kissing and licking his way up each inch of my skin as he pushes my shirt higher. I reach down to thread my fingers in those dark, disheveled locks as I arch into his touch. The pulsing between my thighs is unbearable, almost painful now, and I need *more*.

Right when he exposes my black bra, his phone rings from his back pocket. He reaches behind to silence it, and then he's back, unhooking the front clasp of my bra. I hold my breath as he starts to peel the fabric away from my skin, my nipples already sensitive and hard as rocks from anticipation. Jesse scrapes his teeth against the swell of my breast as my bra falls to my sides, exposing me completely. I shiver, arching into him, but then his phone rings again.

"Someone better be dead," he snaps, sitting back on his heels to fish his phone out of his pocket. When he sees the name flashing across his screen, his entire demeanor changes. His eyebrows pull together, his expression grim. He looks from me to the phone, then back to me again, regret written all over his features. *Regret that he's hooking up with me?*

"I have to go."

"Is something wrong?" Something better be wrong. I'd accept a sick relative. A dead pet. Things happen.

"I…" He frowns at his phone again, and it slips from between his fingers, landing at my feet. I don't see much, but I do see a name. A very feminine name.

My mouth pops open for half a second before I snap it shut. Did I just get traded in for a better option? I suddenly feel cold. Like a bucket of ice water was dumped over the fire that was building inside me. I avert my eyes, pulling my shirt down to cover my tits that are still wet from his mouth.

"Al—" he starts, but I stand and scoop his shirt up off the floor before tossing it to him. Giving him my back, I reach under my shirt to fix my bra, feeling stupid. *So* goddamn stupid. I don't turn around, and he doesn't try to explain. After a moment, I hear the door open and shut behind him, leaving me alone with my bruised ego.

Stupid, stupid girl.

CHAPTER FIVE

Jess

Two months later

"WHAT THE FUCK WAS UP WITH TRAVERS?" my teammate, Riley, asks, scrubbing a towel across his wet hair. Despite Travers ignoring the plays I told him to run and trying to sabotage me anytime I got the ball in my pocket, we won the game tonight.

"Still pissed he didn't make co-captain, I guess." I shrug. Lacrosse is a real douchebag's sport. Lots of rich, preppy, entitled assholes in polo shirts and fuckin' boat shoes. They don't like it when someone like me comes along, and Travers has had it out for me since day one. He likes to bait me into fighting him in hopes of getting me kicked off the team, since he knows I'm already on Coach's shit list.

I look over toward Travers who's smirking at me like a cat that got the canary. Like he's in on something I'm not, and I don't like it. "There a reason you're smiling at my dick, Travers?" I ask just as I drop my towel. The entire team turns his way, everyone erupting in laughter.

The smirk falls off his face, his cheeks turning red.

Riley laughs, turning back to me. "Hurry up. I want to

get back to the house before everyone shows up and drinks all the good shit."

If it's a weekend, it's a safe bet that there will be a party at Riley's. If we win a game, it's not even a question.

"Shep!" Coach shouts, prowling through the locker room, not so much as pausing to greet the team. "A word."

"What'd you do?" Riley frowns.

"Fuck if I know." A look at Travers' smug face has me feeling even more on edge. Coach has given me several warnings about my temper, so I tamp down the urge to hit him as I cross the short distance to Coach's office.

"Shut the door," he instructs from his place behind his desk. "Sit down." He points to the blue plastic chair in front of his desk. He's silent for a minute, rubbing at his forehead as he looks down at his cell phone, seemingly conflicted. As the silence stretches, my palms start to sweat.

"You missed another practice this week."

I stand stock-still, waiting for him to deal the blow that I know is coming. To be honest, I'm surprised I lasted this long.

"You got anything to say?" he asks.

"I had an emergency—"

"What about last week?" he asks, cutting me off. "And the week before that? Your grades are suffering. You're missing classes and practices." He ticks off my transgressions on his fingers. "You're distracted on the field."

When I say nothing, he leans forward, folding his hands on the desk. "Are you in some kind of trouble? Is this too much pressure?"

I clench my jaw so tight it feels like my teeth are going to crack. Pressure? Yeah, you could say I'm feeling the fucking pressure. Funny thing about lacrosse scholarships—they don't cover shit. I can barely afford to be here. Working is prohibited while I'm on the team, so I've had to resort to finding *creative* ways to make money. It's damn near impossible juggling it all.

"No trouble," I grit out.

"I can't work with you if you don't give me something," he says, his voice tight with frustration. This isn't convenient for him. It's probably the reason I've gotten away with breaking the rules so long, and the reason he waited until after we played one of the toughest teams to broach the subject.

"All right," Coach stands, his voice resigned. "You're suspended for the season. Take the rest of the year to get your shit together."

I knew it was coming. Practically dared him to kick me off the team. Disappointment settles over me, and it's almost a relief. I've been waiting for the other shoe to drop. This life wasn't meant to be mine. It never felt real anyway. College. *Sports.* This shit isn't me, no matter how hard I try.

When I leave the office, the rest of the team has cleared out. Everyone but Riley, and judging by his dejected expression, I'm guessing he heard enough to know what went down.

"Just like that?" he asks, hands braced on his sides.

"Just like that," I confirm. He scoffs as I walk past him to clear out my locker.

"Did you even try to fight it?"

"No."

"Why the fuck not?"

I slam my locker shut, slinging my bag over my shoulder. I force a casual stride as I make my way outside. Riley jogs to catch up to me, and I know words are coming out of his mouth, but I don't hear anything once my eyes lock onto Travers. He glances up, cocky expression plastered to his mug before blowing me a kiss.

I flex my fingers, wanting nothing more than to knock his fucking teeth out. And now, I don't have any reason to reel it in.

I drop my bag, prowling straight for him. He stands his ground, confident that I won't possibly do anything to get myself in even hotter water. What he doesn't know is that I'm already done, and I'm prepared to go out with a bang. I see the moment the fear sets in. He tries to conceal it, but his eyes widen once he realizes I'm not stopping. I send my fist into his jaw as hard as I can, and he drops like a sack of fucking rocks.

"What the fuck!" he shouts, cupping a hand under his chin to catch the tooth he spits out. *Well, whaddya know? My wish came true.*

"Shep!" Coach hollers, marching toward us. "Get the fuck out of here!"

I huff out a humorless laugh before spitting on the floor next to Travers. "I'm gone."

CHAPTER SIX

Jess

"**Y**OU *WHAT?*" MY SISTER, LO, SHRIEKS. I CURL my fists at my side, forcing myself not to react. I knew she wasn't going to take the news well. Should've done it over a phone call to give her a chance to calm the hell down before I got here.

"I dropped out," I say again.

"I heard you. I just can't figure out how you could do something so goddamn *stupid*," she snaps. She starts walking around her living room, picking up random things and roughly putting them away. It's what she does when she's mad. She's an angry cleaner. And finding out her little brother is dropping out of college when she worked so hard to make it happen is right at the top of the list of things that would piss her off.

"Changed my mind," I say simply. Lo stares at me as if I've lost my mind, her eyebrows pulling together as her expression morphs from shocked to infuriated. She doesn't speak, and a silent Logan Shepherd is the one thing I've learned to fear, which says a lot considering I grew up in the worst part of Oakland where drive-bys and break-ins were a weekly occurrence.

"Lo," I say, stepping forward, but before I have a chance

to explain, the front door opens and her boyfriend, Dare, walks in. His eyes dart between us, taking notice of the look on Lo's face.

"Fuck."

"Nice to see you, too," I mutter.

Dare makes his way over to the kitchen and tosses his keys onto the counter before grabbing three bottles of beer from the fridge. He looks up at me and I give a slight shake of my head, silently conveying to him that this calls for something stronger. He raises an eyebrow and puts the beers back, opting for a bottle of Jack from on top of the fridge. I nod, and he curses under his breath, knowing this isn't going to be pretty. The last time I broke out the whiskey, I ended up drunk, naked, and bleeding in his hot tub.

Dare unscrews the cap, taking a big gulp straight from the bottle, before walking it over to me. Lo is still staring daggers at me, jaw clenched tight, as I take a swig. It burns my throat, warming my insides as it goes down. Dare makes his way back over to Lo and presses a kiss to her forehead, but her eyes stay pinned on me, arms folded across her chest.

"Someone going to tell me what the fuck happened?" Dare asks. Lo ignores his question, directing her words toward me.

"After everything I sacrificed."

"Figures you'd make this about you," I say, working my jaw back and forth. I knew she'd be pissed, but she'll get over it. We've been through worse. It's always been us against the world. Drug addict parents. Drug *dealing*. Abuse. Poverty. Countless fights over the years. None of it has ever been enough to make Lo turn her back on me. That's not what we do.

"Is it not about me? I dropped out to take care of you. I made sure you got to school every day. I made sure you had food and a bed to come home to."

"I didn't come here for another Lo lecture," I say, my voice devoid of any emotion.

"No," she agrees, her eyes shining with unshed tears. "You just came here to tell me you're pissing away your shot. You came here to tell me you're going back to the fucking life we had to crawl our way out of."

I swallow hard, the guilt hitting my gut like a brick. "I got kicked off the team, okay?" I shout. Her mouth snaps shut.

"It was only a matter of time, right?" I take another swig. "I'm not meant for that life anyway. I'm not meant for college. Besides, you have Dare to take care of you now." My meaning is clear. She always said I was the only one who could amount to anything. I was supposed to be our ticket out of that life, but Dare swooped in like a goddamn Disney prince, fixing all our problems.

Something flashes in Lo's eyes, but before she can respond, I pick up the duffle bag at my feet, shrug it over my shoulder, and raise the bottle of Jack in Dare's direction. "I'm taking this."

"For such a smart kid, you're being a dumbass," Dare says, disappointment written all over his face. I bob my head. *Fair assessment.* Lifting the hand with the bottle, I give them a salute before walking out the door.

CHAPTER SEVEN

Allie

THE ONE GOOD THING ABOUT WORKING NIGHTS AT Blackbear Bar? The fact that I get to be in charge of the music selection. Green Day blares from the speakers as I make my rounds, making sure the remaining customers are set before last call. I applied the day I met Dylan here, and the manager, Lo, hired me on the spot.

As soon as the last person pays his ticket, I crank the music louder. Technically, we're open for another hour, but it's Thursday, so it's probably safe to start closing down. Jake, the owner slash bartender, shakes his head, amused, as he holds out the bowl of suckers, knowing my routine. I pluck out my favorite flavor—butterscotch—before I set to wiping down the tables.

"You can take off, Allison," Jake tells me as he slaps a stack of bills onto the bar top for me. "I'll take care of it."

"You sure?" I ask. I don't want to skip out early. I'm still the new girl.

Before he gets the chance to answer, the door flies open. I startle, head whipping in the direction to find a group of people stumbling in. They're loud and, by the looks of it, drunk. My eyes widen before narrowing with annoyance when they meet a familiar pair of hazel ones.

Jesse fucking Shepherd. Some girl is curled around his bicep, and I can't tell whether she's using him to hold herself up or if she's just trying to send a very clear signal that she's interested.

He sends a smirk my way, but I roll my eyes, already annoyed. Embarrassment rolls through me when I think about how he left me that night, but I straighten my spine, unwilling to show any signs of weakness or insecurity. In fact, he did me a favor that night. The embarrassment I'm feeling now is only a fraction of how I'd feel if I let things go any further.

"We're closing soon, Jess," Jake informs him, but Jesse simply swaggers up and parks his ass in a booth, his friends following suit.

"We're celebrating," he explains with a hollow smile.

I look over to Jake who gives me a reluctant nod, letting me know to go ahead and serve them. I grab a couple of menus and head over to their table, trying to keep my face neutral. "What can I get started for you guys?" I ask after I take the sucker out of my mouth. I should've ditched it, but I can't do it now without it being awkward. Not having anywhere else to put it, I place it back in my mouth and stare at my notepad, waiting for their orders.

"I want some fuckin' fries!" one of the girl slurs. Then, the group of seven hurls their orders at me all at once. Everyone except Jesse. Finally, I look up from my order pad to meet his eyes.

"Allie Girl." He smiles, but it's not his usual, carefree smile that I remember. This one doesn't quite reach his eyes. But then I remind myself that I don't care.

"It's Allison," I correct. "What do you want?" I aim for unaffected and end up coming off snappy instead.

"This, for starters." He plucks the sucker out of my mouth before popping it into his own. My eyes widen, and he leans back against the booth with a raised brow, daring me to react, so naturally, I do the exact opposite, even though his demeanor throws me off.

"How's Halston?" a guy asks, and I realize it's Sullivan—or Sully. He and Halston ended up hooking up that night, which served as the perfect diversion to distract her from questioning me about what happened with Jesse. I never went back to the party. I put on my headphones and fell asleep to the sound of Jimmy Eat World in my ears until Halston waltzed in at four A.M., looking freshly fucked and giddy as hell about it.

"She's fine. I'll get these orders in." I turn without giving them a chance to respond.

"You know Jess?" Jake asks when I approach. I shake my head.

"Not really." I'm definitely not explaining to my boss that I almost hooked up with him, especially since finding out that Lo is his sister. Halston filled me in, but I don't know how I didn't see it before. They both have the same thick, unruly, dark hair and hazel eyes, except Jesse's are more green than brown. *Not that I stared deep into his eyes or anything.*

"Want me to take them?" Jake asks, flicking his chin toward Jesse's table. I glance behind me to catch him staring straight at me, much to the dismay of the drunk yet beautiful girl draping herself across his lap.

"I got it," I insist. I refuse to let Jesse know he's gotten to me in any way. It was probably just another weekend for him. Why should it be any different for me?

"I'll just get their drinks then," Jake insists. I nod,

excusing myself to the bathroom, away from Jesse's prob- ing stare. Once inside, I push the lock in and lean against the door. I catch my reflection, fighting the urge to fluff my hair on his account. My face is free of makeup, save for the red tint of cherry lip balm coating my lips. I tug at my white cotton uniform shirt that hugs my body tighter than I'm used to. I roll my eyes at myself, straighten my shoul- ders, and head back out into the lion's den.

"What are you doing home on a week night?" I hear Jake ask. I pause in the hallway, not yet visible, waiting to hear his answer.

"He's back for good," Sullivan supplies, and their drunken group cheers excitedly.

What? The thought of him being here permanently sends a jolt of something through me. I don't know if it's dread or anticipation. I peek around the corner and Jesse has that fake smirk plastered to his face again.

"That's why we're celebrating," the girl next to him in- forms Jake, rubbing at Jesse's shoulder.

"Welcome home, man," Jake says, giving him the man clap slash handshake thing, but Jesse's eyes betray him. He's not happy. Why am I the only one seeing this? *Or maybe he's just drunk.* That's probably it.

I hang back until I hear the sound of plates clanking together and sliding across the expo window that tells me their order is ready. Grabbing a tray, I load it up and head over to Jesse's table.Once everyone has their food, I look back to Jesse.

"You sure you don't want anything?" My voice is un- intentionally softer than it was just a minute ago, and his eyebrows pull together, assessing. "The kitchen is about to close," I add, forcing indifference into my tone.

As if he senses that I can see through his little charade, he curls a hand around the back of my thigh, his fingers burning a hole through my thin black leggings. "I'm not hungry for food."

I scowl, slapping his hand away. "Asshole."

"I asked for lemon with my water," the girl next to him snaps, seemingly upset that Jesse's attentions have shifted from her to me.

I huff out a sardonic laugh. I pause, looking at her, but my words are for Jesse. "I'm not interested."

I spin around before either one of them can respond and Jake's already armed with a side plate with a couple of lemon slices, heading in their direction.

"Does the offer to leave early still stand?"

"Get out of here. I'll see you tomorrow."

CHAPTER EIGHT

Allie

"**D**ID HE SAY ANYTHING ELSE?" HALSTON ASKS, wrapping my hair around the thick barrel of a curling iron.

"He just asked how you were," I tell her for the third time.

"And you just said 'fine'?"

"What was I supposed to say?" I shrug as she lets a hot curl fall onto my shoulder before scooping up another piece.

"I don't know," she admits. "But something better than that."

"What's up with you guys?"

She frowns, looking perplexed. "I think I like him."

I arch a brow. Halston loves boys, but she doesn't usually *like* any of them for more than a couple of seconds. "So, what's the problem?"

"He's texted me a few times wanting to get together."

"*And*?" I hedge.

"He wanted to do daytime things. He invited me to lunch. What the hell am I supposed to do with that?"

I laugh, rolling my eyes. "I don't know, maybe date him?"

"Boys like him don't date. At least not exclusively."

"So, we're going to this party because?" She runs her fingers through my hair, breaking up the loose waves and shaking them out.

"Because I'm a glutton for punishment," she answers matter-of-factly.

"Same," I say, standing to inspect myself in the mirror attached to her dresser.

"Think he'll be there?" Halston asks, and I know she's referring to Jesse.

I shrug. "He lives here now. Anything is possible." I told her about running into Jesse and Sullivan at Blackbear, which led to me telling her a very watered-down version of the events that took place that night.

She stands next to me, checking us both out in the mirror. "We look hot," she announces. "We're going to go to this frat house, get drunk, have fun, and pretend they don't exist."

"You're the boss."

This party is much bigger than the last one. It's dark as hell, the only lights coming from the black lights that cast a purple glow around the house.

"I spy Jell-O shots!" Halston shouts over the music. We make our way toward the kitchen through the neon-painted bodies, and she plucks two glowing blue cups off the counter. I toss one back, the lukewarm consistency wiggling down my throat.

"Did you know this was a black light party?" I ask Halston. I never seem to know about these parties, but she's always in the loop.

"Nope." She shrugs. "But I'm into it."

The sliding glass door leading to the backyard opens, and even in the dark I can tell it's Jesse walking through it, Sullivan and a pack of hot chicks right behind him.

"Fuck," I mutter. Halston, however, has a different reaction. Her eyes light up with mischief as they approach the kitchen. When Jesse notices me, his face splits into a wide smile, his teeth glowing white against the black lights.

"Miss me, Allie Girl?"

"It's Allison. And not even a little."

"You wound me." He clutches his chest dramatically, bringing my attention to the illuminated words written there. *Kylie was here* is streaked across his skin with an arrow leading down his well-defined abs, past the cut V of his hips, all the way to his crotch.

"Classy," I remark, peeling my eyes away.

"It's a gift." He shrugs unapologetically.

"Hey, Halston." Sullivan looks her up and down with heat in his gaze.

"Oh. Hey," she says nonchalantly, barely sparing him a glance before catching my hand in hers. "I love this song! Let's dance."

I snort out a laugh as she pulls me into the crowd of bodies. She throws her arms around my neck, glancing back toward Sullivan behind me.

"I thought you wanted to see him."

"I'm not going to let *him* know that," she shouts close to my ear. "Trust me. I know what I'm doing."

Some random guys join us, and Halston leans into the chest of one of them, putting on a show for Sullivan. When I try to spot his reaction, I catch eyes with Jess, and I'm surprised to see him glaring at me. *Hard*. I feel my brows scrunch together, confused by his reaction, but I shake it off. The friend of the guy Halston's dancing with moves closer to me, curling his free hand around the small of my back.

"Nooope." I laugh, sliding out of his grasp. He's cute, but I'm not in the mood to be groped by a drunken frat boy tonight. Or ever. He's persistent, though, and before I know it, he slides in behind me, plastering his front to my back. I can feel his excitement through his jeans and I whirl on him, shoving his shoulders with both hands. The drink in his right hand sloshes over the rim, splashing his shirt with beer.

"The fuck?" he slurs angrily, holding his arms out, looking down at his torso to assess the damage.

"No means no." I smirk. Out of the corner of my eye, I see Jesse standing behind him, off to the side. His arms are crossed, jaw clenched. *Did he see the whole thing play out?*

"Whatever, you're fucking ugly anyway." Someone laughs, and then Halston is next to me, grabbing my arm in silent support. He weighs his options, knowing he has an audience now. "Bitch," he mutters, turning to leave. As soon as his back is to me, he comes face to face with Jesse who cocks a fist back before sending it straight into his face. Drunk Guy falls backwards into me and takes me down, thanks to the floor that's slick with alcohol.

To my horror, the music stops, and the lights turn on. Drunk Guy cups his nose, blood running between his fingers and down his wrist. "What the hell, Shep?!"

Jesse lunges toward him, grabbing him by his collar with both fists and throwing him off of me before landing another punch. Sullivan appears, pulling Jesse from Drunk Guy.

"Jesus!" Halston yells, pulling me up from the sticky floor. My skirt and legs are wet, and I lost a boot somewhere.

"You're out!" Sullivan shouts, pointing to the door.

"I didn't do shit—" Drunk Guy starts, but Jesse goes for him again, and Drunk Guy flinches, thinking better of arguing, and heads for the door.

Everyone's eyes are on me now, filled with everything ranging from pity to curiosity. I hear mumblings of *who is she? What just happened? Are they together?* I feel my cheeks heat, hating the unwanted attention.

"What the fuck are you looking at?" Jesse shouts, turning in a circle. "It's a party. Start fucking partying."

The music starts back up, the lights are cut, and thankfully, everyone goes about their business when they realize the drama is over. Jesse runs a hand through the hair that's fallen onto his forehead before bending at the waist to pluck my boot out of the crowd. When he extends his arm in offering, I snatch the boot from his grasp before shoving my foot into it, turning to leave without a word.

Jesse is hot on my heels. Once I make it to the porch, away from prying eyes, I spin around to face him. "I didn't need your help," I snap. I've dealt with way worse. If I can handle handsy guys at bars and concert venues, I can easily handle a sloppy schoolboy.

"Don't flatter yourself. That wasn't for you," he says.

"Oh, really? You just decided to pick a fight for the fun of it?"

"I, uh, I'm just gonna…" Halston trails off, wiggling a manicured nail toward the party before slipping back inside.

"That's exactly it. I was spoiling for a fight. An opportunity presented itself, so I took it."

I take him in, contemplating my next words. He seems different. His hair is longer than it was a few weeks ago. Unkempt. But it's beyond his appearance. Something inside has changed, too. I just don't know him well enough to know what that *something* is.

"Next time you're looking for trouble, leave me out of it."

CHAPTER NINE

Jess

"**W**HAT THE FUCK ARE YOU LOOKING AT?" I ask the freshman taking money at the door who witnessed Allie telling me off. He quickly averts his eyes, moving to stand at the edge of the porch at the top of the stairs.

I feel like a fucking tool watching Allison's back as she walks away from me. What I said was mostly true. I *have* been spoiling for a fight, but I do a damn good job of internalizing my shit. Until it comes to her, apparently.

The minute Daniels laid his hands on her, I knew there'd be trouble. Girls like Allison aren't here to get laid. I knew by her body language that day in her dorm that casual sex wasn't something she made a habit of. I stood back and watched as she pushed him away, letting her handle it. She's not my problem. Not my *girl*. She reminds me of Lo, the way she carries herself. The way she uses sarcasm as a shield. And when Daniels called her ugly and a bitch to boot, I didn't think. I just swung.

Allison wasn't swooning or preening like a peacock like the other girls would be. She stood there in the bright room with one shoe on, while everyone stared at her like some sort of zoo animal. No, she wasn't basking in the attention. She was embarrassed. And angry. *Very* angry. Seemingly at me.

Probably has something to do with how you parted ways, dumbass.

I had her tits in my mouth, then I bailed on her, and from the looks of things, she isn't interested in picking up where we left off. She's pissed. I get it. But it's not like I could've called to apologize if I wanted to. I wasn't exactly thinking clearly enough to get her number when my future was being flushed down the shitter.

I dig into my jeans pocket, pulling out my smokes before lighting one up. I all but quit for lacrosse. Now I can do whatever the hell I want, and *fuck*, I feel free. *Lookie there, another silver lining.* I hear my name being yelled, and I turn around to see Kaylee and Kylie impatiently waiting for me, dressed in tight white tank tops and short skirts with neon handprints all over their tight little bodies, and matching pouts on their faces. I take a drag, holding up a finger to let them know I'll be back in a minute.

"Five bucks," I hear the freshman tell someone.

"Just here to get my girl."

I smirk, feeling sorry for the poor bastard who has to rescue his girlfriend, but when I turn to face him, he looks familiar with his lip ring and the plugs in his ears. I narrow my eyes, trying to place him.

"Sorry, man. Five bucks," the freshman repeats. Dude works his jaw in annoyance before shoving past him. He stops short when I block the doorway, crossing my arms and blowing the smoke from my cigarette toward him.

"Problem?" I ask.

"You," he accuses, his eyes slanting with recognition. I raise my brows at his tone.

"Me." I chuckle, swinging my arms open wide.

"I'm here for Allie."

The smirk drops from my face when it clicks. This is the guy from the bar. The one who touched Allison's body with the familiarity of someone who knows it intimately.

"Rules are rules." I shrug, just to be a dick, flicking my cigarette behind him. The freshman stomps it out for me.

"You're either going to go get Allie or you're going to let me in," he informs me.

"And what you're *not* going to do is come to my fucki—"

"Leave him alone, Jesse," Allison snaps from behind me, cutting me off. I turn to face her. Her cheeks are flushed, eyes hard. A smart-ass retort is on the tip of my tongue, but something in her expression holds me back. She breezes past me, her sweet scent wafting behind her.

"Thanks for coming, Dylan." *Dylan*. Dylan the Douche.

"You good?" he asks, looking her up and down, as if inspecting her for damage.

"Yeah. Just wet," she mutters as Dylan ushers her down the steps with his hand on the small of her back.

"I have that effect on women," I call out just to piss her off.

She glares at me over her shoulder, flipping me off as Dylan tightens his grip on her waist.

"Call me!"

Dylan opens the passenger door of his old school Dodge Challenger, and Allison slides in before he closes it. I watch her through the window, my hands shoved into my front pockets. A pair of slender hands circle my neck from behind, sliding down my chest, and then Kaylee or Kylie's lips nibble on my ear. I hold Allie's stare, the corner of my lip quirking up when I see the frown painting her pretty features. But she can't look away, and neither can I.

"Let's go upstairs," Kylie, the more aggressive of the two best friends, whispers before scraping her teeth across my earlobe. The Challenger roars to life and I sever our connection, if only to be the one to look away first.

Fuck it. I was craving someone in Doc Martens and a perpetual attitude, but... "You'll do."

It's bright. Too fucking bright. Eyes closed, I stumble out of bed, tripping over someone's high heel on the way to the window, and jerk the curtains shut. *Much better*. I sit on the edge of the bed in the spare room at Sullivan's house, propping my elbows on my knees and running my hands through my hair as I piece together the events of last night. After Allison left, I pounded shots, having fun with Kaylee and Kylie before I was too drunk to function. I sent them packing moments before falling into bed and passing the fuck out.

Head pounding, I slap around on the nightstand, feeling for my lighter and the half-smoked blunt I left there last night. I light it up, letting the smoke fill my lungs and ghost it, holding it as long as I can before a cough sputters out. I lie back, one arm behind my head, the other pinching the blunt to my lips once more, as I watch the rotating blade of the ceiling fan. The familiar buzz makes its way through my body, making me feel warm and heavy, and I'm just about to pass out again when my phone goes off.

I fumble around, finding it tangled in my sheets. "What?" I answer, without even checking the screen. My voice sounds rough as fuck, like I smoked eighty packs of cigarettes last night, and I clear my throat.

"Wake up, fucker," says Dare, my sister's boyfriend.

"What time is it?" I scrub a hand down my face.

"Noon. Your sister needs you at Blackbear. One of her servers quit and Sutton's out of town."

"What does that have to do with me?"

"Because she needs your help," Dare says in that calm, yet menacing tone of his. "You owe her this at least."

I roll my eyes, knowing this is Dare's way of forcing us to patch things up. I haven't talked to my sister since storming out of their house. We're both stubborn as fuck, but our wars don't usually last long. In a life full of chaos and drama, Lo has been the one constant. It's always been us against the world. When we're at odds, everything feels off-kilter. I weigh my options. I could tell him no and keep this beef going. Or I could do her a solid and use this as a way to clear the air. Plus, I can't pass up the opportunity to fuck with Allison if she happens to be there. *Unless she's the one who quit.*

"Time?" I grumble.

"Now." Then he hangs up. Yeah, he's pissed at me.

I stub out my blunt and snatch a towel from the back of a computer chair. I head for the shower, ignoring the voices trailing from downstairs. There're always stragglers after a big party, and this morning is no exception. I take a piss, rubbing a hand across my chest as I take in my reflection. I have neon paint, lipstick, and glitter coating every inch of my torso. I jump into the shower and scrub that shit off in record time. I throw on a pair of black jeans and a white tee, then walk downstairs, taking the steps two at a time.

I take the last drag of my cigarette before putting it out in front of Blackbear. I've been stalling, but I have to face Lo sooner or later. She's going to question me about where I've been and what I've been doing in between leaving school and coming here. I fucking hate lying to her, but I can't tell her that. She wouldn't understand. It's the one area in which we've never seen eye to eye.

I push the door open, walking straight through the crowded dining area to the kitchen. A frazzled Lo stops in her tracks when she sees me, a tray in each hand, lopsided ponytail, and hair in her face. She cocks her head to the side. "What are you doing here?" she asks, suspicion lacing her tone.

"Dare said you needed help," I supply. I should've known he didn't tell her. Lo has way too much pride to ask for help. There's no way she'd let Dare do it on her behalf.

"Well, he lied. You can go back to your downward spiral, or whatever the fuck it is that you're doing." She doesn't give me a chance to respond before she walks away, dropping plates off at her tables. When she comes back to the kitchen, I see a flash of hurt in her eyes, and I know I put it there. It's the main reason I didn't come back to River's Edge right away.

I clear my throat. "I'm sorry, okay? I fucked up."

She appears to weigh her options before her shoulders sag. She closes the distance between us and pulls me in for a hug, and I squeeze her back for a second before we both let go.

"You're an idiot."

"I know."

"We're going to talk about this later."

"I know," I repeat.

She tosses me a rag before turning around to grab a big gray tub, then shoves it into my abs. I grunt, curling my fingers around the sides.

"Now go bus some tables."

CHAPTER TEN

Allie

"**A**PPARENTLY, THESE EGGS WERE SUPPOSED TO be over easy," I say, pressing up on my toes to see through the pass-through window into the kitchen. "Sorry, Pete." I wince. The lady at table seven ordered scrambled, but changed her mind, and Grumpy Pete's the only one back here, cooking for a full house.

"Not what the ticket says," Pete grumbles.

"I know. I'm sorry," I say again.

"Yeah, yeah."

I tap my fingers against the counter, keeping my body close to the counter in the narrow walkway to let the other servers by. I feel heat against my back, and before I can react, a low "boo" is whispered into my ear. I lean forward as much as I can, jerking my head to see who I already know is behind me.

"Jesse," I greet, my voice flat.

"Try to contain your enthusiasm, Allie Girl." He smirks down at me. He smells like a distillery mixed with lingering traces of smoke, but there's a faint, familiar scent underneath it—his soap or maybe his shampoo. It takes me back to the night at the dorm, and an image of his mop of dark hair nuzzling against my chest and my nipple in his mouth pops into my mind, unbidden. I push it away, along with the embarrassment that never ceases to follow whenever I think about it.

I shift to the side, wishing my order was up. *How long does it take to fry a freaking egg?*

"Are you stalking me now?" He has the audacity to ask. I look over at him, rolling my eyes.

"I work here," I deadpan. "If anyone's stalking, it's you."

"Nah. My sister called in a favor. Spending time with your cheery self is just an added bonus."

I send Jesse a bratty smile, and finally Pete slides the plate of eggs toward me. I don't waste any time snatching it up. "Thanks, Pete!" Pete grunts in response.

I avoid Jesse as much as I can for the rest of my shift, even though my eyes are begging to disobey me, seeking him out of their own volition. I can't seem to escape him. Is this how it's going to be now that he's back? I still don't know *why* he's back. Lo hasn't mentioned it, and there's no way in hell I'm asking questions. She doesn't even know I *know* him.

At the end of the day, I shoot a quick text to Dylan, letting him know my shift is over. He's supposed to meet me here once I'm off. I stuff my phone into my pocket and head into the back room to grab my bag, but I halt in the hallway, hearing Jesse's voice.

"Does it matter?" he asks, irritation evident in his tone.

"Does it *matter* where you've been disappearing to? Not really, no, but the fact that you won't tell me says you're in some kind of trouble." That's Lo, and she sounds exasperated.

"Not in any trouble," he clips out. "I don't need rescuing anymore, Lo. I can take care of myself."

"Yeah, you're doing a real bang-up job, Jess. First, you mysteriously have enough money for a truck, then you're dropping out of school? I'm missing something here. Fill in the blanks."

Jesse doesn't respond, and then all of a sudden, he's prowling out of the back room, heading straight toward me. I push off the wall, trying to act casual. Not expecting anyone to be lurking around the corner, he comes close to knocking me over but stops short, centimeters from me. His hands catch my upper arms, steadying both of us. I expect some sarcastic remark, something about trying to cop a feel, maybe, but it doesn't come. I make the mistake of looking up. His tortured eyes meet mine for long seconds, his jaw clenched.

Something in his eyes gives me pause. A flash of the human behind the persona. *This* is Jesse. The fun-loving, hotshot lacrosse player? That's Shep. But then something shifts. Those eyes go vacant and a slow grin spreads over his face.

"If you wanted to touch me again, all you had to do was ask."

Annnnd, there it is.

"Not happening." I roll my eyes, shoving past him. Lo is sitting at the small table, sorting through a stack of papers.

"You okay?" I ask. I don't want to pry, but I don't want to be a jerk and not ask either.

She huffs out a laugh. "Just another day in the life."

"What's all that?" I ask, gesturing to her papers, grabbing my backpack off the hook.

"I had the crazy idea of going back to school. It's not like I'm not busy enough as it is."

"It's not crazy at all. What do you want to go for?"

"I need to get my GED, for starters. Then I was thinking about maybe getting a business degree."

"Really? I'm taking some business courses at Kerrigan."

"No shit?" she asks, surprised.

"Yeah, it's more geared toward music management, though."

"I'd expect nothing less," she says knowingly. I tend to monopolize the music selection here. In my defense, no one else seems to care all that much.

"Well, don't go finding some hotshot job anytime soon. I need you here."

I scoff. I don't think she'll have to worry about that. This town isn't exactly booming with job opportunities. Plus, I like Lo and I like working here, despite recent developments. "Deal."

I leave Lo to it, making my way out to the dining area. Like magnets, my eyes are drawn to Jesse. He pushes a hand through his hair before digging his phone out of his pocket, scowling at the screen like it personally offended him. After overhearing the conversation between him and Lo, I'm even more confused than ever. Curious. And you know what they say about curiosity…

Jesse pockets his phone and lifts his eyes to catch me staring. I fight the urge to look away. My gaze bores into him, but he's looking at me just as intently. My teeth clamp down on my lip, ignoring the stirrings of…*something* I feel in my stomach.

"Albert," I hear Dylan say from my left, breaking the spell. I whip my head in his direction.

"I didn't see you come in," I say, standing to hug him.

"Can't imagine why," he deadpans, pulling me into his warmth. My eyebrows draw together in confusion as I pull back.

"What?"

"Nothing." He sighs. "I just don't like that fucker." He flicks his chin.

"Who, Jesse? You don't have to worry about that."

"Good."

"Is there something I should know?" I ask, legitimately confused.

"You're like my little sister, Al." I huff out a laugh and look away. *Your little sister that you made out with,* I want to say. "I just want to make sure you're... I don't know. Safe."

"Are you hungry?" I ask, changing the subject. I get the feeling Dylan feels a sense of responsibility toward me. I don't know if it's because he knew my dad or what, but I don't want to be a burden on him, and I don't want what we have to change. Back home, I didn't have any real friends. I don't want to lose him. I want things to go back to the way they were. *Before* the funeral.

"Nah. I ate earlier."

I nod, feeling uncomfortable with Dylan for the first time in our relationship. Needing to break the awkwardness, I reach for his hand on top of the table. His dark eyes lift to mine through thick lashes.

"Are we okay?" My voice sounds small even to my own ears, and I mentally kick myself for sounding like such a girl.

Dylan frowns. "What kind of question is that?"

Discomfort rolls through me at what I'm about to say. "We haven't really talked about what happened—"

"Don't." Dylan's nostrils flare and he shuts his eyes. "You were grieving. I was upset. That's all it was."

"Agreed," I say firmly with a nod. "I don't want it to change things."

"We're fine. Listen, I gotta meet the band…" he trails off, dropping my hand before he stands.

"Yeah, okay. Let me know when you play next?"

"Sure. You need a ride?" I should say yes, but asking a favor from him feels weird right about now. I'll call Halston to pick me up instead.

"I've got one."

He gives me a brusque nod before turning to leave.

When my marketing class is over, I slide my laptop into my backpack, then check my phone to see what Halston wants. I could hear my phone buzzing from my bag all through class. Three missed calls and one text.

Halston: Call me after class. It's important.

I frown, typing out a quick response.

Me: Everything okay?

Halston: Someone snitched.

Shit. I don't need to ask for clarification. We knew this was a possibility. I hitch my backpack onto my shoulder and make my way across the small campus. When I get to the dorm room, Halston is sitting on her bed, legs crossed, puppy dog eyes directed at me.

"What happened?" I ask, dropping my bag to the floor as I kick the door shut behind me.

"Stephanie happened," she mutters.

"But Stephanie knows the deal," I say, confused. Stephanie is the RA, and she has to know I've been staying here. She saw me in a towel, carrying my shower caddy down the hall, for fuck's sake.

"Apparently, someone complained, so she couldn't look the other way anymore."

"Are you in trouble? I can tell them—"

"No." She shakes her head. "Nothing like that. They just gave me a warning. I'm just worried about *you*."

"Well, thank fuck for that." The last thing I want is for her to be punished for trying to help me out.

"What are you going to do?"

I shrug. "I'll probably call Dylan." I hate depending on him, but I have two more months before my grandparents' vacation rental is free, and there's no way I can afford to stay in a hotel. Halston wiggles her eyebrows at the mention of Dylan.

"Can you take me with you?"

I laugh, lifting my suitcase from the closet and plopping it on my bed. "If you want to live in a party pad with piss-sprinkled toilet seats and moldy food in the fridge, by all means…"

"Okay. Maybe I'll just visit," she says, scrunching her nose in disgust. Truthfully, it's not *that* bad. But not even her love for boys can outweigh her high-maintenance tendencies. Halston comes from a rich family, so I'm not sure why she even bothers with dorm living.

Halston helps me throw most everything into my suitcase. I only fill my backpack with essentials—an extra outfit, toiletries, phone charger, and, of course, my trusty CD player.

"I'll be back for that," I say, flinging my arm toward my suitcase.

"You'll be back *every day*," she corrects.

She throws her arms around me, smashing my face to her chest. "Can't. Breathe."

"I wish you could stay." She pouts after releasing me.

"Halston," I say, reaching up to grasp both of her shoulders. "Get it together. I'm moving out of the building, not out of the country."

"I know." She rolls her eyes. "But I'm bored already."

"Call a boy," I say dryly. "Better yet, call *Sully*."

"If you insist," she says with a dramatic sigh, flopping onto her bed.

Half an hour later, Halston's dropping me off at Blackbear. I haven't heard back from Dylan, so I figure I'll wait here until he calls me back. I'll just commandeer a booth, turn up my headphones, and work on an assignment that's due next week.

"What are you doing here?" Lo asks, looking up from the barstool, the chewed tip of her pen tapping against her chin.

"Got some time to kill," I explain, patting my backpack. "Mind if I steal a booth?"

"Knock yourself out." She laughs.

"Thanks."

I find the booth in the most secluded part of the bar, set my stuff up, and open Photoshop. But for some reason, I can't seem to focus on the project at hand—which happens to be a mock flyer for a non-existent band.

I stare at the screen of my phone, considering calling my mom and coming clean about my living situation, but I can't bring myself to pull the trigger. I'm not ready for the lecture and the guilt trip that is sure to come along with her help. My mom is one of those people who expects you to worship at her feet for the simplest of favors. She once gave me a ride to a concert in downtown LA, and I swear, I still hear about how she got stuck in traffic, and that it was what she got for trying to do something nice for someone.

Never again.

No, I won't call her and beg for help, but calling just to check in won't hurt. Lying to her about my living situation has been easier than I expected. We've only spoken a handful of times since I've been here. Out of sight, out of mind, I guess. Before I can talk myself out of it, I scroll through my call log and click on her number. I play with the sugar packets on the table as her phone rings. And rings. And rings. Just when it's about to go to voicemail, she picks up.

"Hi, honey," Mom sing-songs. Even though we don't have the best relationship, her voice still feels like home. I can picture her sitting in a hammock, smoking weed, and meditating outdoors. My stomach twists in an unexpected way, and suddenly, I want to go home. I want LA sunshine and the beach and my *home*. Except, home isn't there anymore.

"Hi, Mom."

"Everything okay?"

"Yeah, I'm just getting some homework done. Classes and work are kicking my ass."

"That's great, sweetie," Mom says in a distracted tone, and I know she's already checked out of the conversation.

"Yeah. Hey, I was thinking. What if I came and visited you guys? Spring Break is coming up soon." *You guys* meaning Mom and her new boyfriend. My mom uses men as a life raft. I didn't think this one would last more than a few weeks, but here we are, nine months later and they're shacked up together.

"I'm sure you're busy living your life, Allison. I know I'd be living it up if I had a house on the water when I was your age."

"I want to," I insist. Losing a parent at a young age has a way of making you hyperaware of your loved ones' mortality. Even though we don't always get along, she's all I have left.

My mom hesitates, telling me all I need to know. "Listen, we don't have the house quite readyyet, and you know airfare to Hawaii is expensive, especially on such short notice…" She lists off her excuses. "Maybe once we're settled, we can figure something out. If it's meant to be, it'll be."

Ah, her favorite response. I huff out a humorless laugh. Being rejected by the person who brought you into this world feels like the worst kind of betrayal. "Sorry I called."

"Allison, don't be—"

I hit *end* and toss my phone to the table. How I share DNA with that woman, I'll never know. She's flighty and love-obsessed. I'm grounded and wouldn't recognize love if it hit me in the face. She loves pretty dresses and makeup. I love my Docs and vintage band tees. But she's my *mom*. My dad would have moved mountains for me. He promised me the moon, shared his love of music with me, and the only thing he loved more than performing was me. Mom, on the other hand… She loves me, but I don't think she loves being my mom. When I was younger, she insisted on having me stay with her for the majority of the time. I thought, *hey, she must love me if she's fighting for me,* but now I know it was because the thought of being alone is utterly fucking unbearable to her.

I put my headphones on, turning the volume all the

way up as I focus on my screen. I refuse to dwell on my mother, who is in Hawaii living her best life. Meanwhile, I'm over here technically homeless. I'm not bitter at all. I'm not sure how much time has passed when a hand waves in front of my face. I startle, looking up to see Lo.

I take my headphones off, tucking an unruly strand of hair behind my ears.

"Want anything to eat before I tell Pete to head out? It's dead tonight, so I'm going to close up early."

"Oh," I say, shocked by how late it's gotten. "I'm good. Let me just…" I save my work, then start to gather my things.

"You're fine. Stay as long as you want. Just lock up for me before you go, yeah?" Lo drops her keys onto the table in front of me.

"Are you sure?"

She looks at me with an eyebrow arched. "Why wouldn't I be? I have a spare set at home anyway."

I shrug. I don't know the rules about these things. "I'll be done soon."

"Stay however long you need."

I look past her, seeing her boyfriend Dare waiting for her at the door, sporting a plain white tee, arms full of colorful ink, brooding expression. Jesus, that guy is hot in that intense, intimidating-as-fuck kind of way. He owns Bad intentions, the tattoo shop next door, so they're back and forth a lot.

Once Lo is within reach, he grabs a handful of her ass, pulling her toward him for a kiss. She melts into him, laughing as she bites into his lower lip. He groans, getting lost in her before his eyelids pop open, landing on me. I look away, cheeks burning, and then he's tugging on her hand, pulling her outside. I wasn't watching them because I'm some kind of perv. I guess I was just trying to understand. It's not that I don't think love exists. On the contrary, actually. Love is real. Powerful. It has the potential to destroy you. To start wars and end lives. Love is a weapon. Love is dangerous, and I want nothing to do with it.

I watched how love made my mom the happiest person in the world. Then she became the *craziest* person in the world. And when my dad died, the *saddest* person in the world, even though they hadn't been together for years. Don't even get me started on the men who've come and gone since. I've found my mother sobbing on the bathroom floor, unable to work, eat, or function more times than I can count. All because of some guy. Why would anyone subject themselves to that kind of emotional torture? I promised myself at a young age that I'd never be like her. I'd never let love make me crazy.

Pushing those thoughts away, I look down at my phone, deliberating my next move. I'm low on options. I could call Dylan. *Again.* I could try to find a hotel room in my budget for tonight only—not likely in this tourist town.

Or...I could simply stay here. Lo *did* say I could stay as long as I want. What's the worst that could happen? I stand, walking toward the entrance, and flip the lock. Pete must have left when I was stuck in my thoughts, not bothering to say goodbye. *Typical.* I raid the kitchen, looking for something small and simple to ease the burning pit in my stomach. I settle for a banana, tossing the peel into the trash. I munch on it, flipping all the lights off around the bar, leaving only the back room on.

Once I'm finished, I set the alarm on my phone, so that I can be out of here long before people show up, and crawl back into my booth, curling into a ball on my side. I lift my hood over my head and pull my sleeves down to cover most of my hands in an effort to get warmer. Fingering the cracked leather bench, I start to form a mental game plan, but I don't get far before my eyelids grow heavy and sleep takes over.

CHAPTER ELEVEN

Allie

FOUR DAYS I'VE BEEN SECRETLY SLEEPING AT Blackbear, and even though Dylan has since returned my calls, I haven't clued him in on my living situation. It sounds crazy, but I'd actually rather sleep in a booth than stay at his party pad. It's quiet at Blackbear. Private. I can eat, sleep, do my schoolwork, and stare at my journal, willing the words to come without interruption. The only thing I can't do is shower, but I was able to sneak into the dorms a couple of times. I know I need to figure something else out. The longer I stay, the more likely it is that I'll get caught. I feel guilty for taking advantage of Lo when she's been nothing but nice to me, but I'm not hurting anyone.

I'm walking through the quad on my way to my next class, the ground still frozen solid, even though the sun is trying to peek out for the first time this year, when I hear someone shout from behind me.

"Hey," a boy with a blond buzzed cut says, jogging up to me. He's wearing a flannel over a Vandals tee and fitted jeans. Chuck Taylors on his feet. "Allison, right?" he says, smoothing a flat hand over his short hair.

"Yeah," I say slowly, trying to figure out if I've met him somewhere before.

"Garrett." He points to himself. "We're in music marketing together," he supplies, reading the question mark on my face.

"Oh, right."

"You like Gutterpunk?" he asks knowingly.

"How did you—"

"Lucky guess," he jokes, pointing at my binder full of various band stickers.

"I'm surprised anyone in this town knows who they are."

"I'm surprised anyone in this *generation* knows who they are," he tosses back.

"Touché." I laugh, knowing it's true. Gutterpunk is a sloppy punk band—as the name suggests—from the nineties. With them being from Huntington Beach, everyone knew who they were back home.

"Did you know they're playing a secret show this weekend?"

"Here? No way."

"Way. They're playing at The Lamppost, if you want to go together, maybe?"

My lips twist, contemplating. I don't know him, but we have a class together. That has to count for something. Plus, he clearly has good taste in music, so he's automatically cooler than ninety-five percent of the people I've met here.

"Or we can meet there, if that's less weird." He gives me an out, no doubt sensing my hesitation.

"Let's do that." I smile, genuinely excited to go. I haven't been to a show since…well, since my dad was alive. "Where's The Lamppost, though?" I've never heard of it before, and my dad knew of every venue in a two-hundred-mile radius.

"If I told you, it wouldn't be a secret, would it?" He raises a brow. "Give me your number. I'll text you the address Friday night."

I'm way too intrigued to say no. I take his phone from his proffered hand. "And how do you know about this place?" I ask as I type my number in, suspicion lacing my tone.

"I know people," he says cryptically. I can't tell if he's pulling my leg or not, so I don't comment.

"I'll see you Friday then." I slap his phone into his palm and he flashes me a smile.

"It's a date."

I open my mouth to argue, but he cuts me off, walking away from me backwards. "It's a figure of speech. Relax."

Right. *Not everyone is hitting on you, Allison.* I spin around, heading for my next class.

Class goes by quickly, and then I meet up with Halston to hang out for a little bit before I head back to Blackbear.

"I'm going to start charging you rent," Lo jokes, and I stop short, nerves bubbling in my stomach. "I'm kidding, Allison." She laughs. "You're my best employee. I wish everyone was as dedicated," she says loudly for Jesse's benefit, who's sitting at the bar with a plate of food.

"I don't fucking work here."

I eye the bowl of suckers next to him, and he follows my gaze, smirking when he realizes my thought process. Instead of handing them to me like a decent human, he slides them closer to himself, daring me to get close enough to take one. We haven't spoken since the day I overheard him arguing with Lo. He hasn't been around much, but on the rare occasion he is, he hasn't so much as looked in my direction.

"Well, you should," Lo says, her voice monotone.

I leave them to their bickering, walking past the bar toward the back room. But Jesse sits sideways on his stool and throws out an arm, stopping me with the bowl of suckers at my stomach. He raises a brow when I don't immediately dig in.

I roll my eyes, quickly finding the brownish label I'm looking for, then move past him. I hear him chuckle behind me before Lo's chastising follows.

"Don't even think about it," Lo warns.

I can't see Jesse's reaction, and if he responds, I don't hear it.

"I mean it. Leave her alone. If you fuck this up, I'll be even more short-staffed."

She doesn't need to worry about that.

I don't hear the rest of the conversation, but when I come back out front, ready for my shift, Jess is gone. I let out a sigh of relief. Or maybe it's one of disappointment.

CHAPTER TWELVE

Jess

"**W**HERE THE FUCK ARE YOU GOING?" SULLY asks as I swipe my keys off the counter. Not having a place of my own is getting old fast. You'd think I'd be used to it after twenty years of bouncing from shitty apartment to even shittier apartment, never knowing when my mom would skip paying rent to support her drug habit instead.

"Not in the mood tonight," I say, referring to the kick-back-turned-party taking place around us. I'm sick of this whole fucking scene. He nods, knowing what I mean. He's probably the only one who knows the real me.

"Hit me up tomorrow."

Walking outside, I make a beeline for my truck, not stopping to make small talk with anyone lingering in the front yard. I don't know where the hell I'm going, but I throw the gear in drive, laying on the gas. I'm on autopilot as I drive through town, wondering how everything got so fucked up. I've been staying at Sully's, not wanting to look Lo in the eye and have to lie to her every goddamn day, but the longer I stay there, the better going home sounds.

I'm about to pass Blackbear and Bad Intentions, and at the last second, I jerk the wheel, skidding into the dark parking lot. Empty. Quiet. Fully stocked with liquor. I don't know why I didn't think of it sooner.

I park, killing the engine, then jump out, fishing my keys to Blackbear from my pocket as I approach the door. A light shines from somewhere in the back, and I cup my hands on the glass of the door, trying to see inside. When I don't see anything out of the ordinary, I shrug it off, turning the lock, then I close the door behind me. Someone must've forgotten to turn it off earlier. I go straight for the bar, grabbing the bottle of Jack from the shelf. I don't get the lid off before I hear a faint noise from somewhere behind me. I pause, listening, scanning the dining area.

Quietly setting the bottle onto the bar, I start to move in the direction it came from. Just when I think I'm trippin', I hear it again. A soft moan. My eyes snap toward the sound and I see something hanging off the edge of one of the booths. Grabbing my phone, I turn the flashlight on, seeing a foot. A woman's dainty ass foot with black-painted toenails. *The fuck?* I trace up the body attached to said foot with my flashlight, only to realize it's *Allison*. She's lying on her side, headphones covering her ears, fists tucked under her chin, lips slightly parted.

What the fuck is she doing here? At first, I think she must've fallen asleep after her shift, but as I take in the scene in front of me, I know it's more than that. Her open backpack is on the table with her toothbrush lying on top of a wad of clothes, and her boots with socks stuffed inside are on the floor next to her. I tamp down the urge to wake her up and ask what the fuck is going on and shoot off a text to Sully instead.

Me: Text your girl and find out where Allison lives.

Not thirty seconds pass before my phone vibrates in my hand.

Sully: Now?

Me: ASAP.

Minutes pass as I stare at her sleeping form, waiting for a response. Her hair is in a messy wad on top of her head, strands sticking out every which way. I can hear the faint sound of the song playing on her CD player that's propped on top of the table. She looks so fucking serene, like she doesn't have a care in the world, even though she's posted up in a goddamn bar.

My phone vibrates in my hand again, lighting up with a text.

Sully: She was staying with Halston at her dorm until the RA kicked her out. Halston says she's staying with some dude now.

Interesting. I work my jaw, having a good idea who "some dude" is. The only question is, why isn't she there? Why is she sleeping in a fucking booth instead of a cushy bed? *Trouble in paradise?* I back away quietly as I came, as I start to formulate a plan.

"You hiring homeless people now?" I ask sarcastically. "You're more desperate than I thought."

"What are you talking about?" Lo asks, a frown marring her features, making her look more like our mother than I'd ever admit out loud. Those are fighting words.

"You didn't know?" I play dumb. "Your girl Allison's camped out in Blackbear right now, and from the looks of it, she's been staying there for a while."

"Allison? As in Allison Parrish, my server, Allison?" Lo seems shocked, but then I see the moment realization dawns in her eyes. "She's stayed late almost every night this week. I figured she just needed a place to study, so I gave her keys." She shrugs. "Doesn't she live with her dad? Maybe shit hit the fan at home."

"Her dad?" I didn't realize she *had* a dad. I mean, everyone has a dad—except us, of course—but she's never spoken about him and I've never seen him. I figured she was here by herself for school. "No clue. I barely know the chick." Sort of the truth. I know her body, but I don't know shit about *her*.

"Yeah, when I first started at Blackbear, she used to come in with her dad all the time. Haven't seen him in a long time, though," she adds as an afterthought. "Maybe I'm mixing customers up. But I could've sworn…"

I shrug. "Either way, you've got a stowaway." I grab an apple from the bowl on her counter, taking a big bite before turning to leave, now that I've planted that little seed of information. Lo can't resist helping an underdog. It's an unfortunate side effect of growing up the way we did.

"When are you going to come home, Jess?" she asks grudgingly. I know it killed her to be the one to ask.

"I don't know. *Is* this my home?"

"What the fuck kind of question is that?" She's pissed, and for some reason, it takes a weight off my shoulders. She's with Dare now, all fucking coupled up. I'm not trying to be a third wheel. I was supposed to be gone, making a life for myself. Instead, I ended up right back where I started with nothing to show for it. I have no one to blame but myself—least of all Lo—but I still find myself feeling bitter.

Truth is, I'm not sure I'm ready to come back. Sully's is getting old, but at least I can drink and smoke and fuck and coast in peace. No one to call me on my shit. No one to guilt-trip me. No one to look at me with disappointment in their eyes.

Lo comes up behind me, spinning me around by my elbow. I focus on a spot on the wall behind her, not meeting her eyes. "Your home is wherever I am. It's always been that way, always will be. If you want to go fuck off and do your thing, fine. But you always have a home with me. School or no school. Dare or no Dare. Whether we're fighting or not. It's you and me."

She says that now, but if she knew where I've been and what I've been doing, she'd feel a hell of a lot differently.

Lo pulls me in for a hug and I let her, resting my chin on the top of her head. I fucking hate when she does this, making me feel my emotions and shit. I pull back, clearing my throat.

"Stay—or go—but I'm going to bed. Apparently, I've got a squatter to deal with in the morning."

I bob my head and turn for the door. She looks disappointed that I'm leaving, but I'll be back. *Sooner than she thinks*.

"Oh, and Lo?" I say, one hand on the doorknob. She looks at me in question. "Don't tell her I told you."

Her eyebrows pinch together, perplexed.

"Shit's embarrassing."

She nods, her eyes softening like I'm some fucking saint. "I won't tell anyone about that bleeding heart you got there either."

I roll my eyes, giving her the middle finger, hearing her laughter trailing after me.

CHAPTER THIRTEEN

Allie

"**G**OOD MORNING, SLEEPING BEAUTY." THE DRY voice cuts through my sleep and I jump up, pushing the headphones off my ears, heart racing, to see Lo sitting on the seat opposite me.

Fuck. Shit. Fuck. I wince, my neck hurting from the position I slept in and my left ear sore from the headphone pressing into it all night.

"Relax," Lo says, both hands cradling a mug. "Coffee?" She slides a second mug toward me. I eye it, hesitating.

"Are you mad?" I ask sheepishly. I consider saying that I simply fell asleep. But I've been caught. Might as well not add insult to injury by lying about it.

She exhales audibly, cocking her head to the side. "Depends. Are you going to tell me what's going on?"

I take a sip of the coffee—*the black coffee*—trying to choke down the bitter taste to buy time. Lo waits patiently, big, expressive eyes boring into me.

"My grandparents have a vacation rental here, and they said I could stay there while I go to school."

"Mhm," she prompts, folding her hands under her chin and listening intently.

"They rented it out to a retired couple, and apparently

forgot about it. By the time they figured it out, I was already packed and ready to go." Not to mention, my mom had already sold the house and was on a plane to Hawaii. But I keep that part to myself. "I was staying with a friend at the dorms, but someone complained and, well… here I am." I shrug.

"Where's your dad?"

My chest squeezes at the mention of him, and I hope to hell I don't do something stupid like start to cry. Grief is a weird thing. You think you're doing fine. You think you're *over it*, for lack of a better phrase, but the smallest thing can have you choking on despair. Scents. Places. *Songs.* Nothing is worse than being blindsided by a song, and with my dad, there's a song for every occasion. "Alison"—my namesake—by Elvis Costello, "Good Riddance" by Green Day, the song I chose for his funeral, and pretty much anything by Radiohead are some of the biggest offenders.

When I don't answer right away, Lo continues. "You *did* used to come in with him, right? Or am I crazy?"

"You're not crazy," I say, trying to keep my voice light and easy. Unaffected. "I didn't think you remembered us. He was in a car accident last year. He didn't make it."

"Shit," she breathes. "I'm sorry. I never know what to say in these situations. Other than *that sucks.*"

I huff out a laugh. "That it does."

"And your mom?"

I sigh. "My mom…is a complicated creature."

"I get that more than most," Lo says bitterly.

"She thinks I'm at my grandparents' vacation rental, and my grandparents think I have other arrangements until their place opens up."

Lo nods, appearing to consider something. Her lips

twist as she studies me for long seconds, before seemingly coming to a decision, slapping her palms down onto the table.

"What?" I ask, narrowing my eyes at her.

"You do now."

"I do now *what*? I'm not following."

"Have other arrangements. Get your crap. You're coming with me." She stands, gathering my stuff.

"Wait. You're not suggesting—"

"That you stay with me? Yeah, I am." Her eyebrow is raised in a challenge.

"That's super nice of you and all, but I can't."

"I know that I was in your position not too long ago, and someone took a chance on me when I needed it the most. Without him, I don't know where I'd be right now."

"Dare?" I ask. I don't know their story, but it doesn't take a detective to put the pieces together. Lo nods.

Still, I can't stay there. Jesse being the biggest reason. Besides the fact that I'd have to see him way more than I'd like to, how would that make me look? Like the stalker of the century, that's how. *Hey, I know we almost hooked up and then you ghosted me, but I'm going to move in with you and your sister. Hope you don't mind!*

Not happening.

"Look, I really appreciate it, but I'll figure something else out." I stuff my CD player into my backpack and Lo flattens her lips, like she wants to tease me about it, but refrains.

"Listen, I get it. You don't want to take handouts. But it's temporary. Your situation has an expiration date. You're my friend. I fail to see the problem here."

"I don't know." I sigh, rubbing at my forehead. It's

tempting. Really tempting. But it also feels like asking for trouble.

"You can stay in my brother's room until we get the spare room set up."

I give her an incredulous look, instantly shaking my head. Lo smiles her wide smile, laughing at my reaction. "I should probably mention that Jess doesn't currently live there."

Oh. *Oh*. I assumed he did. Well, that changes things. Slightly.

"Okay," I concede. "It's just for two months. I promise."

"Deal. Let's go."

"What, *now*?"

"Yeah. From the looks of it, you could use a shower," she says bluntly, pointing at my crazy hair and wrinkled clothes from the day before.

"I have to get to class." I laugh, trying to smooth down my bed head with my hands. I'll have to settle for brushing my teeth and a quick change of clothes in Halston's dorm.

"You have my number?" Lo asks, and I nod. Of course I do. I work for her. "Let me know when you're coming over."

"Are you sure Dare will be okay with this?"

"You let me deal with that."

Super comforting. Note the sarcasm. I swing my bag onto my shoulder and slip into my shoes before hurrying toward the door. If I leave now, I can make it on foot without being late.

"Allison," Lo shouts my name just as I'm pushing the door open. I pause, turning to face her.

"What's up?"

She gestures to her chin. "At least wipe the drool first."

"How well do you know this chick?" Dylan asks belatedly. I told him I was moving in with Lo about an hour ago, and he just blurted it out. Clearly, he's still thinking about it. I tilt my head to see him better from my position—lying on the couch with my head on his lap—as we watch some Quentin Tarantino movie.

"Well enough." I lift a shoulder. He peers down at me, those dark eyes framed by thick lashes. Silver hoop in his lip glinting in the light cast by the TV.

"Any roommates?"

"Just her boyfriend." I don't mention the fact that Lo is Jesse's brother since he seems to have some weird beef with him. I sit up and face him, crossing my legs on the cushion. "Why have you been so weird with me lately?" I finally ask the question that's been bugging me.

Dylan works his jaw, his eyes locked onto the screen, not meeting mine. "I haven't."

"You've been ignoring me," I accuse. He doesn't deny it. "And now you're getting all big-brother-y on me."

He huffs, shaking his head. "What?" I push, needing him to give me something, but getting Dylan to talk to me is like pulling teeth. I know he had it rough growing up, and whatever he went through has made him more guarded than Fort Knox.

"I've just got a lot on my mind."

"Like what?"

"Not important. So, you want a ride? Show me your new place?" Dylan helped me grab the rest of my stuff from Halston's dorm after class, so it's already in his car.

"Sure." I know he's changing the subject, but I let him get away with it. For now.

"Are you sure this is okay?" I ask. Dare's on a stool, sketching something out at the counter while Lo cooks. It's all very…domestic. I feel like an interloper, standing in the middle of their kitchen with my hands in my back pockets, not having a clue how to act or what to do. This right here is why I'd rather be at the restaurant.

"Would you stop asking that?" Lo says, turning away from the stove to point her spatula at me. "It's not a big deal." When Dare doesn't say anything, she plucks a grape from the bowl next to her and pegs him in the head with it. He looks up at her with a scowl and she raises both eyebrows, jerking her head in my direction.

"Better you than Adrian," he says, barely sparing me a glance. I don't know who Adrian is, but I'll take it. Lo snorts.

"This is not an either/or situation. Once Adrian catches wind of her being here, you really think he'll stay away?"

Dare drops his pencil onto the pad of paper and stands, making his way over to Lo. He cages her in, both hands braced on the counter behind her. I'd probably shit my pants if I were her, but she simply smiles, wrapping her arms around his neck. "Just another reason we should get away for a while. Just the *two* of us," he says pointedly.

"You know I can't right now."

"Why not?" he pushes, and I get the feeling this is an ongoing conversation.

"I'm just going to grab a shower," I say awkwardly, hitching a thumb behind me before I slink away.

"Towels are under the sink!" Lo yells after me.

After hightailing it upstairs, I go to Jesse's room—my room for the time being—and sit on the edge of the bed. "This is weird," I mutter to myself as I take in my surroundings. The walls are stark white and bare, free of any holes, telling me he didn't have any pictures or posters on them. Back home, my walls were painted black—one of the few times having a hippie, carefree mother who allowed me to express myself came in handy—and almost completely covered in posters of my favorite bands, album covers, records, and pictures from concerts. My room told a story about my life and who I am. This room is devoid of any personality. This room tells no story.

Morbid curiosity taking over, I stand and open the drawers of the black dresser. They're all empty. I check the nightstand next, finding nothing but a pack of condoms. I slam the drawer shut, turning for the closet. Sliding the white wooden door open, I find a beat-up skateboard with the grip tape peeled halfway off the deck. I turn the board over to see faded stickers of various skate brands and *Jesse* carved into the wood in jagged letters.

Lacrosse player. Asshole. Playboy. *Skater?* How many personalities does this guy have?

I grab a change of clothes from my suitcase before slinging it and my other bag into the closet, then head for the bathroom for a shower. A shower that I don't even have to wait in line for.

Home sweet home.

The first three days at Lo and Dare's, I felt awkward and on edge. I kept looking over my shoulder, as if Jesse was going to pop up at any moment and I'd have to explain why and how I'm in his sister's house but, thankfully, he doesn't come. He may not be here physically, but his face is everywhere I turn, taunting me. In the hallway next to my room hangs a framed diploma, a scholarship letter with his Lobos logo, and a picture of him and Lo at his graduation, cigarette dangling from his lip, appearing aloof as always, but the happiness shining through his eyes is unmistakable.

The refrigerator is full of pictures, too. Most of them are of Jesse wrestling and playing lacrosse, but there's one photo that always gives me pause. It's a young Jesse, sitting on a tattered couch with a southwestern print. His too-long hair hangs in front of one eye as he holds a skateboard on his lap. Jeans ripped at the knee, once-white socks that are almost black on the bottom, and no shirt. The carpet around him is stained and the table in front of him is cluttered with dirty dishes and various takeout boxes. His eyes are purple underneath, and he's way too skinny, but he smiles like he doesn't have a care in the world.

Other than the guilt of feeling like I'm hiding something from Lo by omitting the truth about my history with her brother and having to be reminded of his existence at every turn, I like staying here. Both Lo and Dare work a lot, and I have a lot more time to myself than I thought I would. Like right now, they're both closing tonight, so I have the house to myself. Plucking a black bikini from my bag, I make quick work of getting changed. Lo told me to help myself to the Jacuzzi in the backyard, but I didn't want to risk using it when other people were around.

I grab my phone and wrap my towel around myself before heading downstairs. When I don't see or hear anyone, I make my way through the kitchen and out the back door. Once outside, the night air chills my skin, and I shiver, hurrying to open the top of the Jacuzzi. I spread my towel out on the closed portion of the cover and hit shuffle on my playlist. I rarely ever listen to music on my phone, but headphones and hot tubs don't mix. "Criminal" by Fiona Apple starts to play as I twist my hair up into a messy bun. I dip my toes into the blissfully hot water and slowly submerge the rest of my body.

I fiddle with the controls until the jets come on, then sit with my back to one of them, my head resting on the ledge. I close my eyes, singing along, as I feel my body start to loosen with each minute. I don't know why or how it happens, but suddenly, Jesse pops into my mind uninvited. My subconscious and I don't get along, because this seems to be her favorite pastime—torturing me with memories of the night I'd rather forget ever happened. I can almost feel him on my skin, feel his hips shifting between my legs before pressing against me.

I'm pathetic.

With the hot water on my sensitive skin, the jets vibrating against me, and thoughts of Jesse, I start to feel a familiar stir between my legs. My pulse quickens, and I squeeze my thighs together to ease the ache.

Hot tongue flicking against my nipples. Hazel eyes peering up at me.

Fuck it. It's been too long since I've had any kind of release. Maybe if I give my body what it wants, it will stop reacting to Jesse like a bitch in heat.

My hand snakes down below the bubbles, finding the

heat between my legs. I rub myself through the fabric of my bathing suit, slowly at first. I allow myself to imagine it's Jesse touching me, my legs parting slightly. My hand moves faster, my breath coming in quick, short pants. Biting my lip, I feel my orgasm building. I hold my breath, waiting for it to wash over me…but then it slips just out of reach. *Gone.* Just like that.

"Ugh." I let out a frustrated growl, slapping at the water.

"Need a hand?"

My eyes fly open to see Jesse standing in front of me as I jolt up, water splashing everywhere before I sink below the bubbles from the jets. The lingering arousal coursing through me is instantly replaced with dread, my stomach twisting and ears burning with embarrassment.

"What the hell! What are you doing here?" I shout, folding my arms over my chest.

"What am *I* doing here? Last I checked, this is my house."

"Not anymore!" I reach behind me for my towel, but I come up empty. I spin around, knowing I left it right here.

"Looking for this?" Jesse taunts, dangling my towel from his fingers. Oh God. If he was out here long enough to snag my towel without me noticing… I can't even finish that thought.

Calling on counterfeit confidence, I stand and step out of the hot tub, ignoring the light-headedness I feel, and march up to him. "Towel," I demand, holding my hand out.

"Come get it." When I get close, he pulls his hand back, forcing me to come closer. I step forward, my wet chest nearly touching his. I'm dripping on him, leaving a puddle at our feet, but he doesn't back down, and neither do I. I reach for it, but he smirks, raising his arm above his head. I roll my eyes and press up onto my tiptoes. My chest rubs against his and his eyes lock onto where our bodies meet. I take the opportunity to jump up, finally jerking the towel from his grasp.

"I win." I smile, quickly wrapping it around me, forcing myself to take unhurried steps as I walk away from him.

"I just wanted to see your tits bounce, so who's the real winner here?"

I look over my shoulder to scowl at him.

"You played your role perfectly, though," he praises.

CHAPTER FOURTEEN

Jess

THE MOMENT ALLISON'S OUT OF SIGHT, I ADJUST MY dick that strains against my pants. I knew she'd be here alone, so I couldn't resist coming over to see my little plan come to fruition with my own eyes. But the boner gods were really smiling down on me, because I never thought I'd find her getting herself off. Half-naked. Wet. *Fuck.* I got the first good look at her body, because that night in the dark dorm? Didn't even come close to doing her justice. Small, hourglass figure. Fat ass. Don't even get me started on those tits.

After zero deliberation, I seek her out. I already spotted her stuff in my room when I got here, so I head for the stairs. *So much for always having a place to come home to.* But I'm not complaining. In fact, it makes this all a little sweeter, knowing she's already in my bed. I take the steps two at a time, then push the cracked door of my bedroom open. Allison's already dressed, another baggy shirt that falls mid-thigh. Bare legs. Her hair is still up high on her head, the still-wet baby hairs stuck to the skin of her neck.

"Remind me again why I can't fuck you."

"Maybe because you say things like that," she says, nose scrunched, cheeks red.

"You're blushing," I accuse. She's actually fucking blushing.

"I'm overheated."

"Obviously." I take a step closer.

"From the Jacuzzi," she deadpans, rolling her eyes. She scoops her wet bathing suit off the floor before walking into the attached bathroom and tossing it into the hamper.

"You keep telling yourself that."

When she comes back into the room, she stands on the opposite side of the bed, putting distance between us. "Look, I'm sorry if it's weird that I'm here. Your sister doesn't like to take no for an answer—"

"Runs in the family."

She ignores my interjection. "And it's just temporary. She doesn't know about our..." she rambles, trailing off as she gestures between the two of us.

"*Our...?*" I prompt, eyebrow raised.

"Our...transgression."

"Transgression? Is that what we're calling it?"

"Well, what would you call it?"

"Blue balls. I'd call that blue balls." She snorts out a laugh, rolling her eyes. "Do I make you uncomfortable?"

"Despite your best efforts, no."

"You're a terrible liar."

"Can I ask you a question? One you'll actually answer with a serious response?" she asks, ignoring my accusation.

"Shoot."

"Why *did* you leave like that? I mean, you seemed into it, and then..." Her hand falls, slapping against her thigh.

I give her a lazy smirk. "Is that what you think? That I just lost interest?"

"What the hell was I supposed to think?"

I move around the bed, eating up the distance between us. "Leaving before I got the chance to fuck you will go down as one of my biggest regrets. My dick is still mad at me."

She laughs, shaking her head.

"I'm serious. I got a phone call that I couldn't ignore." The same kind of phone call that eventually led to me getting kicked from the team. The same kind of phone call that is forever fucking up my shot at a normal life. "Now that that's cleared up, ready to finish what we started?"

"Not happening."

"Why the fuck not? I want you. You obviously want me."

"Oh, *obviously*, huh?"

"If I touched you right now, would you be wet for me?"

"And there you go again. You can't just say things like that."

"Why not?"

"I don't know," she admits.

"Because you like it?"

She doesn't have a response for that.

"That night was a momentary lapse of sanity. And now that I'm staying with your sister, I just think it's best if we don't… I don't know." She fumbles to find the words. "Complicate things."

"What's complicated about it?"

"Sex is always complicated."

"Whatever you say, Allie Girl."

"So, we're on the same page?"

"We're not even reading the same book."

She sighs, plopping down onto my bed. "Please. I really need this to work out."

"What are you doing here, anyway?" I don't tell her that I played a part in getting her here. I know what it's like to not know where you're going to sleep that night, or when you're going to get your next meal. I don't know Allison's situation, but the fact that she was sleeping in a booth tells me it isn't all sunshine and roses.

"It's only temporary."

"You said that part already."

She glares at me. "I was living at the dorms with Halston without permission. I got kicked out, but in two months, I'll have a place to stay." She gives me a bratty smile, crossing her arms. "Happy?"

Two months of living with Allison? *This should be fun.* "Ecstatic."

CHAPTER FIFTEEN

Allie

"THIS IS THE LONGEST DAY IN THE HISTORY OF ever," I grumble to Halston, who's sitting on the bench next to me. After my run-in with Jesse, I couldn't sleep. My body was buzzing with the unfinished orgasm, while my mind was buzzing with thoughts of him. Why is he so persistent? Why me? I tossed and turned all night.

"Well, wake up. It's Friday, and your ass is mine."

"Shit. I forgot."

"Forgot what?"

"I have plans tonight. I totally spaced it."

"With Jesse?" she asks, nudging my shoulder with hers.

"Nope."

"Dylan?"

"Nope."

"Then who? You don't have friends."

"Garrett."

"Who the hell is Garrett? How many boyfriends do you have?"

"Zero." I laugh. "He's just a guy in my marketing class."

"I can't believe you're going on a date and didn't tell me."

As if on cue, I spot Garrett walking through the quad, heading right toward us.

"First of all, it's not a date," I correct. "Second of all, pipe down because he's coming over here."

With all the subtlety of a bulldozer, Halston whirls around to check him out before nodding in appreciation. "He's cute in that grungy, fuck-him-to-piss-off-your-parents kind of way."

She's not wrong. He's wearing a white thermal with a black zip-up hoodie over it, a beanie covering the short blond hair that I know is underneath, and a smirk on those upturned, full lips.

"Hey, Allison," Garrett says, stuffing his hands into his front pockets.

"Hey." I smile up at him, using a hand to shade my eyes from the sun. "This is Halston."

"Garrett," he greets her with a jerk of his chin. Polite, but not overly enthusiastic. *Interesting.* Everyone wants Halston. "So, you still coming tonight?" he asks, rocking back on the heels of his worn Chucks.

"I think Halston's going to take me," I say, bumping her shoulder with mine.

"Actually," she pipes up. "I can't make it. I have this thing."

"What *thing*?" She doesn't have a thing.

"You know." Her eyes widen, wanting me to play along. "Anyway, you should have Garrett here take you."

Garrett scrapes his teeth along his lip, eyebrows raised. "You have my number. Let me know if you want me to pick you up."

I nod, and he walks away, probably feeling uncomfortable after that painfully obvious lie.

"Real smooth."

Halston laughs, throwing her head back. "He's hot. Have fun on your date."

"It's not a date!" I whisper-shout, not wanting to chance him still being in earshot. I stand, slinging my backpack over my shoulder.

"Does he know that?"

"Yes." I think.

I dig through my suitcase in search of a clean shirt, flinging clothes behind me. Most of my stuff is still in my grandparents' garage, and I make a mental note to do some laundry soon. I pull out a white NOFX tee and bring it to my nose, making sure it passes the sniff test. *Bingo*. I shrug it on over my head, then check myself out in the bathroom mirror. My shirt falls below the hem of my black shorts. Black tights. Burgundy Docs. Good enough. This isn't a date, after all. It's a show with a friend at what is most likely going to be a crammed, dirty, smelly venue.

I toss my wavy hair up into a high ponytail, swipe a few strokes of mascara onto my lashes, and I'm done. I hear the front door slam downstairs and I pause, listening. Both Dare and Lo are at work, and it being Friday night, I don't expect either one of them to be home this early. I pocket my phone and grab my small black purse, fixing the strap across my chest. I scoop my dad's jacket off the bed and tie it around my waist before heading down the stairs. Once I'm near the bottom, I peek around the corner, attempting to see who's here.

Movement by the fridge catches my eye, and then it slams shut, revealing Jesse. Why does he have to be so obnoxiously attractive? Backwards hat. White tee. Gray sweats. *Don't look at his crotch. Do not look at his crotch.*

"Are you looking at my dick?"

I jerk my eyes away at the sound of his voice. "What? No."

Jesse smirks, rounding the counter and heading for the couch. "Wild Friday night?" I ask, eyeing his setup. There are bags of chips, sodas, beers, and… *Are those Dum-Dums laid out across the coffee table?* Netflix is pulled up on the flat screen.

"Didn't feel like going out." He shrugs, plopping down onto the couch, legs spread wide. I sit on the arm of the couch, reaching forward to steal a sucker. I don't waste any time unwrapping it and taking a lick. Jesse watches my mouth intently and I try not to squirm under his attention.

"What are you watching?" I ask, if only to break the silence. Jesse clears his throat and adjusts his sweatpants, making no attempt to hide the bulge there. Why do my eyes keep wandering toward his crotch? I don't particularly like dicks. I haven't even seen very many of them in person. It's not like I'm a connoisseur.

"Not sure yet. You pick."

Me? Does he want me to watch a movie with him?

The doorbell rings, not giving me a chance to answer. I set my sucker on the wrapper on top of the table while Jesse stands, beer in hand, and makes his way for the door. *Garrett.* I sent him Lo's address after I got home, letting him know I'd need a ride after all.

Jesse swings the door open, revealing a slightly confused-looking Garrett. "I'm here to pick up Allison," Garrett says, leaning back to check the number on the house, like maybe he got the wrong address.

"Hey," I say, stepping into view. Once he sees me, his mouth quirks up into that mischievous grin of his as his eyes scan my body. "Nice choice," he says, pointing toward my shirt.

Before I can respond, Jesse shuts the door in his face. I jump back, shooting him a glare before I open the door again. "I'll be out in a second," I explain, holding up my finger. "I'm just going to grab my stuff."

He nods, luckily not appearing to be too offended, heading for the truck parked in front of the curb.

"What the hell was that?" I ask Jesse.

"He bored me."

"So you slammed the door in his face? Instead of walking away? Since, you know, he's my guest and all."

"Pretty much, yeah."

"Oookay," I drawl. "I'll see you later then."

Jesse doesn't say anything, so I turn for the door.

"Boyfriend?" Garrett asks when I climb into his truck.

"God no," I say, laughing. "He does like to make my life hell, though. I hear relationships do that to people."

Garrett pulls out onto the street and reaches forward to turn the music down. We spend the rest of the way talking about our favorite bands and listening to music. Garrett is easy to be around and could quite possibly be my musical soulmate. We're a good forty-five minutes away when he swings into a dark parking lot. No lights. No signs.

"Did you bring me here to kill me?" I look over at him with an eyebrow raised.

"Where's the trust?" He climbs out of his truck, rounding the hood before he's opening my door and helping me out. "Come on."

Garrett leads me toward the entrance, and if it wasn't for the faint sounds of a bass guitar floating from the building and the parking lot full of cars, I might think he was taking me to some rapey abandoned building. Once inside, it looks like a normal venue. Two bars on each side of the floor, stage up front—though no one is up there yet.

"Drink?" Garrett asks over the music, gesturing toward the bar to our right with the shorter line.

I pull him closer, trying not to announce it to the entire bar. "I'm not twenty-one." Garrett laughs. "No one is. They don't give a fuck here." Taking my hand, he pulls me through the crowd where a chick with a blue bob and a spiked leather choker mans the bar.

"Whatcha havin'?" she asks, leaning over the counter that separates us.

"Whatever you have in a bottle," I say. I'm not picky.

"Two," Garrett adds, holding two fingers up.

I dig into my purse, trying to find the loose cash that I know is floating around somewhere, but Garrett beats me to it, slapping a twenty down onto the bar.

"Thanks," I tell him. *Not a date. Not a date.*

"Let's get a good spot," he says, gesturing toward the stage. There's a solid crowd here, but I'm surprised there aren't more people. We weave through the staggered groups of bodies, easily making our way toward the front. Out of the corner of my eye, I see a man approach. I turn to face him, taking in his pressed jeans and untucked white button-up.

"Well, look what the cat dragged in," he says with a smile in his voice.

"Victor," I say, smiling in return. He brings me in for a hug, and when he pulls back, I see the pity in his eyes, even in the dimly lit venue. "Sorry to hear about your Pops," he says, uncharacteristically solemn. Victor is maybe mid-thirties, but he's a perpetual child. The only time his serious side comes out is when it comes to business. Or, when he's extending his condolences, apparently.

"Thanks," I say so quietly I don't even know if it's audible over the noise. "This is—"

"Garrett," Victor answers for me. They slap hands in greeting. "Glad you could make it," he says, and if I'm not mistaken, it's sarcasm I detect in his voice.

"The lady needed a ride," Garrett says with a shrug.

"Yeah, well, the *lady* is a family friend, so be good to her." Victor points a stern finger at him.

His phone flashes in his hand and he looks back at me. "I have to take this, but find me before you leave, huh?"

I nod, and then he turns around, disappearing into the crowd. When I look back to Garrett, his eyebrows are at his hairline.

"What?"

"How do you know Victor?"

"He's a friend of my dad's." I keep it vague, not wanting to have the whole *dead dad* conversation right now.

"You just keep getting more and more interesting." He smirks.

"I'm just full of surprises," I deadpan. My cold fingertips remind me of my untouched drink, and I bring it to my lips, letting the cool liquid slide down my throat.

Suddenly, the lights lower, the music over the speakers cuts out, and a guy with a faded electric guitar—Squier, by the looks of it—takes the stage.

"We'd love to play a show for you guys, but unfortunately, it seems our drummer has decided that now is a good time to chat up a hot chick."

I laugh, scanning the crowd, but I'm surprised when

Garrett throws up a middle finger and shakes his head. "Hold this for me?" he asks, handing me his bottle.

"Uh, sure," I say, feeling more than a little confused. Garrett gives me a sheepish smile before effortlessly pulling himself up onto the stage.

"We'll get him back to you in about twenty minutes," the guy with the guitar says, pointing his finger at me and sending a wink my way.

Garrett takes his seat behind the drum kit, clicking his sticks together to start the song off. The band—consisting of two guitar players and one bass player—seamlessly follows suit. I bob my head as the song pulls in the crowd around me. Their sound is good—really good. They're that perfect blend of pop punk with enough of an edge to be distinguished from boy band status. Catchy chorus and lyrics, fast tempo. I'm impressed. Garrett has sweat dripping down the side of his face, the biceps I didn't know he had flexing with each hit. *Why the hell didn't he tell me he was playing tonight?*

By the time their set is over, I've finished both mine and Garrett's beer. After clearing off the stage, he waves me over. I cut through the bodies that have started to disperse, making my way over to him.

"Why didn't you tell me?" I slap his shoulder.

"I'm full of surprises," he teases, throwing my earlier words back at me.

"Apparently." I laugh.

Victor appears from behind me, clapping Garrett on the back. "Good set," he praises.

"You guys were pretty amazing," I agree.

"Yeah?"

"Hell yes. But why are you playing this shitty venue? This could've been a much bigger turnout."

"You think?" Victor asks. I turn my attention to him.

"One hundred percent."

"What would you do differently?" he asks, crossing his arms.

"I'd make a kickass flyer, then start by blasting it all over social media. Target the college kids. Even if it's not their typical scene, this town is small. Everyone would show up simply due to the lack of things to do around here."

"Is that all?"

"No." I shake my head. "I'd also ask the owner about having half-priced drinks for the first hour. The only thing we like more than alcohol is cheap alcohol."

Garrett smothers his smile with his hand, and I look between them, confused.

"What?"

"This is my venue," Victor says gruffly.

"Oh." Shit. "I'm sorry—"

"You think you could do it better?" he asks, cutting me off. "Call me, and I'll let you try your hand at it."

"Really?" I ask cautiously. He pulls out a card, handing it to me.

"Tonight was a trial run for me. But you have good instincts, and even more importantly, you're from the right generation."

Speechless, I take the card that sits between his first and middle finger.

"Get her home safely," he tells Garrett.

Garrett salutes him, and then Victor's gone.

"What...the hell just happened?"

"Surprises, Allison. Full of surprises."

For the rest of the night, Garrett and the lead singer of his band, Mark, stay close to me, drinking and talking shit. Gutterpunk plays, and they're the same old sloppy punk band I remember, even though they've got to be pushing fifty by now.

"Thanks for tonight," I say as I almost lose my footing on the uneven walkway outside Lo's house. Garrett grips my arm as I right myself, and I laugh at my clumsiness. I'm not *drunk*, but I'm feeling a little buzzed. But it's a good buzz. Warm and fuzzy and *happy*. Garrett is fun to be around, and I don't get the impression that he's interested in me, so my guard is down. It feels good.

"I'll see you Monday?" I scrounge for my key in the small purse that hangs by my hip. But before I can locate it, the front door swings open. A familiar tall blonde appears in front of me, lipstick smeared and eyes wide with surprise before her face transforms into a slow, devious grin. *Victorious* would be the word I'd use to describe it. Sierra. Again.

I narrow my eyes at her as she swings the door open wider, allowing me the opportunity to see Jesse zipping his jeans. She watches me closely for a reaction. One that I won't give her.

"Well, this was fun," I say lightly before turning back to Garrett. My stomach is swirling with something that feels a lot like disappointment—or maybe the alcohol is starting to rear its ugly head and I'm about to be sick—but I don't show it. "Thanks for the ride," I say. Sierra trots past me, knowing she's not getting the reaction she wanted. Garrett looks over my shoulder, taking in the scene behind me before meeting my eyes. "Call me if you need anything."

I nod, giving him what I hope is a convincing smile,

before closing the door. Taking a deep breath, I turn back around. Jesse sits on the couch with his thighs spread wide. No shirt. Hands crossed behind his head like he doesn't have a care in the world, but the tension in his jaw tells me otherwise. Who hooks up in the middle of the living room when people are home? Jesse fucking Shepherd, obviously.

"You're gross."

"It's a gift."

"Your sister is right upstairs," I whisper-shout, gesturing above us.

"She's seen worse. Trust me."

I scoff, shaking my head. Jesse cocks his head to the side, inquisitive, before he stands, eating up the distance between us. "Why are you really mad, Allie Girl?" He twirls a lock of hair from my ponytail in his fingers. "Is it because I was hooking up with someone on the couch, or because you wish it was you?"

"Neither," I grit out. "Maybe it's because you tried to get with me approximately five minutes before hooking up with someone else."

"Oh, that's rich," Jesse says, taking a step back. "Considering you were just doing the same fucking thing with Kurt Cobain over there," he says, flinging a hand toward the door. I clamp my mouth shut before I can deny it. I don't owe him an explanation. Jesse's eyes narrow into slits, assessing. "Unless you didn't."

I roll my eyes, turning to leave, but he blocks my way.

"You didn't, did you? How long has it been, Allie? Is that why you were touching yourself in the hot tub?"

Oh my God.

"That's none of your business," I say, feeling my face burning.

"I mean, you *have* had sex, right?" His eyebrows jump toward his hairline.

"I've had sex!" I yell, before remembering where I am and what time it is. Lowering my voice, I continue. "I have lots of sex." Jesse smirks, like he doesn't believe me. "Like…a lot. All the time." Jesus Christ, why can't I stop talking? *You're making it worse, Allison.*

"So let's have sex then. Right now. If you're such a pro," he challenges.

"No."

"Why not?"

"Because I don't like you, for starters."

He chews on his lip for a minute before speaking again. "Liar."

"And you couldn't pay me to touch you after being with her."

"You sure about that?"

I shake my head, annoyed. "You're a lot more obnoxious than I remember."

"And you're a lot bitchier than I remember."

"Manwhore," I shoot back.

"Guilty." His lips curve into that infuriating cocky grin of his. I snort, shaking my head before moving past him without saying another word.

This time he lets me go.

CHAPTER SIXTEEN

Jess

I SIT BACK ON THE COUCH, SCRUBBING A HAND THROUGH my hair. When Allison left with that douchebag in the flannel instead of hanging out with me, I felt stupid as hell. I smoked a blunt and had a few beers before trashing the candy and shit I brought over. Lo and Dare came home around midnight, but Allison was still out. I was staring at that goddamn sucker she left on the table, brooding like a little bitch, when I got a text from Sierra. She's been hitting me up since I've been back, but I never responded. I try to avoid her brand of crazy like the plague. Until tonight. You'd think she'd have moved on, considering that little mishap with her sister. Apparently, that only increases the appeal for her.

She pulled out all her best moves, doing the most to impress me. But all I could do was stare at that stupid fucking sucker taunting me from the coffee table. How Allison's tongue licked at it, how her lips wrapped around it. Whatever Sierra was doing down on her knees wasn't cutting it. Like an asshole, I told her to leave. She only sucked harder.

I leaned forward, grabbed Allie's sucker, and stuck it in my mouth before leaning back on the couch, arms crossed behind my head as I closed my eyes, pretending it was her mouth around me. If I was solo, that thought alone would get me off, but this felt all wrong. It pissed me off, knowing that Allison had gotten into my head and under my skin enough to ruin a perfectly good blow job.

"What's wrong?" Sierra asked, wiping her mouth with the back of her hand when it was clear that something wasn't working.

"I think we're done here," I said, feeling tired and high and nowhere near coming. My dick was hard, but it wasn't for her.

"Let me help you," she said, trying to sound coy as she pushed back on my shoulders and reached under her skirt to slide her panties to the side.

"I said we're done here."

Pride good and wounded, she righted her dress, swiped her purse off the floor, and stormed toward the door.

"You should see a doctor for that little issue," she said.

"It's not me. It's you," I said flatly.

She growled, flinging the door open, only to reveal Allison and her little hipster boyfriend out front. Allison's face changed when she took in the scene in front of her. Her expression went from shocked to...hurt, if I wasn't mistaken. It was subtle, but I saw it. I should have told her that it didn't get that far. That she managed to cockblock me without even being here. But I was too busy relishing in the fact that she did want me on some level. She just needs a little push.

I hear the shower start above me, the water rushing through the pipes, interrupting my thoughts. I groan. This is torture. Pure fucking torture. The only girl I want, in this moment, is naked right upstairs. And I can't have her. Probably not anytime soon, after tonight.

I feel my phone buzz somewhere underneath me, and I stick my hand in the crack between the cushions until it finds the cool, hard case of my phone. Turning it over in my palm, I see a text on my screen.

Tomorrow. 5741 East Baker Rd. 10P.M.

I clench my jaw, simultaneously hating being under someone's thumb while itching for the thrill that's sure to come. Plus, I could use the extra money. I punch out a reply.

I'm in.

As if I have a choice in the matter.

Allie

I went to bed feeling irritated, but when I woke up Saturday morning and found the trash can full of unopened snacks, I felt a twinge of guilt, which is ridiculous. I couldn't have known he planned that for me. And if he wanted to hang out, he could have—oh, I don't know—asked me?

The next few days go by without any more Jesse sightings. I try to casually ask Lo where he's been during my shift at Blackbear Sunday, but she laughs and says it's better that she doesn't ask. At first, I was glad I didn't have to face him, but when Thursday rolls around, and he still hasn't shown his face, the disappointment sets in. I find myself wondering where he disappears to. And why isn't he in school? Why is he so hot and cold with me? But mostly, *why the hell do I care*?

"Albert." Dylan snaps his fingers in front of my face.

"Sorry." I shake thoughts of Jesse from my head. "What were we talking about?"

"The show," he reminds me, tuning his guitar while we sit at his kitchen table.

"Right. So, there's this new venue called The Lamppost. I went with this guy from school Friday, and you guys have to try it out. The place is massive. You remember Victor from The Cold Snap?" I ask, and he nods.

The Cold Snap was a hole-in-the-wall venue in town that Victor owned. I don't know what happened, but it's a sandwich shop now. "He owns it. Turns out, he doesn't have the first clue as to how to throw an event."

"Shocker," Dylan says, full of sarcasm.

"He gave me his card—"

"He has a card?" Dylan laughs, his beer bottle halting at his lips.

"I know." I smile. "Anyway. He wants my help with the next one. And naturally, I thought about you."

"Sounds fun."

I nod. "I have a good feeling about it. You in?"

Dylan nods. "Our schedule's not exactly full. Can we play your song? You can sing it with me."

I shoot him a look as if he proposed kidnapping the president. There's a better chance of me doing just that than getting up on a stage and singing, no matter how small the crowd. "You're high. That's not happening."

Outside of singing to whatever my dad plays—*played*—on guitar, and the occasional song with Dylan for fun, I'm no singer. It's not what I want to do. Songwriting? Maybe. Owning my own venue, or even producing music? Definitely. I always thought I'd do it with my dad. The plan was to open our own place together when I graduated college—hence the music business major—but now, everything seems like one giant question mark.

"When's the last time you wrote, anyway?"

"Not in a while." I used to write in my journal daily, and not just lyrics. My every thought, frustration, hope, and dream. Since my dad died, I haven't written a word. Writing about it means thinking about it, and thinking about it means *feeling* it.

"It'll happen," Dylan says, reading my thoughts. I bite down on my lip, swallowing hard.

I reach for his beer, taking a swig before pasting a smile onto my face. "So," I say, slapping the table, "let me hear what you've been working on."

The front door swings open, and we both swivel our heads around at the sound. Hunter, the bassist for their band The Liars, walks in wearing only a pair of basketball shorts and a backwards hat. He's six-foot-four—I know this, because somehow, it always ends up being the topic of discussion—and has to be at least two hundred and fifty pounds. Between his ginormous frame, his tattoos, and his beard, chicks cling to him like cellophane. Caleb, the drummer, is right behind him, clothed and a few inches shorter, but never lacking in the female department with his blond hair and blue eyes. Total boy band material. That face was made to grace the bedroom walls of teenage girls everywhere.

Caleb has a girl riding piggyback and another few pour in behind him.

Hunter smacks a girl's ass, and she twirls around. "Don't you have a girlfriend?" She giggles.

"Nah, she died," he says, sporting his best puppy dog eyes, bottom lip jutting out.

The girl gasps, her smile dropping. "I'm so sorry. How did it happen?"

"Plane crash."

"Oh my God…"

"Help me forget?" Hunter pulls her to his front and kisses her. Hard.

Dylan looks over to me, raising a brow, knowing that's a load of shit. Hunter's ex is alive and well. "I guess we're partying."

"Can't." I pout. "I have class tomorrow."

"Allie!" Hunter shouts after he comes up for air, like he hasn't seen me in years. "What's up?" he asks, dipping down to hug me in the chair where I sit. I laugh, circling my arms around his neck, and he takes the opportunity to lift me up, spinning me around. It's impossible to be in a bad mood around Hunter.

"Allie Cat," Caleb says, shucking the girl off his back, letting her land on the couch before coming in for a hug of his own. "What are you guys up to?"

"Trying to talk your lead singer over here into playing a new venue."

"I'm in," Hunter declares, clearly unconcerned with the specifics.

"Fuck yeah," Caleb agrees. "As long as it's not during finals."

Hunter and Dylan share a look, and I know it's because they feel like Caleb has one foot out the door. The band isn't his life, like it is for Dylan and Hunter. I get the impression that Caleb is just passing time with the band until he graduates.

"Talk him into it," I say, flicking my chin toward Dylan. "I've gotta go."

Dylan stands, reaching into his front pocket for his keys. "I'll be right back," he tells the guys. "I'm gonna take her home." The girls, now all three huddled up on the couch, eye fuck Dylan as we walk through the living room, but he doesn't so much as acknowledge their existence.

"So, how are you liking your new digs?" he asks, once we're on the road.

"It's good for now," I say, leaving it vague. "Getting to school is a pain in the ass, but it's free and Lo's cool."

The distance between Dylan and Lo's house is only a couple of miles, but with the windy roads through the woods, it feels much farther. "Turn here," I say, pointing. Once we're pulling into the driveway, Dylan turns to me, looking like he wants to say something.

"All—" he starts but stops when another vehicle swings into the driveway next to us. A black truck. And out comes none other than Jesse fucking Shepherd.

Dylan works his jaw and I close my eyes, dropping my head back against the headrest. "He doesn't live here," I say. I don't owe Dylan an explanation, and he has no say in where I decide to stay or whom I decide to spend my time with, but for some reason, I get the impression that his feelings are hurt.

He bobs his head, not saying a word. Jesse, obnoxious as always, opens the passenger door.

"Going in?" he asks, ducking down so his face is visible. I shake my head at him, trying to convey that now is not the time.

"Go inside, Allie," Dylan says, starting the engine back up. I look over at him, but he stares ahead, not meeting my eyes.

"Fine. Be a baby." I step out of the car, sidestepping Jesse when he tries to help me. I hear Dylan pull out of the driveway before he flies down the road.

"You really have a knack for showing up at the wrong time," I mutter.

"It's part of my charm."

I snort. "Whatever you say."

"He has a lip ring. What is it, 1999? I did you a favor."

I roll my eyes, pushing open the front door, noticing a duffle bag and a pile of clothes on the floor inside. "What's this?" I ask, kicking the bag.

"My stuff." He moves past me, bending over to throw his duffle bag over his shoulder.

"What are you doing?" I ask, even though I have a pretty damn good idea of where this is going.

"Putting my shit upstairs," he says, like the answer is obvious, walking up the steps.

"Why?"

He pauses mid-step, looking at me over his shoulder with an infuriating grin. "Because I'm your new roomie, roomie."

"What?" I ask, charging up the stairs after him.

"You heard me."

"But why?"

"You ask a lot of questions." Jesse passes my door, then the bathroom, before opening door number three. I follow him into the room I've never been inside before. Another empty room, this one doesn't even have a bed. *Because I have his bed.*

"It's convenient, don't you think?" He tosses his bag into a corner unceremoniously before turning back toward me with a smirk, hands on his hips.

"Excuse me?" I cross my arms over my chest, ignoring the way my stomach flips at the way he's looking at me.

He moves toward me, and instinctively I step backwards until my back is flush with the door. "I want you. And I'm sick of playing this game."

I swallow hard, feeling the warmth of his skin without even touching him. "That's not why you're here," I say, calling his bluff.

"No," he admits. "But it definitely sweetens the deal."

"You had your chance. The offer's expired."

"Is that so?" he asks, moving closer. "And what's changed?" He pinches my chin between his finger and thumb and tilts it up so I'm forced to meet his gaze.

"Everything." I don't know why my voice comes out as more of a whisper. I can't think when he's this close. I notice a faint red mark on his cheekbone. Without thinking, I reach forward, brushing my thumb over it. Jesse sucks in a breath before clamping his mouth shut. When my brain catches up to my actions, I drop my hand to my side. "What happened?"

"It's nothing," he says, but his voice is huskier than it was a second ago. He clears his throat, taking a step back.

"Want to know the best part about being roommates?" he asks, the playful demeanor firmly back in place. How does he do that? Shift gears so effortlessly? Better yet, what made him learn?

Jesse opens a door off to the right, waving me over. Hesitantly, I walk over to see—*oh my God.*

"We get to share a bathroom." He bounces his eyebrows.

"Joy," I deadpan, walking through, opening the opposite door that leads to my room. I saw the door to his room, obviously, but I thought it was a damn linen closet.

"We could conserve water? Shower together?"

"Not happening."

"Every drop counts."

I slam the door without a response, hearing a muffled chuckle behind me.

After doing some schoolwork, I grab a towel from my room. I brush my teeth and take a quick shower—making sure to lock the adjoining door—then throw an oversized shirt on. Crawling into bed, I pull the covers over me, then reach for my headphones and CDs from my nightstand. I flip through the square black case with doodles from my silver Sharpie decorating the front and back before finding my sleep mix. I pop it in and snuggle into my pillow as "Mix Tape" by Brand New croons in my ear.

Keeping my thoughts from drifting to the boy on the other side of the bathroom is a feat damn near impossible. Why is he so persistent? And what happened to his face? The more I get to know him, the higher my list of questions piles up. I hate that I'm starting to see him in a different light. He was this one-dimensional, manwhore of a jock before, and now, there are layers. Layers that I want to peel back, even though I know I'll get burned in the process. How am I going to resist Jesse Shepherd when we're under the same roof for two whole months?

And as I'm weighing the pros and cons of giving into temptation, I also give in to sleep.

"WHAT'S SO FUNNY?" LO ASKS, AS I'M smiling down at my phone during my shift.

"My grandma seems to have just figured out how to use emojis," I explain, showing her my phone screen. She messaged me to let me know I could access the garage where all my dad's things are, followed by every heart, rainbow, and flower available.

"Damn." She laughs. "She's better with that shit than I am. I repel technology."

"That's sad, Lo."

"This coming from the girl who rocks a portable CD player?" She shoots me a look, moving past me with her hands full of plates.

"Touché."

"Finish up with your table, then take your break," she instructs, jerking her chin toward the elderly couple who's been taking up residence in my section for going on three hours, yet has ordered nothing besides two coffees and the soup of the day. Spoiler alert: it's creamy tomato bisque. It's *always* creamy tomato bisque.

"I could be waiting a while." I sigh.

"Look on the bright side. Doesn't look like they've got much time left," Lo jokes.

"You're going to hell." I smother a smile.

Thankfully, the couple doesn't stay much longer. I put in an order with Grumpy Pete for a grilled cheese and eat it at the bar, making small talk with Lo while she serves up drinks. Glancing at the clock, I realize I have a few minutes of my break left, so I can't resist leaning forward to grab a butterscotch sucker out of the bowl.

"Anyone ever tell you, you have the taste buds of an eighty-year-old?" Jesse asks, coming up behind me. *When the hell did he get here?*

"Let me guess. You're a cherry fan." Everyone loves cherry. "Such a cliché."

"I've been known to enjoy a few cherries in my day," he agrees suggestively, throwing an arm around my shoulders. *Gross.* "But my favorite happens to be strawberry."

He plucks the sucker from my mouth, then sticks it into his own. My eyes follow the movement, and I have to peel them away. My stomach swirls at his nearness.

"There's a whole bowl right there," I point out. "Get your own."

"Where's the fun in that?" He winks then bites into it, eating the whole thing. Lo looks between us with her arms crossed, a mix of suspicion and amusement in her narrowed eyes. I stand from my stool, putting some distance between us. I wipe my greasy hands on the black apron tied around my waist before grabbing my plate.

"Break's over." The last thing I need is for Lo, or anyone for that matter, thinking there's something going on between Jesse and me.

"By the way, we're leaving early," Lo calls after me. I turn to face her.

"On a Friday?" I ask, confused.

"One of Dare's friends from out of town showed up this morning, so we're going to have some people over tonight."

"Oh, cool. I can stay with my friend Dylan tonight—"

"Why would you do that?" Lo cuts me off. Her eyebrows pull together in confusion at the same time Jesse's eyes harden.

"I don't want to intrude."

Lo throws her head back, laughing, before she walks over to me, throwing an arm around my neck. "She doesn't want to intrude," she mocks, putting emphasis on the word *intrude*. Jesse smirks, but he doesn't say anything.

"It's a kick-back, Allie, not a private meeting. And by *we*, I meant *you and me*. Jake's closing tonight. It's time you meet the family."

I give her a skeptical smile. Why does it sound like I'm about to be jumped into a gang, or introduced to the mob?

"Unless you've got better things to do," Jess taunts, no doubt sensing my unease. The creases in his forehead deepen as he waits for my response.

Challenge accepted.

"Nope. I'm wide open." I shrug. "Sounds fun."

"We're out of here in an hour," Lo announces before smacking a kiss to my cheek.

Jesse's eyes bore into me until Lo's out of sight, and we're locked in some silent staring contest. I don't know what it's about, but I do know that I won't be the one to back down. I stare right back, crossing my arms over my chest defiantly. Jesse breaks first, huffing out an amused laugh. He moves past me, his chest skimming my folded arms as he leans in close to my ear. I hold my breath, suppressing the shiver that's fighting its way through me, but my traitorous heart doesn't get the message. "See you at home."

"How do you know my brother?" Lo asks, looking over at me from the driver's seat.

"What?" I ask, thrown off by her question.

She lifts a shoulder. "I've noticed the way you two go back and forth. It just seems like you guys have known each other for a while."

"We met briefly a couple months ago, but we didn't exactly get off on the right foot." That's putting it lightly, but she doesn't need to know the sordid details.

"Ah," she says, nodding. "He's a good kid once you get to know him. The only thing bigger than his ego is his heart."

I laugh, knowing the ego part is true at least.

"He's been dealt a shit hand in life," she goes on, seemingly lost in her thoughts. "He's sort of in a weird place right now." She swings into the driveway, cutting the engine and then looking over at me. "Anyway, I just wanted to make sure you guys were cool."

"We're fine," I assure her, keeping my tone light.

"Good," she says with a nod, but I get the feeling that she's worried about him for some reason. Maybe it's the fact that he seems to have dropped out of school. Maybe it's because he disappears for days at a time. Maybe it's because his mood seems to flip-flop more often than I change my underwear. "Now let's go inside."

As soon as I open the door to hop out of her SUV, I hear music coming from inside the house. We make our way to the front door and Lo pushes it open, revealing a house full of people, some I recognize, some I don't.

"Come on," she says, pushing me between my shoulder blades and closing the door behind us. A guy with tan skin, full lips, and a mischievous grin notices our arrival first. He breaks away from his conversation with a blonde girl who sits on the lap of a guy who has his hand tucked between her thighs, as if anchoring her to the spot.

"Hey, Lo-Lo," he says, pulling her into his arms for a tight hug.

"Try again," Lo says, immediately shutting him down.

He laughs. "Still working on a nickname for you," he says with a shrug.

"Work harder. Because that one is not happening."

"Noted. You brought me a present?" he says, looking me up and down with brown eyes so light they appear golden. He's gorgeous. And clearly trouble.

"She's too young for you," Lo says, snapping her fingers in front of his face. "She's staying with us for a while. Adrian, this is Allison. Allison, this is Adrian. He likes to sporadically show up unannounced to piss Dare off."

"Allison and Adrian. We already sound good together," he says, taking my hand and bringing it to his lips.

"Oh, you're good." I laugh, pulling my hand back. For some reason, his brand of flirting doesn't put me on edge like Jesse's does. Maybe because it's so overt that I know it's all in good fun. *Or maybe it's because you haven't been near naked with him between your thighs.*

Lo grabs ahold of my hand, tugging me away from Adrian. I follow her lead toward the kitchen. She grabs two beers out of the fridge, handing me one before she's being pulled into another hug. This time by the blonde girl I saw when I walked in.

"No baby tonight?" Lo asks, leaning a hip against the counter.

Blonde Girl inhales deeply. "My mom's in town. It's our first time leaving him. I don't know who's more worried, Ash or me." She looks over toward the couch at the guy she was sitting on before who's sitting there bouncing his knee as he takes a swig from his beer. "Twenty bucks says he's going to check the time on his phone in five, four, three, two…"

Sure enough, he digs into his black jeans pocket before pulling his phone out and flipping it over, glaring at the screen.

"Wow." Lo laughs. "Daddy Asher is not fucking around."

"I'm Briar, by the way," she says to me, her smile as warm and bright as fucking sunshine.

"Allison," I say, shaking her hand.

"Where's Dare?" Lo questions, scanning the living room. There's a guy in swim shorts with tattoos from his neck to his ankles, another guy who looks like him without as many tattoos, and a couple of brunettes, but no Dare in sight.

"Do you really have to ask?" Briar laughs, grabbing another beer from the fridge. "He's hiding upstairs."

I'm not the least bit surprised by that. Dare is about as sociable as I am. The only difference is, he doesn't try to be polite about it. He's unapologetically anti-social.

Briar returns to her spot on the guy's lap, and I almost laugh at the sight. It's like seeing an angel perched atop the Grim Reaper. *A really attractive Grim Reaper.*

"I'll be right back," Lo says, heading for the stairs. I nod, standing awkwardly at the counter for all of ten seconds before I decide to head out back for some fresh air. I slip out the sliding door unnoticed, the cool night air hitting my face. Spring is coming, but the nights are still cold. Thankfully, no one else is out here. I rub the chill out of my upper arms, walking across the deck to the set of table and chairs. I scroll through my phone and see a missed call from my mom. I stare at the notification for a minute before finally tapping on it. I'm surprised when she answers almost instantly.

"Hi, honey," she says in that sing-song voice of hers.

"Hi, Mom. You called?" I pluck a bottle cap from the table, absentmindedly spinning it.

"How's school? How are you liking the lake house?"

Alarm bells ring in my mind. My mom doesn't do small talk unless she wants something.

"It's fine." It's not like I *need* to lie to my mom about where I'm staying. What can she do from Hawaii? But for reasons I don't even want to analyze, I don't want her knowing. It's easier this way.

"That's nice," she croons. "Can you hear the waves?" she asks. "It's so peaceful here."

"Mhm." I won't make the mistake of inviting myself there again. I wait for her to get to the point of the phone call, but when she asks generic question after generic question, I start to think maybe she really did just call to check in and see how things are going. That maybe this is her making a genuine effort. My mom and I, despite our monumental differences, are…fine. Not particularly tight, but not necessarily distant either. She loves me in her own way. I never doubted that. We just don't *click*. My dad and

I clicked. We were two peas in a pod from day one. But now, with all things considered, if she's trying, then maybe I should, too.

I relax, leaning my back against the canvas cushion of the chair, propping my Docs up on the edge of the table. "How's Hawaii?" I ask, then cringe at my lame attempt at making conversation.

"It's perfect," she says with a dreamy voice, and I try to ignore the way my stomach twists at her words. *Perfect.* As in, she's *perfectly* happy without me. "I do need a favor, though."

And there it is.

"What?" I ask tightly, my guard creeping back into place like a coat of armor.

"I seem to have misplaced my divorce papers," she says sheepishly. I roll my eyes. *My mom lost something? How unlike her.*

"Shocker."

"I was thinking, when you go through—"

"I told you I'm not ready to go through Dad's things yet," I snap, feeling myself shutting back down at the direction this conversation has taken. My dad's entire life has been reduced to a pile of boxes in my grandparents' garage. I know I need to go through them, but every time I think I'm ready, something holds me back.

Mom sighs, and I can picture her pinching the bridge of her nose. I can almost bet that she'll be self-medicating her impending "migraine" in the form of a joint right after this phone call. "Allie, it's been almost a year. It's time. I know you don't like talking about him, but you have to heal, baby. I miss him, too."

I scoff, shaking my head. "He might have been another

notch in your bedpost, but he was my *dad*. It's not exactly something you just get over." It's cruel, but it's true. My mom is addicted to love, and James Parrish was just her drug of choice for a short time.

"Don't say that," she admonishes. "I loved—"

"I have to go."

"Allie—"

I hang up the phone before she can throw some cliché, hippie-dippy bullshit quote my way, like *the only way to get over the pain is to go through the pain*. I toss my phone down. Bracing my elbows on the edge of the table, I use both hands to push my hair back and out of my face and take a deep breath.

"So stupid," I mutter to myself. I can't believe I almost fell for her act. She's not interested in a relationship with me. She's still the same old self-serving, self-involved person she's always been. How silly of me to think the death of my father would have changed things.

A faint crunching sound catches my attention and I whip my head around, seeking out the source. Along the black iron fence that separates the sand from the yard stands a form that I recognize, even with the pitch-black sky as the only backdrop. A beer bottle hangs from one hand and the cherry from his cigarette seems to float in the dark as he brings it to his mouth with the other hand. He sucks, causing it to burn brighter. I can tell he's facing me, but he says nothing as he watches me…watching him. *How long has he been there? More importantly, how much did he hear?*

I look back toward the glass door where everyone is drinking and laughing and having a good time. I should go back inside, but after that little chat with my mother, the last thing I feel like doing is socializing with a bunch of strangers. Then I glance back over my shoulder at Jesse. He flicks his cigarette to the ground before stomping it out, then bends over to pick up the case of beer at his feet. "Wanna get out of here?"

I know it's not a good idea. Encouraging him will only blur the lines, and boys like Jesse need boundaries. Very clear, very bold, written in stone, type of boundaries. Even as I tell myself all the reasons I should turn around and go back inside, I move toward him, unable to resist the pull. Call it morbid curiosity.

"What, no headphones tonight?"

"Ha-ha," I deadpan, but in reality, I did consider running upstairs to grab my CD player before I came out here, but the benefits didn't outweigh the risk involved. "Where are we going?"

Jesse unlatches the gate with one hand and steps onto the sand. I chew on my lip and look back toward the house, second-guessing my decision to bail on Lo. *Technically, she bailed first.*

"She'll be occupied for a while," Jesses says, reading my thoughts. "Trust me. She won't even notice you're gone."

I snort. He's probably right.

"Grab a blanket," he instructs, pointing the beer bottle in his hand toward a teal and black striped blanket with white fringe on the ends that's thrown across one of the chaise loungers. I cock an eyebrow.

"Get your mind out of the gutter. It's to sit on."

"Right." I pluck the blanket from the chaise, wrapping it around my shoulders. "Lead the way," I say, sweeping a hand out in front of me. He tosses his empty bottle toward the grassy area, then grabs two more, handing me one.

We sip our beers, walking in silence, with the angry waves in the lake as the only sound. The cold sand gets inside my boots, and I stop, handing Jesse my beer. He holds both our bottles in the same hand as I kick off my boots. I bend over to peel my black knee-high socks off before stuffing them inside my shoes. When I straighten, Jesse is staring at my exposed legs. His eyes flick up to mine and he shrugs, as if to say, *You caught me. So, what*?

"There's a spot right up here."

I nod, following his lead. It's so much different than I expected. The lake itself looks big enough to be an ocean, but the sand is rough against my feet, as opposed to the fine, soft sand I'm used to. And instead of palm trees and little shops, there's nothing but pine trees and wooded areas behind us. Eventually, he peels the blanket from my shoulders before spreading it out onto the sand. Goosebumps break out across my naked arms, but the alcohol is creeping in slowly, starting to warm me from the inside out.

Jesse sits first, his elbows propped on his bent knees, the brown bottle dangling between them as he stares out onto the dark lake. I drop my boots onto the sand before sitting next to him, hugging my knees and looking up at the sky. "I'll never get used to that."

Jesse follows my gaze. "What, the stars?"

"Yeah. You don't see this in the city."

I pinch a handful of sand between my fingers, then let it sprinkle back to the ground, my chin resting on top of my knees.

"Wanna tell me what that was about back there?" he asks, taking me by surprise. Leaning my cheek onto my knee, I look over at him, assessing.

"What, I can't ask questions?" he asks, eyebrow raised.

"Not those kinds of questions."

"Okay. Let's start small," he says, cracking open another bottle. He holds one out for me in silent offering. I take it, feeling the condensation on my fingertips. "We'll take turns."

"Sure." I laugh.

"There's a catch," he warns.

"With you, I'm sure there always is."

Jesse cuts his eyes at me, mid-drink, but ignores my comment. "If you don't answer, you have to drink."

I shrug. "Easy enough."

"I'm not talking favorite colors and shit either. Real shit. Shit no one else knows."

"Fine."

Jesse smirks, clanking his bottle to mine. "What's with you and the emo kid?"

"That's what you start with?"

"Answer the question."

"Fine." I roll my eyes. "If you're referring to Dylan, he's a friend and *only* a friend."

"Has he always been only a friend?"

"My turn," I say, ignoring his question. I know exactly what I want to ask him. I don't want to start off too personal in case he follows suit, but I can't bring myself to wait. "Why aren't you in school anymore?"

Jesse works his jaw, a dark look clouding over his features, making me instantly regret asking him. "Got kicked off the lacrosse team."

"Why?"

"My turn," he says, throwing my words back in my face. "Do you ever fantasize about that night?"

I don't miss how he deflects by turning the

122

conversation to something sexual in nature, but I feel my cheeks burn nonetheless, and I'm grateful to the night sky for concealing it. Instead of answering him, I tip the bottle to my lips, drinking the entire thing. I throw the empty bottle onto the sand and turn back to find Jesse looking at me with heat in his eyes, his bottom lip trapped between his teeth.

"I guess I got my answer. I do, too, if you were wondering."

"I wasn't," I lie. "Where do you disappear to?"

Jesse narrows his eyes at me before opting to chug instead.

"Interesting," I muse, trying to act nonchalant, when in reality, his reluctance to tell me only makes me more curious.

"What's up with the CD player?"

"My dad gave it to me on my fifth birthday." I smile at the memory. "Most kids would be getting a bike or—I don't know—dolls. I got a portable CD player and a Jimmy Eat World CD. I've had it ever since." I laugh. "Not as convenient as everything else these days, but I still prefer it. I guess I don't do well with change."

Jesse snorts.

"What about you?" I look over at him. "What were you like as a kid?"

He looks out at the black lake. "A punk. A white boy from the hood who couldn't stay out of trouble." I think about the picture I saw of him with the skateboard, unable to imagine that sweet little face getting into trouble. "Got kicked out of school a lot. Lo saved my ass, though. On more than one occasion." He takes a long pull of his beer. "She raised me. Our mom was always more concerned about getting her next fix than remembering she had mouths to feed."

"I had no idea," I say quietly. "I thought you were just some spoiled, lacrosse-playing, party-loving manwhore."

Jesse barks out an unexpected laugh at my blunt admission. "I guess that's what I became when I moved here." He chews on his bottom lip for a minute, seeming to think something over before he speaks again. "It's funny. You can't handle change, and I feel like all I've done my whole life is adapt to it. I don't know what the fuck *consistent* even feels like."

I study him, once again sensing that there's more to him than his persona. I want to swim in his depths, uncover every little hidden piece that the rest of the world doesn't get to see.

"Like a chameleon," I muse.

"What?"

"You adapt to survive."

"Seems I'm not the only one."

My eyebrows pull together in confusion.

"Someone incapable of adapting wouldn't move to a new town, all alone," he explains.

I lift a shoulder in response, but I don't elaborate. *They would if they didn't have any other options.*

We go back and forth, round after round, him avoiding all questions to do with what he does and where he goes when he's not here, me avoiding anything about my parents. The more we drink, the more sexually charged our questions become. I don't think Jesse even expects me to answer. I think he just likes to watch me squirm. We aren't even drinking when we opt not to answer anymore. We're just drinking to drink. Eventually, we're both lying on our backs with a graveyard of beer bottles around us. Jesse pulls out something that was tucked behind his ear, and the familiar smell tells me it's not a cigarette.

"How many girls have you been with?"

"We're really doing this? It's a little early on in the relationship to have the numbers discussion, don't you think?" His voice is raspy as he speaks, and then a second later, he lets out a cloud of smoke between us. He holds his hand out to me in offering, a brown blunt pinched between his thumb and forefinger. I shake my head. He shrugs, taking another hit.

"Not in a relationship," I correct.

"Honest answer? I don't know."

"Ballpark." I look over at him, one arm folded behind his head, the other holding the blunt an inch from his lips, forehead creased in concentration. My eyes have long adjusted to the dark by now, and I don't know if it's the alcohol talking, but it hits me out of nowhere that Jesse Shepherd is fucking beautiful.

"More than ten. Less than thirty?" He sounds anything but sure, but my stomach twists with unexpected jealousy, so I decide not to push for a more concrete answer. "What about you?"

"Pfft. Way too many to count," I joke. Jesse chokes, a plume of smoke rushing out of his mouth, and I can't help but laugh.

"You're a liar," he accuses.

"Nuh-uh. I've been with tons of girls."

"You're *so* funny," he drawls.

"I know." I feel my smile stretch across my face, but it falls when I notice how he's looking at me. "What?" I ask defensively.

"I want to try something," he says.

"Okay…"

"Come here."

I roll onto my side, heart pounding, but he hooks a finger into the belt loop of my jean shorts, pulling me until I'm straddling him. I brace my hands on his chest, my thighs cradling his torso. His free hand skates up my leg, and my head swims at the feeling.

"You're cold," he rasps, his voice sounding thicker than it was a second ago.

"I'm burning up," I argue. The cold can't touch me now. Between the lust and the alcohol, I'm on fire. The corner of his lip ticks into an almost-smile.

"You trust me?"

I nod, and then he brings the blunt to his lips once more, taking a long pull. Holding it in, he crooks his finger in a "come here" motion. I know what he wants to do, and with the position he chose, I have to be the one to make the move. Liquid courage fuels my movements as I lean down, my fingers bunching up his hoodie, then I press my lips to his. They're softer than I remember. He parts them, gently blowing until the smoke fills my mouth. I breathe it in, then pull back, looking down at him as I let it out. His hand tightens on my thigh, and the air is charged as we stare at each other. Jesse swallows hard, and I shift my hips a little lower, feeling how turned on he is through his jeans.

"You trust me?" It's my turn to ask. Jesse scrapes his teeth along his bottom lip as he flexes his hips upward, then nods. I bring both hands to either side of his face tentatively before lowering my mouth to his once more. When my tongue peeks out and flicks into his mouth, Jesse groans, wrapping a hand around the back of my neck to deepen the kiss.

All pretenses and inhibitions go out the window as our tongues slide together, my pulse beating wildly in my neck. Jesse's hand starts to tremble, and for some reason, I find it endearing. Like maybe he's just as affected as me. The tightening between my legs becomes almost unbearable, and I shift my hips, trying to assuage the feeling.

"Fuck," Jesse groans into my mouth. I pull back, lifting the hem of my shirt, but Jesse's hand covers mine, stopping me. His nostrils flare, eyes hard. He looks like he's in pain. "Stop." His voice is curt, but his thumb circles my exposed navel, as if to soften the blow of his harsh words.

My jaw goes slack when I realize he's rejecting me for a second time. I scoff bitterly, letting my shirt fall back into place before pushing his hand away roughly. "Unbelievable." I lift my leg, rolling off of him, then make quick work of putting my Docs back on.

"Allie—"

"Don't talk to me."

Jesse rolls his eyes, shaking his head as if I'm simply being a petulant child. From the corner of my eye, I see him lift his hoodie over his head a second before it lands on my head. I fling it off me onto the sand. *Might as well play the part.*

"Put it on."

"No."

"Goddammit, Allie. Wear the fucking sweatshirt."

The temperature has dropped since we've been out here, but the chill I feel has absolutely nothing to do with the weather. Jesse bends over to retrieve the sweatshirt before he takes matters into his own hands and pulls it over my head. When I realize he's going to try to dress me like a toddler if I don't comply, I reluctantly shove my arms through and then stand.

"Was that so fucking hard?"

I don't respond. Instead, I walk away as fast as I can without running, leaving him to collect the boneyard of bottles behind me.

CHAPTER EIGHTEEN

Allie

MY HEADPHONES ARE RIPPED FROM MY EARS AND thrown onto the table in front of me. "Hey!" I yell. "Spill it," Halston demands.

"How did you find me here?" I mutter, bitter that she found me. After I got back to Lo's house, the party was still going strong, so I grabbed my forgotten phone off the patio table and called Halston to come rescue me. I got a free pass from her interrogation last night in my sad, drunken state. But I knew all bets would be off today. So, here I am, passing the time in the library on a freaking *Saturday*, working on an assignment that isn't due for two weeks, before my shift at Blackbear starts.

"You don't have friends. Where else would you go?"

I open my mouth to say Dylan's, but she stops me.

"And Dylan doesn't count."

"I have other friends," I grumble.

Halston shoots me a look before pulling out a chair and makes herself comfortable, her folded hands resting on top of the table, a waxed to perfection eyebrow arched in expectation.

I sigh, shutting the screen of my laptop. "I almost hooked up with the enemy last night."

"If you're referring to the fucking god you're living with, that's a slight exaggeration, don't you think?"

"Whatever, Judas."

Her eyes roll toward the ceiling. "I see we're rolling with the dramatic theme. What happened?"

I debate on how much to divulge. Halston won't judge, but more than that, I'm genuinely baffled by his behavior, and I could use some advice from someone with more experience in this department. Shoving my pride aside, I decide to tell her everything. Every single detail from the very first night we hooked up in her dorm to last night.

"It just doesn't make sense. He pursues the shit out of me, and then when we're *right there*—" I smack the table for emphasis, earning a glare from a nearby student with thick, black glasses with round frames. "He pulls back. Twice, now. Am I some kind of a game to him? Oh God, what if I'm a bet?"

"What?" Halston laughs at my outlandish rambling.

"You know, like those teen romance movies circa 2002. The popular guy goes for the nerd slash loner girl and she fucking falls for it, only to learn she was just a bet all along."

"First of all, you're not a nerd. You're a hot chick with questionable fashion sense. Big difference."

"That's really comforting. Thank you for your sage words of wisdom. Really, I feel so much better now."

"Jesus, Allie." Halston's eyes grow wide. "You really like him!" she accuses, her voice increasing in volume. The same kid from before shushes us, but we ignore him.

"That's ridiculous." I scoff, shaking my head in denial, and this time, it's my voice that's rising in pitch.

"Can you two airheads go ponder the meaning of life somewhere else? Some of us actually have work to do."

"Pack it in, Potter!" Halston growls, glaring at him. "Or I'll tell the librarian what you're really doing over there." She points a manicured finger, gesturing at his screen, as a devious grin spreads across her face.

His cheeks turn tomato red and he snaps his mouth shut.

"That's right," she taunts. "I saw your screen when I came in. I'm pretty sure watching anime porn on school grounds is frowned upon."

A laugh spills out of me as he fumbles to pack his things up, tripping in his haste on the way out.

"You wouldn't care if you didn't like him," she continues, as if nothing happened.

My smile slips a little. "Okay, so maybe I like him a little," I admit. "It's just a crush. It's not a big deal."

"Exactly. So, why not ask him what's up with the Jekyll and Hyde act?"

"Uh, because then he'll know how I feel…"

"Pretty sure you showed him exactly how you felt when you threw that little hissy fit last night."

"Whose side are you on?" I bristle at her words, even though I know she's right.

"Hey," she holds up her hands in mock surrender, "I'm not saying I wouldn't have done the exact same thing and kicked him in the balls to really drive my point home. But don't write him off without hearing him out. That's all I'm saying."

"Well, he's not exactly beating my door down to explain."

"You don't have a door. You're homeless."

"You're an asshole," I say, but I can't hide my smile.

"You love me."

"I do. Anyway, enough about my crap. What's up with you? Have you been talking to Sullivan?"

She lifts a shoulder. "Here and there." I try to read her expression to no avail. Seems I'm not the only one keeping secrets. "Are you staying for Spring Break?"

"Yep." It's not like I have anywhere else to go. "You?"

"I wish." She sighs. "My parents are forcing me to go to some bullshit vineyard for the week."

I scrunch my nose. That sounds like my idea of hell. "At least your parents want you around." I didn't mean to say that out loud, and the look on Halston's face is exactly why. I didn't mean to make her feel guilty.

"Are we hanging out before you go?" I ask quickly in an effort to get the look of pity out of her eyes.

"What time do you work tomorrow?"

"Evening shift."

"I'll pick you up around eleven. We'll get pedis—my treat—and drink champagne."

"Yay," I deadpan, waving an invisible pom-pom.

I manage to make it through my shift at Blackbear unscathed. I didn't think Jesse would pass up an opportunity to harass me, but he never showed. He's probably moved on to his next willing victim by now.

"Why are you pouting?" Lo asks. I look up to see her watching me, propping a hand on her hip.

"I'm not pouting."

"You're scowling."

"I'm a scowler," I say, lifting a shoulder. "I'm not exactly Little Miss Sunshine if you haven't noticed," I joke, but her pinched lips and narrowed eyes tell me she's not buying it.

"Where'd you disappear to last night?"

I straighten, clearing my throat. "Halston called. Boy trouble. I went to stay with her."

"Mhm."

"You went upstairs. Jesse said you'd be a while."

"Whatever's got you upset wouldn't have anything to do with why Jess has been stomping around, slamming every door in the house, would it?"

I shake my head, not wanting to outright lie.

"You're a shit liar," she says. "But I'll let you keep your secrets for now."

Once Lo lets me off the hook, the rest of my shift goes quickly. It's just Grumpy Pete and me closing and naturally, I get full control of the song selection, so the day isn't all bad. By the time I get home, Dare and Lo are upstairs watching a movie, and Jesse is nowhere to be seen. After a quick shower, I don't bother putting on more than underwear and an old Metallica shirt that's five sizes too big. It's probably older than I am, and it's faded from black to a dingy gray color, but the material is soft and it's my favorite thing to wear to sleep. I crawl into bed, too tired to bother with my headphones tonight.

I don't know what time it is or what wakes me, but it's still dark when I tiptoe down the stairs to get some water. My bare feet pad across the cold wood floor as I head for the kitchen. Grabbing a black cup with a neon pink heart with the words *Bad Intentions* through it, I turn for the fridge, using the dispenser to fill it up. Faint laughter hits my ears half a second before the back door to my left slides open, scaring the shit out of me.

Three girls in barely-there bathing suits clumsily barrel inside, dripping wet and drunk, if their incessant giggling and shushing is anything to go by. "I told you they weren't together," the one girl I do recognize says, her voice sounding smug. *Sierra*. I tiptoe backwards into the hall, a sick feeling rolling through me. *Are they talking about me?*

"How do you know?" another girl asks.

"The fact that he was practically dry humping me in the hot tub was my first clue," Sierra says dryly.

I'm not with Jesse. The last thing I want is a relationship—*with anyone*. Why should I care about who he's hooking up with? I have no claim to him. So why are my eyes burning with unshed tears, and why does my stomach feel like it's suddenly full of lead? I take a step backwards, not wanting to hear any more, when I bump into something. Or some*one*. A hand comes around my mouth, muffling my yelp.

"Shh," Jesse says. I fight against his hold, not wanting his hands anywhere near me, but his arms band around me in a vise grip.

"Doesn't mean anything," another voice chimes in, and I stop my struggling, if only to avoid drawing their attention. "He doesn't exactly strike me as the monogamous type."

"I don't really give a shit, to be honest," the devil in the form of a Victoria's Secret model says flippantly. "As long as he gives me that big, fat—"

Having heard more than enough, I bite down on Jesse's fingers, causing him to hiss, but he doesn't pull away. He pushes me forward, my chest pressed against the wall. I attempt to kick him in the balls, but it's a fail from this angle, and he simply arches out of the way. "Stop and listen," he growls into my ear. I blow a piece of hair out of my face.

"Why?" I whisper. Why the hell does he *want* me to hear this? "I fucking get it, okay?"

"I wonder if he's good in bed," one of them muses. "Just because he has the equipment doesn't mean he knows how to use it."

"Please." Sierra scoffs. "Of course he does."

I jerk against his hold once more as hurt morphs into anger. Anger is good. Much better than feeling sad. Jesse tightens his hold, bringing his lips close to my ear. "Just listen," he says, his voice soft, almost apologetic. Like he knows exactly what he's doing to me by making me hear this shit.

"And Jesse doesn't care that you're going for his friend?" This is from another voice I don't recognize.

I freeze in Jesse's hold, realization setting in. *They're not talking about him.* When he senses me soften, I feel Jesse's smile against my neck. The stretched-out collar of my oversized shirt hangs loosely off one shoulder, and he skims his lips back and forth on my exposed skin.

"Once he sees someone else playing with his toy, he'll want it back." She laughs.

"No, he won't," Jesse argues low in my ear. His hand leaves my mouth, trailing down toward the hem of my shirt. I stiffen, but don't object as he reaches under, softly stroking my thigh before cupping me between my legs. "I have exactly what I want in the palm of my hand."

"Where is he, anyway?" one of them asks.

"I don't know. He said he was going to make a drink, but he never came back out."

"He found something better to do," Jesse says while a single finger traces me through my underwear. I gasp, my head falling back onto his shoulder. The sound of "Bad

Guy" from Billie Eilish floats in from the back door that they neglected to close as he continues his ministrations. Soft, teasing strokes, enough to drive me crazy, but not enough to get me off.

"He's probably hooking up with that girl upstairs," one girl jokes. She has no idea how close to the truth she is.

"Ew, Allison? Please. That frigid bitch couldn't handle him—"

"She feels nice and warm to me," Jess counters, slipping his fingers beneath my underwear. I gasp at his touch. "Wet, too." His voice grows thick. "So fucking wet."

"Jesse, we shouldn't—"

"She's way too uptight," Sierra continues, and her minions laugh on cue. Jesse slides a finger inside me, causing me to gasp again.

"Uptight? Nah. Tight? Very."

A moan slips free from the back of my throat and my eyes pop open, hoping to hell no one heard.

"Shut up," Sierra hisses sharply. "Did you hear that?"

"Hurry up and make the drinks. He said his sister and her boyfriend are upstairs."

I let out the breath I was holding when I hear them clanking around in the fridge. Jesse spins me around, my back hitting the wall with a soft thud. His wet hair hangs down on his forehead and his black swim shorts are damp, but his plain white tee is dry. I catch myself pouting at the knowledge that he was in the hot tub with those girls, even if nothing happened, but then he's lifting me up, my legs wrapping around his waist, before prowling toward the hall bathroom. He kicks the door shut, not bothering to be quiet, and then his mouth is on mine.

My hands fly into his wet hair, too wound up to

maintain any semblance of playing it cool. Jesse flips us around so that my back is pressed up against the door. Using it for leverage along with his hips, he slides both hands up my sides until he's cupping me through my shirt, flicking my nipples with the pads of his thumbs.

"Jesse," I breathe, trying not to push my chest into his hands, unable to put my thoughts into words, so I settle with, "Please." *Please don't stop. Please don't walk away. Please make me feel good.*

"I'm not fucking leaving this time, Allie," Jesse rasps, reading my mind as he flexes his hips into me.

"Good."

He dips down to kiss my neck, pushing my shirt up in the process, but I stop his wandering hands with mine as a thought occurs to me. "Wait."

"What?" he says into my neck in between licks and kisses.

"I don't want you to touch her if we're doing this."

"Fuck her," he says, going back in for more. I arch my neck, my head falling against the door.

"I mean it, Jesse. Her or anyone else. When you're done with me, tell me first." I try to sound firm, but I sound vulnerable, even to my own ears and I hate it.

He pulls back, hazel eyes lifting to mine, regarding me with something I can't quite put my finger on. My stomach swirls with nerves, waiting for his response. I bite down on my lip, feeling completely exposed under his scrutiny, unsure of what's going through his mind—of what he's going to say—but he shocks me when he says, "Same goes for you."

I give a small smile, nodding in agreeance. Jesse wastes no time, gripping my ass and spinning me around before he plants me on the sink. I squeal when the cool granite hits my exposed, overheated skin, but he smothers the noise with his mouth when he kisses me again. Deft fingers find the heat between my thighs once more, moving my panties to the side. When he finally fills me with them, I bite down on his shoulder to keep from crying out.

Jesse groans, pumping harder. I grip his upper arms and rest my forehead on his shoulder, looking down at the way the thick veins in his forearm bulge with the movement. "Fuck, Allie." I feel myself clench around his fingers at his words and he curses again before pulling his fingers from me.

He drops to his knees and hooks his fingers into the waistband of my black underwear before sliding them down my legs. My heart jumps in my chest, equal parts excited and anxious for what's about to happen. Once they reach my ankles, I point my toes so they fall easily to the floor.

"Spread your legs for me."

My face heats at the command, but I do it nonetheless. Jesse stares between my legs for long seconds, and I fight the urge to squeeze them shut.

"Fucking beautiful," he says before leaning forward. His nose grazes my leg on his trail upward. He plants little kisses in the insides of my right thigh, then my left, and everywhere in between, ignoring the place I want him most. I'm practically shaking when his tongue finally meets my center, taking one, long swipe. My hips buck forward of their own volition, my knees lifting. Jesse grips my shins, spreading me farther as he licks at me, and I'm drunk on the feeling, drunk on *him*. My sweaty palms slip on the counter and I fall back onto my forearms, squeezing my eyes shut at the sensations running through me. My thighs start to tremble, and when he sucks my clit into his mouth, I nearly fall apart.

To my complete and utter horror, he stops too soon, wiping his mouth with the back of his hand. "I want you to come on my cock." Once again, his blunt words take me by surprise. My wide eyes must show my hesitation, because he gives me a lazy smirk.

"I'm not going to fuck you for the first time in a bathroom, Allie." I swallow hard, nodding, even though he's given me absolutely zero reason to trust him. Jesse tugs the string to his swim shorts. Using my feet, I push them down his hips. His length bobs between us, thick and hard. I gulp at the sight, unable to stop myself from staring, suddenly forgetting all the reasons I should deprive myself of having sex with Jesse fucking Shepherd.

Jess pinches my chin between his finger and thumb. "If I'm going to have any self-control, you're gonna have to stop looking at my dick like that."

"Sorry." I don't know why I apologize, but my nerves are on another level right now. Still holding my chin, he leans in, kissing me deep and slow. I lean back on the palms of my hands, parting my legs to let him in the space between. His fingers curl around the nape of my neck, his thumb resting on my cheek as his warm, hard flesh meets my soft. We both suck in a breath, and Jess rolls his forehead against mine, his eyes squeezed shut. He lines himself up with my center before thrusting upward, sliding through my slick heat. I jolt at the feeling, and his grip on my neck tightens.

"Goddamn, Allie. If not fucking you feels this good, I can't imagine the real thing."

His words spur me on and I rock my hips, sliding along his length, causing him to groan. Letting go of me, he pulls back to grip my hips, then tugs, making me shift down even farther. My ass hangs off the edge of the sink now, and he hooks his hands under my knees, holding me in place.

"Oh my God," I breathe, my head suddenly feeling too heavy to hold up. I'm not even attempting to be quiet at this point, his company long forgotten. Jesse releases my right thigh for half a second to lift the hem of his shirt, stuffing it under his chin in one swift motion. His eyes are fixed on where we're connected, his abs flexing with each thrust.

"I could slip inside you so easily right now," he says, the thick head of his cock nudging against my entrance, teasing.

I can't form a response. All I know is that I want more of this. I'm so close.

"Lift your shirt and show me those perfect fucking tits," he orders. I feel myself clench at his words, and the smug look in his eyes tells me he feels it. His blunt words usually embarrass me, but when we're like this, nothing turns me on more. Resting my weight on one elbow, my hand makes its slow descent. My fingertips curl around the bottom of my shirt before I peel it up, exposing my chest, the cool air hitting my almost painfully hard nipples.

"Hottest thing I've ever seen in my life," Jesse says, his voice strained. I feel myself pulse against him, wondering what would happen if I tilted my hips and took him inside me. Jesse's movements grow rougher, and I hold my breath as I feel the sensation building.

"I think I'm close," I confess, my body tensing with the impending orgasm. Jesse leans down and sucks a nipple into his mouth, and that's all it takes to send me over the edge. I cry out, my legs shaking as my arms give out. I'm flat against the counter as Jesse holds my spent legs, his length rubbing against my sensitive clit as I jerk with aftershocks. He gives one final hard pump of his hips, and then he curses as warm liquid spills onto me.

Gathering me in his arms, he lifts my boneless body. Mustering up every ounce of my strength, I wrap my limp legs around his waist. He lowers me to the soft rug before slumping into me, his sweaty cheek resting against my chest, and I know my heart must be pounding in his ear. Neither one of us speaks as our breathing evens out. I'm too afraid to break the spell, to go back to pretending not to like him. *I think the jig is up.*

Jesse peels himself off me, reaching behind his neck to tug his shirt over his head before bringing it between my legs. The move is thoughtful. Unexpected. My brows tug together as I watch him, once again, trying to figure him out.

"Allie—" he starts, but someone knocks on the door. My wide eyes fly to Jesse's, full of panic, but he looks cool as a fucking cucumber.

"No one can know," I blurt out. When this thing with Jesse ends, and it will, I don't want to look like a fool.

Jesse's expression goes blank, his eyes flat. "Give me a minute," he barks at whoever's on the outside of the door.

"What the fuck, Shep? Have you been taking a shit this entire time?"

Sully? Oh my God. That's who Sierra was talking about? I narrow my eyes, ready to shove him off me, but he must anticipate my reaction, because he straddles my waist, pinning my wrists to the floor. "Halston knows."

What? I highly doubt that's true.

Another knock.

"I said give me a fucking minute!"

"Pinch it off already!"

Jesse shakes his head, annoyed. Once we hear Sullivan's retreating footsteps, Jesse hurries to explain.

"They have an understanding."

"There is no way Halston would be okay with this."

"It was her idea," he says, lifting a single brow. "I'm going to go get rid of these assholes. Give it two minutes, then you can leave."

I nod wordlessly, feeling ridiculous and awkward as I lie here exposed. Jesse obviously doesn't have the same hang-up. He stands, gloriously naked, still half-hard, without a care in the world. He bends over to pull his shorts on, letting them hang loosely off his hips, showcasing that ridiculously cut Adonis belt. I sit up, tugging my shirt down over my knees as I scan the floor for my underwear in an attempt to look anywhere but at him.

"Two minutes," Jesse reminds me with his hand on the doorknob. I nod again, tucking a wayward piece of hair behind my ear.

Once he's gone, I do as I'm told, waiting a couple of minutes before I make my escape. I peek out into the hall, and when I don't see or hear anything, I tiptoe back upstairs. The clock on my phone reads *2:17 A.M.* I contemplate calling Halston, but I decide to wait until morning. No need to ruin her night if what he says isn't true.

"Two minutes" soon turns into twenty. I can hear them partying down there like nothing happened. Then thirty minutes passes, then forty-five, and finally, somewhere around the hour mark, I accept the fact that Jesse's not coming. I tell myself it's a good thing. This thing between us isn't serious, and I'd do well to remember that. I hear a loud squeal followed by a splash, and I pull a pillow over my head to block out the sound. How the hell do Lo and Dare sleep through this shit? I flip my blankets off and stand to flip the lock on the door before climbing back into bed. There's no way I'd be able to sleep with it unlocked knowing those assholes are downstairs.

My body is tired and sated, but my mind is going a mile a minute. I reach for my headphones, hitting shuffle to drown out all thoughts of Jesse. I huff out a laugh when Something Corporate comes on, singing about a girl who's feeling empty and worthless after another meaningless hookup, the irony not lost on me. I hit the *skip* button. *Much better.* Stuffing my CD player under my pillow, I close my heavy eyelids and drift to sleep.

CHAPTER NINETEEN

Jess

EALING WITH DRUNK COLLEGE GIRLS IS LIKE trying to herd cats. They're impulsive, knock shit over while deadass looking you in the eye without a single fuck given, then they rub up against you when they want attention.

Sully talked me into having another drink while he bitched about Halston, which led to two, which then led to smoking a blunt, all while the girls proceeded to get progressively drunker, which brings us to now. Sully and I are standing over near the fence smoking a cigarette while Sierra makes out with the brunette—Jessica, maybe—in the hot tub. Even as I watch their tongues tangle together, their tits pressed against each other, I feel nothing more than annoyance at the fact that they're still here, keeping me from Allie.

Fuck. Allie. Almost fucking her was the best sex I've never had. I don't know what it is about her. Going back and forth with her feels like foreplay and after last night, I knew I'd end up going back for more. Nothing could have prepared me for how good she felt. After experiencing Allie, this shit in front of me? It feels fake as fuck. Fake moans, fake laughter, fake feelings. *Fake, fake, fake.*

"All right," I say, snatching the blunt from Sully's fingers and prematurely stubbing it out on the bottom of my shoe, despite his protests. "Time to get the fuck out."

"What the fuck, Shep? You choose *now*?" He cuts his eyes toward the show the girls are putting on.

"Stop trying to prove a point and go home, man." He may think he wants this, but he doesn't want to be here. Not really. He's all fucked up over the fact that Halston wants to keep things casual, so naturally, he set out to even the score. I'm just waiting for him to realize it.

"I'm drunk as fuck," he admits, avoiding my unspoken accusation. "I can't take them home." I pull my phone out of my pocket, and with a few clicks, I've solved that problem.

"There. Ordered an Uber. You can crash on the couch, but I want them gone." He's the one who invited them without my permission; he can deal with getting them out of here. I'm already going to catch shit from Lo. When she catches wind of this, she's going to think it's me spiraling, when in reality, tonight is a product of Sullivan getting all up in his feelings.

"You heard the man." Sully claps his hands together. "Your ride will be here in—" He looks to me and I check my app before holding up five fingers. "Five minutes."

Sierra's fuming. I can sense it even from here. She doesn't handle rejection well. I don't think she's ever experienced it before me. In a rather pathetic attempt to tip the scales back in her favor, she exits the hot tub, dripping wet as she struts over to Sullivan. Once she's within arm's reach, she presses onto her toes and grips his dick while she shoves her tongue down his throat.

When she finally pulls back, she smiles victoriously at

Sullivan's dazed expression. "Call me," she says before turning around to gather her clothes and purse, her friends following suit.

"Remind me again why they have to leave," Sully says, still watching their asses as they walk through my house toward the front door.

"Because you'll regret it tomorrow," I say, clapping him on the shoulder on my way inside.

"Where the hell are you going in such a hurry?" Sully asks, suspicion in his voice, even in his drunken state.

"Don't worry about it."

Sullivan lumbers in after me, shutting the door behind him before collapsing facedown onto the couch like a sack of potatoes, promptly passing the fuck out.

"Goodnight." I laugh, saluting him. I jog up the stairs, but when I turn Allie's doorknob, I find it locked. The regret's setting in so soon?*Interesting*. I could easily pop the lock, but I decide to go through my still-empty, still bedless room, grabbing a pair of sweats on the way. This time, the bathroom knob turns, and I feel my lips stretch into a smile. She doesn't want to keep me away. She just wants to keep up the pretense of wanting to keep me away. I leave the bathroom door cracked, leaving just enough light to illuminate her sleeping form.

I drop my shorts and quickly pull on my sweats before climbing into bed. She's on her side, facing away from me with her headphones, complete with those ridiculous, puffy, foam pads over the earpieces. I move in behind her, snaking an arm around her waist before I gently peel them from her and toss them to the edge of the bed. "Still playing games, Allie Girl?" I whisper into the dark. She moans in her sleep before rolling to face me and I lift my arm, letting her get comfortable. Her dark eyelashes rest on her full cheeks, her lips pursed in an adorable fucking pout. She looks so innocent when she's not glaring daggers at me. I slide my palm underneath the back of her shirt, feeling her warm skin, and pull her closer. She burrows into me, her face nuzzling into my chest, wedging a thigh between mine.

I'm starting to find that being with Allison quiets every fucking thing I'm forced to face. When I'm with her, I don't think about my endless failures. I don't worry about my mom or Henry, the fact that I'm lying to everyone I know, or the fact that I have zero direction in life. And it's here, with Allie in my bed, that I have the best sleep of my life.

I wake up to the sound of knocking, followed by an earthquake. No, not an earthquake. It's Allison frantically shaking me, her face a mixture of panic and...anger? "What the hell are you doing in my bed?" she whisper-shouts.

I yawn, stretching. "It's actually my bed."

"Allie?" Lo's voice comes from the other side of the door.

"Go!" Allie shoves me out of bed and I hit the floor with a thud.

"Calm the fuck down," I mutter. It's just Lo. "You keep freaking out every time we're almost seen together and I'm going to develop a complex."

"Just a sec!" Allison shouts back, shooting me a look. She stands, pulling on a pair of black sweatpants from her drawer before moving toward the door. She looks at me over her shoulder, motioning for me to go into the bathroom.

"You owe me," I say, standing my ground. She glares, but impatience wins out and she mouths *fine*. I send her a wink before closing the bathroom door.

"Hey," I hear her say. "Sorry, I was trying to find some pants."

"Everything okay?" Lo asks.

"Yeah?" Allison responds, but it sounds more like a question.

"Have you seen Jess? There's a drunk guy on my couch and he's not in his room."

Shit, I forgot about Sullivan.

"Nope," Allie says, and Jesus Christ, she has to be the worst liar I've ever encountered. I roll my eyes, reaching behind me to flush the toilet before I open the door. I make a show out of adjusting myself, like I just went to the bathroom. *Take notes, Allie. This is how to lie convincingly.*

"I was taking a piss. What's up?"

Lo eyes me skeptically, then looks between the two of us. Allie picks at her nails, looking like she'd rather be anywhere but here. *Real smooth.*

"Dare and I are leaving for a while."

"Okay." Since when does she give me a play-by-play of her day? "Have fun, I guess."

"I mean, like, for a week."

"As in a vacation?" I ask, my eyebrows jumping in surprise.

"I guess that's what you'd call it." Her mouth breaks into a wide smile. "I've never been on a vacation."

"When?"

"Now."

"*Now*?"

"It was a surprise."

Ah, now it makes sense. Dare has been trying to get her to go away with him, but she always has an excuse, usually involving work or me.

"Jake's covering my shifts, but they could use you if you want to make a few bucks," she says. "I'm leaving money on the counter for food. I don't care if you have people over, just don't break anything, don't let anyone puke inside, and stay out of my room. I'll have my phone if you need me."

"Jesus Christ, Lo, would you get the fuck out of here already?"

She rolls her eyes, moving through Allison's room to meet me in the doorway. She reaches up to wrap her arms around my neck and kisses my temple. I lock eyes with Allie over Lo's shoulder. She's watching us curiously. She does that a lot, I've noticed. As if she's always trying to figure people out.

"Love you, asshole," Lo says, pulling back before mussing up my already-disheveled hair.

"Love you, too."

Lo worries her bottom lip, and I can tell she's overthinking. She might be living the good life with Dare now, but she still hasn't seemed to figure out that she's allowed to do things for herself. She doesn't know what the fuck to do with herself now that she doesn't have to take care of everyone around her. Leaving for school was supposed to give her a chance to live her life. She sacrificed everything for me, and even though I'm not exactly a team player, I took the lacrosse scholarship.

I did it for two reasons. The first being that I didn't want to let her down—look how well that turned out—and the second being that I didn't want her to put her life on hold any longer. I didn't want to be her crutch. You can take the girl out of the ghetto, but you can't take years of conditioning out of the girl.

There are three kinds of people where we're from. The kind who never get out, the kind who are lucky enough to get out and *stay* out, and the kind that get out for a while but ultimately end up back where they started when they realize they weren't meant for more. Lo always said I'd be the successful one—that it was me who'd dig us out of our world full of drugs and poverty and crime. She thought I'd be the one with the future. She didn't realize that it was her all along. I felt like a fucking imposter when I tried to play the part. I fall into the last category.

"Hey." I snap my fingers in front of her face. Her gaze snaps up to mine. "You're going on a vacation with your boyfriend, not being sentenced to death row. Try to look happy about it."

"I am," she insists.

"I'll be fine. I have Allison to take care of me. Isn't that right, Allie Girl?"

Allison pulls a face, arms folded under the perfect tits I know are hiding beneath that haggard ass T-shirt. "You're on your own."

Lo laughs and slaps my cheek lightly. "Behave. If you get arrested, you're shit out of luck for a *week*. Oh, and you'll get Allison to work if she needs it."

"Noted."

Lo opens her mouth to speak again, but before she can get a word out, we hear a loud *"What the hell?"* come from downstairs.

"Who the fuck is on my couch?" Dare shouts. Allison flattens her lips to hide a smile.

"That's my cue." Lo Laughs.

Once Lo's gone, I lock eyes with Allison, the silence stretching between us as she fiddles with the hem of her shirt.

"Guess it's just you and me," I say, walking toward her bed before lying back down, folding my hands behind my head.

"What are you doing?" Allie's eyes cut toward the door, making sure we're alone before closing it.

"I wasn't ready to wake up. Get back in bed."

"We are not making a habit of this," she hisses. Her words say one thing, but the way her eyes trail down my stomach to the morning wood in my sweats says another thing entirely.

"We'll see about that."

She stands her ground, arms still crossed in defiance. I swing my legs over the edge of the bed, then stalk toward her.

"Stay away," she says, backing up as I advance on her. I pause mid-step, cocking my head to the side as I try to get a read on her. "You don't play fair," she explains. "My brain says one thing, but then you touch me and—" Allie stops abruptly, then clamps her mouth shut, as if she didn't intend to reveal that fun little piece of information.

"And what?" I ask, taking another step in her direction.

"You're a bad influence."

I smirk, taking another step, effectively closing the distance between us. "I've been called worse."

"This isn't a good idea," she almost whispers, her gaze trained on my chest, avoiding eye contact. Her hair, all wavy and wild from sleep, falls in front of her face. I pinch a strand between my thumb and fingers, feeling the soft strands against my callused fingers.

"The best things never are."

Big gray eyes lift to mine, searching. "What do you want, Jesse?" she asks.

"You," I say simply.

"Why?"

"Do I need a reason?"

She tries to move past me with a huff, but I block her path. "I don't know, okay," I admit through gritted teeth. "I just know that I do."

"There are plenty of other willing victims. Go play with one of them instead."

"I don't want them."

"Well, I don't want you," she snaps.

"That might have been more convincing if my cock wasn't still covered in your cum." Her cheeks bloom red with a mixture of what I'm sure is both anger and embarrassment. I turn around, heading for the bathroom, leaving her to seethe in peace. Not bothering to close the bathroom door, I turn the hot water on, then drop my sweats. I step under the hot water, images of last night flashing through my mind. My dick stirs at the thought, and I grip it with a tight fist, giving myself a single stroke. Before I get any farther, the shower curtain is wrenched open.

"Just because my body has a physiological reaction to you doesn't mean I like you."

"Obviously," I deadpan. That sums up about ninety-nine percent of the "relationships" I've been in.

"And say we hooked up again," she starts, her eyes dying to drift south. "It would stay between us?" I should feel victorious, but I can't help but fixate on the last part of her question. She wants me to be her dirty little secret. If I stopped to analyze it, I'm sure I'd be offended.

"Why, Allison, are you proposing a secret, sexual relationship with me?"

"Forget it." She turns to leave, but my hand snaps out, catching her wrist. We lock eyes, tension building between us. I can practically feel her wall going back up, brick by brick. She pushes, I push back, neither one of us wanting to be the first to bend—the first to show something real.

"Say something," she pleads, gaze fixed on my stomach, and not an inch lower. The water from the showerhead is starting to make a mess with the curtain being open, pooling under her bare feet.

"No one has to know," I say the words she wants to hear through gritted teeth. My fingers are still clutching her wrist when her hand moves toward me, flattening against my chest. My muscles tighten under her touch as she tentatively slides her palm downward, exploring. Her eyes flick toward the door, but her hand continues its descent. The tips of her fingers graze my happy trail, and I can feel her warmth radiating from her palm on my cock right before she wraps her hand around me. My eyes close, head dropping back onto my shoulders.

"Sullivan," she says, her voice breathy.

My head snaps back up, the grip on her wrist tightening. "The fuck did you just say?"

She jerks her wrist out of my hand, nearly slipping on the wet floor before righting herself. "Halston's here. I forgot she was picking me up."

I sigh, running a hand through my wet hair to get it out of my face. Allie hurries out the door, leaving me high and dry. And hard. *Fuck you, Sully.*

CHAPTER TWENTY

Allie

I HURRY DOWN THE STAIRS, WANTING TO WARN HALSTON before she's ambushed by the sight of a drunken Sullivan passed out on the couch, but I'm too late. She's standing in front of the couch, arms crossed, eyebrow arched, looking down at him as he scrambles to sit up. Dare and Lo, thankfully, are nowhere to be seen. They must have left already.

"Halston—" Sullivan starts, but she holds up her hand, cutting him off.

"Not my business."

I study her, looking for any signs of deception, trying to gauge how she really feels about this. She turns to me, taking in my baggy sweats, damp shirt, and messy pony-tail. "Tell me you're not going like that."

"I woke up late." I shrug.

She scrunches her nose. "Well, fix it." She laughs.

"Halston, can we talk?" Sullivan tries again.

"Nothing to talk about. You had an itch and I wasn't around to scratch it," she says, the picture of nonchalance. She turns away, heading for the stairs.

"Nothing happened," he promises, standing as if he's going to go after her. But then his blanket falls, revealing the fact he's not wearing pants.

"Jesus, Sullivan." I cover my eyes. "I did not need to see that." He scrambles to cover himself, falling back onto the couch and balling the blanket up on his lap.

"Yeah, sure looks like nothing happened," Halston challenges, with a pointed look before she gives him her back once more. "Oh, by the way," she pauses, one hand on the stair rail, "the next time you're going to lie, make sure the evidence isn't plastered all over Sierra's socials." Sullivan sighs, dejected, raking a hand through his hair.

Once we're in my room, I shut the door behind her. I can still hear the shower running, and I quickly shut that door, too.

"I found out in the middle of the night," I say, walking over to sit on the edge of my bed. "I almost kicked his ass, but Jesse told me you knew. I should've known he was trying to cover his friend's ass."

"He wasn't lying." Halston pops a shoulder, unconcerned. "We have an understanding."

"You're shitting me. I thought you liked him."

"I do."

"Then why…"

"Because we're in college," she points out, like it should be obvious. "And he's Sullivan. He couldn't be faithful if his life depended on it. His type never is." She sighs, moving toward my temporary closet, sifting through the few articles of clothing I've actually managed to hang. "These boys… Their only mission in life is to collect as many conquests as possible."

I bob my head in silent agreement, unease rolling through me. "So, you hook up with him knowing he's hooking up with other girls? Doesn't it bother you?"

Halston glances at me over her shoulder. "Sometimes."

I think back to last night, and how jealous I was when I thought Sierra had been talking about Jesse, and we're not even together. We're nothing. But it doesn't feel like nothing.

"Do you think friends with benefits actually works?" I ask, genuinely curious.

"For some people, sure." Halston settles on a white cropped T-shirt, peeling it off the hanger before tossing it onto my lap. I'm not at all surprised she picked the smallest piece of clothing in there. She squats down to riffle through my suitcase. "The key is to have ground rules."

"Such as?"

"That depends on you and your expectations," she says, holding up a pair of old, ripped jeans before throwing them to the reject pile to join the other pieces she deems unworthy. "My personal rules are no hooking up with other people on the same day, no cuddling, no sleepovers, no unprotected sex, and most importantly, no lying. And Sullivan," she stands, throwing a pair of high-waisted jean shorts at me, "is a liar."

"I'm not wearing these," I say, bunching the shorts into a ball.

"Yes, you are. We're getting pedicures, remember?"

"Fine," I relent, kicking off my sweats, wishing I had a chance to shower after last night's—*ahem*—activities. I pull my shorts up quickly. "Hand me that bra," I say, pointing at the suitcase. Once she hands it to me, I turn away to change. "For what it's worth, I don't think Sullivan got very far with Sierra."

"How would you know?"

I walk back over to my suitcase, plucking a pair of gray socks to go with my boots because I don't even *own* a pair of flip-flops. "I overheard some stuff. She was trying to use him to make Jesse jealous."

"And then I sent their drunk asses home in an Uber," Jess says, standing in the bathroom doorway, towel tied around his waist. I didn't even hear him.

"Knock much?" I snap, trying to appear unaffected by the way he looks, his dark wet hair slicked back, beads of water trailing down his chest.

"Stare much?" he counters. I flip him off, sitting on the edge of my bed to pull my boots on before gathering a jacket and my work shirt to throw into my backpack for later. He returns his attention to Halston, who's pinning me with an accusatory expression. "Even drunker than shit with a chip on his shoulder, he still passed on the opportunity. I wonder why that is?"

Halston shrugs. "He didn't want the herp?"

"Funny," Jesse deadpans. I take advantage of their little tête-à-tête, seizing the opportunity to use the bathroom and brush my teeth. When I come out, they're speaking in hushed tones, but they stop when they see me, Halston glaring at him through narrowed eyes.

"We're leaving," I interrupt their staring contest, tugging on Halston's wrist.

"We're going to talk about what you were doing up with Jesse in the middle of the night. And don't think I didn't notice you failed to inform me that you share a *bathroom*," she says in the loudest whisper known to man as we make our way down the stairs.

"Shut up," I hiss, hurrying down the steps. I don't need Jesse—or Sullivan for that matter—overhearing anything.

Three hours later, my fingers and toes are painted glossy and black, my stomach is full of tacos and margaritas—Halston promised this restaurant wouldn't card, and she was right—and I've successfully managed to field all questions pertaining to Jesse. I didn't outright lie. I simply…downplayed.

"What am I going to do without you for an entire week?" I pout, then lick the leftover salt off the rim of my margarita.

"I think you'll have your hands full," she says pointedly. "I'll be the one suffering. Wanna trade?"

A week with Halston's rich, overbearing parents? I'll pass. "What were you and Jesse whispering about, by the way?"

"Nothing." She plugs the tip of the miniature lime green straw in her drink, then sucks the slush out of the bottom.

I narrow my eyes at her, but before I can press, my phone lights up on the tabletop with a number I don't recognize. I don't usually answer unfamiliar numbers, but this one's local, and my curiosity is piqued. I bring my phone to my ear. "Hello?"

"Allison?"

"This is she." Halston sends me a questioning look, mouthing *who is it*, and I shrug.

"This is Victor."

"Oh." I sit up straighter. "How are you?"

"Can't complain. I wanted to see if you were still interested in throwing an event."

"Yes!" I say a little too eagerly, and his amused laughter rumbles in my ear.

"Not this Friday, but next. Does that give you a sufficient amount of time?"

"I can make that work," I say with confidence I don't

feel. It's the end of the semester, and school is going to take over my life after Spring Break, but I can't pass this up.

"That's what I like to hear. If this goes well, we can talk about a possible summer internship. That is, if you're interested."

"Definitely interested," I say, trying not to squeal like a schoolgirl. "Thank you so much."

"Don't thank me yet. Text me your email and I'll send the information over."

He hangs up without another word, and I relay the details to Halston, whose excitement rivals mine. "Holy shit, Allie! That's cause for celebration. One more drink?"

"When you get back." I check the time on my phone. "I have to get to work, and I think showing up drunk would be frowned upon."

"Fine, party pooper."

"You're just stalling because you don't want to go home."

"That, too," she admits. "But I really am happy for you."

"Thanks." Since moving to River's Edge, I've felt…lost. Lacking direction, and like I don't belong. Having this fall into place is the first thing that's felt right. Maybe I'm right where I'm supposed to be. I tap out a quick text to Dylan, telling him to meet me at Blackbear tonight so I can deliver the good news in person, then Halston drops me off at work. When I show up, Jake, Grumpy Pete, and a couple of other servers are here, but Jesse's noticeably absent. The first part of my shift goes by quickly. I'm on autopilot, thinking of everything from the flyers I want to design to the best way to get the word out.

I'm coming out of the bathroom when a hand darts out, pulling me into the back room. "Whoa," I squeal before I'm pulled into Jesse's chest.

"Hi," he says, wrapping his arms around my waist, resting on my lower back.

"Hi," I breathe, my neck straining in order to meet his eyes.

"We didn't get a chance to finish our conversation earlier."

"I don't think now is the time," I say, glancing over my shoulder to make sure we don't have an audience, my heart kicking up in speed at the tone of his voice.

"Why not?" He bends down to squeeze my ass in his palms.

"Someone could walk in."

"That's half the fun," he says, one of his hands dipping into the gap in my waistband before curling around the curve of my butt cheek.

I sag into him, my pulse quickening. He takes the opportunity to kiss me, and I open for him, allowing his tongue to brush against mine. Suddenly, his hands are gripping my waist as he sits in one of the chairs, pulling me to straddle him, never breaking the connection.

My hands find his face, allowing myself to get lost in the kiss, unable to resist the pull. Something about Jesse makes all of my common sense fly out the window. He smooths his hands up my back as I grind on his lap, his need evident beneath me.

Mustering every ounce of self-control, I pull back, breathless. "We have to stop." I clumsily climb off his lap before wiping the corners of my lips and straightening my clothes.

Jesse gives me a lazy smirk, his eyes promising that this isn't over. I hurry back, avoiding eye contact with everyone I pass, afraid my flustered expression will give me away. When I reach my section, I find Dylan and the guys sitting there.

"Hi," I say, smiling.

Hunter stands to hug me, then pulls back, gripping me by the shoulders. "Why are you all flushed and shit? Are you sick?"

"No," I say quickly. "I'm just excited." Dylan's gaze fixes on something behind me, and I look back to find Jesse standing near the bar, watching us with an unreadable expression.

"I bet you are," Dylan remarks, eyeing Jesse with contempt. Ignoring him, I walk over to hug Caleb.

"I only have a minute," I start, "but I heard from Victor. He asked me to plan a show for next Friday, so naturally..."

"Naturally, you thought of the most talented fuckers you know," Hunter supplies.

"Yes. That." I laugh. "You in?"

"Just name the time and place, baby," Hunter quips.

"I'm in," Caleb agrees.

My smile slips when I see Dylan's expression. He's not the most expressive person I've ever met, but I expected some degree of... I don't know, happiness? Instead, he's absently spinning a butter knife on the tabletop, seemingly lost in thought. "Dylan?" I prompt when he doesn't say anything.

His gaze snaps to mine. "Sounds good, Al. Thanks."

"If you don't want to, I could get someone else," I offer, unable to keep the disappointment out of my tone. I guess I could ask Garrett. "I thought you'd be excited."

"No." Dylan shakes his head. "No, this is great." He stands, his palm flattening on the side of my head before he leans down to press a kiss to my cheek. "I've gotta go. Call me tomorrow. We can talk about the setlist."

I catch his hand when he tries to leave. He pauses, troubled brown eyes meeting mine as he chews on his lip ring. I move in closer, lowering my voice. "Is everything okay?"

He gives me a forced half-smile that's meant to be comforting but feels anything but, and with a clipped nod, he's gone.

"He's been in a weird mood all day," Caleb says, giving my shoulder a squeeze.

"Yeah," Hunter agrees, looping an arm around my shoulders. "It's not about you. You're the fucking best for this."

"Make sure he's okay," I say.

Hunter nods before they leave to catch up with Dylan. I make a mental note to be a better friend to Dylan. I've been so wrapped up in school, work, and *Jesse*, that I haven't noticed that he's clearly going through something. I try to piece together everything I know about him. I know he's originally from the Eastern Shore. I've gathered from some of the things that he's said in the past that he's had some family drama, but he's so tight-lipped. Getting Dylan to open up is like pulling teeth. Not that I'm much more forthcoming. It's probably part of why we get along so well, if I'm being honest. I don't like talking about my shit, and neither does he.

He knows my story, though, and that's the difference. I *know* Dylan. I know all his favorite songs, and that he hates the smell of ketchup with the passion of a thousand burning suns, and that he secretly prefers acoustic to electric. But I don't know his past, or what made him the way he is.

"Allison," Jake shouts, snapping me out of my thoughts. I whip around to find him pointing at a couple who just sat down in my section.

"Shit," I mutter under my breath, then paste a smile on my face before heading over to take their order.

Jesse stayed, bussing tables when he felt like it, but other than that, he sat in a booth, watching me all night. I felt his eyes on me like a second skin the entire time. It wasn't until my shift was over that I remembered Lo wasn't around to give me a ride home, and I didn't make other arrangements.

Naturally, Jesse swooped in the moment he saw the realization set in. I stood in the hall next to the back room, sucker in mouth, backpack on my shoulder. He gave me a crooked smile, dangling his keys. "Need a ride?"

Surprisingly enough, he was quiet on the ride home. He kept checking his phone and tapping the steering wheel with his thumb in an agitated gesture. I wanted to ask him about it, but everything is so…undefined.

Once we pulled into the driveaway, the house was noticeably dark. Jesse cut the engine and neither one of us made a move to get out, the fact that we were alone for a week hanging between us. Jesse reached over, popping the sucker out of my mouth without a word, before sticking it between his own lips.

"I'm going to shower," I said, feeling for the door handle, before I thanked him for the ride. I bolted up the stairs, needing to both put some distance between us and take a much-needed shower.

Which brings me to now, the scalding water beating down on me, and it feels so good that I don't think I'll ever leave. All day, I walked around with Jesse's scent on my skin, serving as a constant reminder of what we did last night. I stay in the shower long after all evidence of our indiscretion has washed away, until the water runs cold. I step out and wrap my towel around myself, my skin flushed and overheated, my body suddenly feeling heavy and exhausted. When I open the door to my room, I'm almost surprised Jesse isn't here waiting for me.

I reach for another baggy T-shirt to sleep in, but then I second-guess my decision. What if Jesse comes in later? *No.* Screw that train of thought. If he can't handle me in my borderline homeless attire, he doesn't deserve what's underneath. I pull the shirt on over my head, throwing on a pair of boy shorts underneath, then head back to the bathroom to finish getting ready for bed. As I'm brushing my teeth, I pause at the sound of Jesse's muffled voice coming from his room. I turn the faucet off and lean in toward his door, quiet as a mouse.

"I told you last time. I'm out." His voice is sharp and angry, brooking no argument, but the person on the other end of the phone obviously doesn't take the hint. "I don't give a shit about that," he snaps. There's another pause before he speaks again. "Lose my number." It's quiet for long seconds again, so I assume he ended the call.

What the hell was that about?

The doorknob turning has me jumping away from the door, heart pounding, toothbrush still in my mouth. Jesse stops short when he sees me, his eyes narrowing with suspicion.

"What?" I ask around a mouthful of toothpaste.

"Nothing." He unbuttons and unzips his jeans, turning for the toilet. A second later, I hear him emptying his bladder as I'm rinsing my mouth with water.

"Ever heard of boundaries?" I ask, scrunching my nose, reaching for a towel to dry my face.

"I know what your pussy tastes like—the answer is fucking delicious, by the way. I think boundaries are a thing of the past with us."

I shake my head, turning toward him with a witty retort on the tip of my tongue, but his open door allows me a glimpse into his room and the words die on my lips. A duffle bag sits in the middle of his floor, but there's not much else. Still nowhere to sleep. The sight suddenly has me feeling guilty for stealing his bed. Sure, he has the couch, but that can't be comfortable, especially for more than a night or two. I'm the interloper. I should be the one sleeping in the living room.

"I can take the couch tonight," I say, taking him by surprise. Jesse chuckles, looking over his shoulder at the empty space before shutting the door.

"You getting soft on me, Allie Girl? Trust me. I've had worse living arrangements."

I cock my head to the side, regarding him. Another little glimpse into his life.

"Don't look at me like that," he snaps, but the words sound contrived. Defensive, but holding little heat.

I shrug, playing it off. "Suit yourself."

He turns for his door, and I turn for mine, shutting it behind me. I crawl into my bed, not even having a chance to reach for my headphones before Jesse appears again.

"What are you doing?" I ask, eying the laptop in his hands.

"Movie?"

I narrow my eyes at him, debating. "Okay."

Jesse moves my bedside table, then angles the laptop so we can both see it. "What are you in the mood for?"

"Nothing sad," I answer. He clicks around, settling on a movie before climbing into bed with me. I'm still sitting, nerves percolating in my stomach, but Jesse opts for a more comfortable position, lying on his side behind me.

"Relax, Allie."

I nod in response. The opening credits for *Zombieland* play on the laptop screen, and it breaks the tension I'm feeling. I laugh softly, moving onto my stomach. My knees are bent, feet crossed in the air, my chin resting on my folded arms. My goal when choosing this position was to put more space between us, but that was a mistake because now, all I'm doing is wondering if he can see up my shorts.

Fighting the urge to look behind me, I focus my attention on the movie. Jesse is on his best behavior for the first half, but about forty-five minutes in, he sits up against the headboard before his hand circles one of my ankles, tugging me toward him. I shift closer until he pulls me into him, my back to his chest.

"What are you doing?" I whisper as his arm bands around me, his palm coming to rest on my stomach.

"Touching you," he says, his voice thick from not speaking.

"Why?" My stomach tightens, my pulse quickening.

"Because I like it."

Okay, then.

After overanalyzing his actions and motives for a solid twenty minutes, I eventually start to relax. Jesse's warmth and his scent work together at making me feel all sleepy and content.

I jerk awake in the dark room, feeling overheated and clammy. Sitting up, I rub my eyes as consciousness creeps back in.

Dad.

The dream felt so real. He was playing his guitar, his hair a little too long and a little too greasy. But he looked happy. Only, when I walked toward him, the distance between us seemed to stretch farther. I started to panic and tried to run toward him, but it felt like I was moving in slow motion against a thousand pounds of water holding me back. My dad was oblivious, still smiling and singing along to his song, but I couldn't hear him. And when I tried to scream, nothing came out.

I bring a hand to my chest to calm my racing heart, batting away a single tear that rolls down my cheek with the other.

"That happen a lot?" Jesse's deep, sleep-thick voice rumbles from behind me, startling me.

I shake my head. "Hasn't for months." I feel him shifting behind me and look over my shoulder in time to see him turn onto his back, crossing his arms behind his head.

"What's it about?"

I bring my knees up, resting my chin on top of them as I debate how much information I want to divulge. I'm feeling raw and split open, my grief a living, palpable thing in this moment. Both the dark room and the fact that I'm not facing him give me enough anonymity to speak.

"My dad," I finally say. Jesse stays silent. Whether it's not knowing what to say or sensing that I need a minute to wade through my thoughts, I'm not sure. "The accident was almost a year ago." The words still feel wrong, even after all these months. "I used to dream about him all the time at first. The anniversary is coming up. Maybe that has something to do with it," I muse, more to myself than him. It's hard to believe the world has existed for almost three hundred and sixty-five days without him. "Sometimes I think the nightmares are better than not seeing him at all."

"That's fucked up," Jess remarks, and I huff out a humorless laugh.

"We're all a little fucked up."

"That's an understatement," he agrees bitterly.

Turning around, I sit cross-legged on the bed. "Tell me yours?"

"My what?"

"Your fuckedupness. I need a distraction," I whisper. I don't want to think about my dad right now. I can see enough to make out his hand pushing through his hair as he blows out a breath.

"What do you want to know?" he grumbles. "My list is longer than most."

"Let's start with something simple. Where are your parents?"

"Fuck if I know." He laughs. "Lo and I moved out here to live with our dad a couple of years ago. Turns out, Henry wasn't even our dad."

"What?" I did not see that coming.

"Yup," he says matter-of-factly. "Poor bastard didn't know it either. My mom won't tell us who the real sperm donor is. Lo thinks she's just being a bitch, but I'd bet money that she doesn't even know."

"Where is she?"

"Probably passed out in an alley somewhere in Oakland."

"Shit," I breathe. "*That* is fucked up."

"It's not even the tip of the iceberg."

"What about Henry?" I ask, hoping there's something good in this story. Jess looks over at me, confusion painting his features.

"What about him?"

"I don't know anything about being a parent, but I don't think all those years just vanish because you're not blood-related."

"Clearly, you don't know my family. He's off the hook." He jerks a shoulder. "Guilt made him attempt to stay in touch, but I did him a favor and cut it off."

I frown. "Maybe it was hard for him, too. Maybe he wants to be in your life."

"Maybe we're done talking about me," he says, abruptly reaching for me before pulling me down the bed and rolling on top of me in one swift motion. "Where's your mom?"

"Ugh," I groan. "That's not the type of distraction I need right now."

He shifts his hips into mine, and I realize he's only in his boxers. He must have ditched his jeans when I was asleep. "What kind of distraction *do* you need, Allie?"

I know he's trying to change the subject, but I give in, needing the same thing. I don't want to think. I don't want to speak. I want to *feel*.

"Halston says we need rules."

"You told Halston about us?" he asks with an arched brow.

"Not really. But she said rules are crucial when it

comes to this sort of thing…" I trail off, the words sounding stupid when I say them out loud.

"Oh yeah? How's that working out for her and Sully?"

"Good point." I laugh.

"I'm not much of a rule follower," he says, brushing a piece of hair off my forehead. "You got something in mind?"

I worry my lip, considering my words. "No lying."

Jesse gives me a sharp nod. "Easy. Done." He kisses my neck, and I arch to give him better access. Goosebumps break across my skin from my neck down to my arm and Jesse's finger follows their path.

"And I want a clean break," I blurt out. He cocks his head to the side, waiting for me to elaborate. "We're just having fun. If one of us wants out, we end it. No hard feelings. No questions asked." I don't want to lose my friendship with Lo, my job, or anything else if this thing goes south. *When. When it goes south*, I remind myself.

"Deal," he finally says. I squeeze his hand in the small space between our bodies to shake on it, but he looks at it with a raised eyebrow. "Don't I get to make any rules?"

I drop my hand back to the mattress. "By all means…"

"No hooking up with other people."

"We've already established that. Anything else?"

He cocks his head to the side, pretending to consider it. "Nope. I think that about covers it."

He flexes his hips into me, and I close my eyes, loving the way it feels. "Jess," I breathe, trying—and failing—to keep from squirming. He leans in, his lips close to my ear.

"Do you want me to make you feel good?" His teeth clamp around my earlobe and tug. I nod in response as he brings a hand down to stroke me on the outside of my boy shorts, applying the faintest amount of pressure. "Say it, Allie."

I stay silent, pushing back on him in response. A single finger slides along my crease, but he doesn't give me more than that. Lust trumps pride when he touches me like this. "Make me feel good," I whisper. "Please."

No sooner do the words leave my lips than he pushes my underwear aside, sliding a thick finger inside me. I gasp at the sudden intrusion, arching my back. He pulls back slightly, and when I open my eyes, I find him watching where we're joined, his eyes hooded.

"Open your legs for me," he rasps. I let my knees fall to the side, and he sucks in a breath. It makes me feel powerful knowing he's affected like this.

Suddenly, his finger is gone, leaving me empty as he sits back on his heels and shoves his boxers down just low enough to free his cock. I can't look away as he fists himself, slowly moving up and down his length. The pulse between my legs throbs, and I have the sudden urge to taste him, but Jesse has other ideas.

"Show me how you touch yourself."

I hesitate, biting down on my lip. I've never done that in front of anyone. Somehow, it feels more personal. *Dirtier.* And I'm surprised to find it only gets me hotter.

I trail my hand down my stomach slowly, stopping between my thighs. I tease my clit through my underwear, loving how Jesse's eyes flare as he watches me.

"Take them off," he says, working himself.

I push them down my legs, and once they're to my knees, he tugs them off, letting them drop to the floor. Planting my feet on the mattress, I spread my bent knees, giving him a better view.

"Fuck, Allie."

Using two fingers, I rub myself in small circles. I don't expect it to feel so good, but I'm already close to the edge, rolling my hips into my touch. I need him to touch me. Kiss me. Anything at this point. Wanting to push him into action, I use my free hand to pull my shirt up before teasing my nipples with my fingertips.

Jess groans, leaning down to swipe his tongue across the hardened tip. My heart pounds faster, blood rushing through my ears as he tugs it between his teeth and pulls.

"Oh my God, Jess," I moan, my hand moving faster. I squeeze my eyes shut, lost in the sensations, when I feel him nudge against my entrance. My eyes fly open, but he doesn't push farther, sliding his head up and down my slit as I continue to rub myself.

Feeling bold, I move my hand down farther, wrapping it around him. He's thick and smooth and hard in my hand. He lets out a strangled curse as he releases his grip. He pulls his shirt up so he can have an unobstructed view as I pump his length. He rocks forward slightly, nudging in a little more before pulling back out.

"Do it again," I urge, needing more.

He repeats the motion, then licks his thumb before bringing it to my clit, applying just the right amount of pressure to send me over the edge. I tighten around his tip, every nerve ending tingling as I come, shuddering beneath him. I feel light-headed and dizzy, my hand around him going slack. He takes over, pumping hard, abs tensing. A few more strokes and he's pulling away abruptly, spilling onto my inner thigh.

Jess and I haven't so much as left the room all day. It's two P.M. and we've been in bed alternating between having more *not sex* and watching movies on his laptop. He never pushed for more. I know what's holding *me* back, but why he hasn't tried to seal the deal is beyond me. It's almost some sort of game between us to see who breaks first, and I'll admit, I'm very close to losing that battle.

Dehydrated and hungry as hell, we finally see the light of day when we decide to grab lunch at Blackbear before my shift starts. The closer we get to the restaurant, the more I start to rethink this idea. It's bad enough that he's always hanging out during my shift and watching me intently. But showing up for lunch together looks an awful lot like a date.

"Relax, Allie."

My gaze snaps up to Jesse's.

"I am relaxed," I lie, and he sends a pointed look at my hands that are twisting in my lap.

"We're living together. Roommates eating a meal together isn't exactly unheard of."

I bristle at his snarky tone. Jess pulls into a parking spot behind Blackbear and cuts the engine.

"I didn't mean anything by—"

He shakes his head. "It's fine. Let's go inside. I'm fucking starving."

I nod, confused by his sudden mood change, then hop out of the truck. Jess stuffs his hands into his front pockets, keeping a healthy distance between us as we head for the entrance. Once we're inside, Jess stops short, eyes fixed on a man at the bar. I pause, looking between the two of them.

"Go eat, Allie," he says to me without taking his eyes off the man at the bar with the backwards Raiders hat.

"Aren't you coming?"

"I just lost my appetite," he says, finally meeting my eyes. "I'll be here after your shift to give you a ride."

"Oh." I fight to keep the disappointment from being written all over my face. "Okay." A million questions racing through my mind, I reluctantly walk away, not wanting to raise suspicion.

I take a seat in one of the back booths, too far away to hear, but close enough to see Jesse.

"Henry," Jake says, standing over me with his order pad. I didn't even notice him approach.

"Huh?"

"That's Henry." He nods toward Jess and the man—Henry, apparently—who pats the stool next to him in invitation. Jesse runs his hand through his hair, hesitating. I can feel the uncertainty radiating off him from here. "He's the closest thing to a dad they've got," Jake explains.

I nod, having gathered that. Not wanting to seem too interested, I pick up a menu. "I'll have…" I say, pretending to scan my options that I know by heart, "a personal pepperoni pizza, a side salad with ranch, and a Coke."

"Sounds good," he says, not bothering to take down my order before walking away.

From the corner of my eye, I notice Henry walk outside, Jesse right behind him. I watch them through the window, Jesse's gaze pointed at his feet as Henry speaks. Jesse shrugs in response to whatever he's saying, kicking around a piece of gravel. They don't appear to be fighting, but I can tell he feels uncomfortable. Right now, I see that vulnerable little boy from the picture. I don't know what's being said, but I know that I have the urge to hug him and make it better. To put that obnoxious, cocky grin back on his face. And the fact that I *want* to do that fills me with unease. He's not my boyfriend—he's not my *anything*—and I need to remember that. I can't let the lines blur because we're *having fun*.

Henry reaches a hand out to squeeze Jesse's shoulder, causing him to flinch. The movement is almost imperceptible, but I catch it, and Henry does, too, if his dejected expression is anything to go by. Then they're parting ways, Jesse going right, Henry going left.

By the time ten o'clock rolls around, I'm running on fumes. I've alternated between trying to answer all the question marks where Jesse is concerned and replaying the events of last night—and this morning—in my head like a movie all day. Every time the door chimed, I expected to see Jess, then chastised myself for it.

I'm absentmindedly wiping down my last table when I hear his voice behind me. "Hey, little girl, want some candy?"

I turn around, eyebrow lifted, to see Jesse holding a bouquet of Dum-Dums, all strawberry and butterscotch, by the looks of it. I flatten my lips to hide the smile that tries to break free.

"Sorry for bailing on breakfast. Lunch. Whatever that was." His hair falls into his eyes, his expression mischievous. I roll my eyes, snatching the bundle of suckers. "Does that mean you forgive me?" he asks, amused.

"Nothing to forgive," I say, feigning indifference, turning back around to finish wiping down the table.

He leans down, his front covering my back as he brings his lips close to my ear. "That's a shame. I was hoping to make it up to you tonight." His fingers rake up the back of my thigh, digging into my tights, and I jump away once they get to the hem of my shorts.

My eyes dart around the crowded room to make sure no one's watching, putting a healthy distance between us. My skin is already on fire from his touch and the promise of what's to come, but I glare at him. "What are you doing?"

"Relax. Everyone's too drunk to notice."

"That's not the point."

"Then get in the fucking car so I can touch you at my leisure because it's been eight hours since I've had you underneath me." His words both thrill me and embarrass me, and I think that's his intent. He wants to throw me off my game and watch me squirm.

I walk toward the back room to gather my stuff, intentionally taking my time. I'm just as anxious to be alone with Jess, but I'm not going to give him the satisfaction of knowing it. When I've got everything, I find him waiting by the door, eyeing me with amusement—as if he knows I'm being purposely slow—with his arms folded across his chest. He pushes against the door with his back to open it, gesturing for me to go first with a flick of his chin.

"How chivalrous."

"Chivalry's my middle name."

"I thought it was Cocky," I say, rounding the corner toward the back parking lot.

"I'll show you cocky," he promises. *Walked right into that one.*

The moment we're inside his truck with the doors closed, we both look at each other, the tension mounting between us. I wet my dry lips and his eyes follow the movement.

"Come here." Jess lunges for me, pulling me over the middle console until I'm straddling him. His hands grip my hips, his thumbs pressing into my exposed skin where my work shirt has ridden up. My hair falls around us like a curtain as I decide to make the first move, leaning down to bring my lips to his. I tentatively lick the seam of his lips before sucking the bottom one into my mouth and giving it a light tug. Jesse groans, his fingers tightening on my hips, but he allows me to continue my exploration without making a move. I bring my hands to his face before kissing his top lip, and when I slip my tongue inside his mouth, he finally snaps into action. Our noses mash together as he kisses me back in full force. Our bodies start moving to a rhythm of their own, nothing but the sound of our harsh breathing in the quiet cocoon of his truck.

Jess dips his hands under my shirt, his warm palms sliding against my skin. He stops just south of where I need him to touch me, but not going any farther. I squirm in his lap, wanting more. Always needing more. *Even in a public parking lot, apparently*. My nipples tighten painfully, and I pull back, pouting.

"What's wrong, Allie Girl?" he taunts, lips glistening, as he pushes my shirt up to expose my black mesh bra that does nothing to hide my current state of arousal.

"Stop playing with me," I demand, but it comes out sounding more like a petulant whine.

"Never," he says before leaning forward to catch my nipple between his teeth over the thin material of my bra.

"Jess," I breathe, letting my head fall back as my hips rock into him. One of his hands holds me in place by my ribs and the other one slides down my back toward the gap in the waistband of my shorts. When he sucks me through my bra, wetness pools between my legs. I've never felt this with anyone, and now that we've started this little game, I can't seem to think of anything else.

Suddenly, headlights illuminate the interior as a vehicle swings into the space next to us. The spell effectively broken, I jerk back, accidentally beeping the horn just as the man in the black SUV steps out. A man I recognize. He turns toward us, eyebrows furrowed as I scramble to pull my shirt back down.

"Allison?" Victor says, squinting at me through the dash.

"Oh my God," I say through clenched teeth, forcing a smile. Victor starts walking toward us, and I'm quick to hop out of the truck before he gets any closer, meeting him in front of the hood.

"Hey," I greet him, hoping like hell he can't tell that I've been dry humping Jesse in the driver's seat. "What are you doing here?" I slide my palms into my back pockets, rocking back on my heels.

"Meeting a buddy for a drink," he says, gesturing inside. "How's the planning coming along?"

"Really good." I instantly perk up at the mention. "I got the perfect band. They're local and already have a solid following, so I have a good feeling about it."

"Sounds promising," he says, looking me up and down, probably judging my disheveled appearance.

Before I can respond, Jesse's out of the truck, sauntering over to us. He curls a hand around my waist, pulling me into his side in an obvious display of ownership.

"Jesse, this is Victor. Victor, this is my friend, Jesse," I say, sending him a pointed look as I inch away from him. Victor gives him an amenable smile, holding out his hand.

Jesse hesitates, eyeing his proffered hand like it's covered in dog shit.

Jesus, Jess, don't screw this up.

Just when I think he's going to leave him hanging, he reaches out to shake Victor's hand.

"Nice to meet you," Victor says before turning his attention back to me. "I have to get in there, but call me if you need anything."

"Will do."

Victor gives a polite nod to Jess—which he ignores—then he's walking away.

"Who the hell was that?" Jess asks.

"Someone who can potentially open a lot of doors for me if I manage to plan an event without screwing it up." I stalk back to the car, annoyed with myself for being stupid enough to get caught in this position, and annoyed with Jess for pulling that caveman shit in front of someone who could play a huge role in my future.

I climb back into the car, and Jesse's in the driver's seat a second later.

"I don't like him," he says, squeezing the steering wheel. "He's smarmy."

"Smarmy?" I huff out a laugh.

"Smarmy as fuck. I don't like the way he looked at you."

"He was looking at me like that because I was having a make-out session in a car like some…" I trail off, searching for the right words, "some horny teenager," I deadpan.

"You *are* a horny teenager."

I cut my eyes at him. "Not helping."

He starts the engine, throwing the gear into reverse. "So, what's this event?"

"You remember when I went to that show with Garrett?"

Jess narrows his eyes, and I take that as my answer.

"I ran into Victor there. He was a friend of my dad's. I didn't know it was his venue, and I may have pointed out some things I could've done better."

I swear I see his lips lift at the corner into an almost-smile.

"He offered me a chance to organize my own event and put that theory to the test."

"That's a big deal, right? Is that what you want to do for a living?"

"I don't know." I shrug. "I know I want to do something with music, so the experience can't hurt. And Dylan's band hasn't had a place to play, so I figured it was a win-win situation."

Jess nods. "When is it?"

I study him, the streetlights illuminating his sharp features. "Next Friday. Why, you suddenly a fan of my kind of music?"

"Hard pass." He scoffs.

"What about you?"

"What about me?" He stares ahead at the dark road, one hand on the wheel. Every few seconds, the streetlights allow me a brief glimpse of his sharp profile, his jaw set hard.

"What's next for the infamous Jesse Shepherd?" I joke, throwing in jazz hands for effect.

His grip on the steering wheel tightens, his knuckles turning white. "You're looking at it."

My smile falls. "So that's it? You're just giving up?" He can't possibly be content to hang around Blackbear *sometimes* working for the rest of his life.

"You don't know what you're talking about."

"I know that you're not who you want everyone to think you are."

He looks over at me. "And who do you think I am?"

"An outsider. Like me." I don't mean to blurt it out, but I do and there's no taking it back now. I don't think anyone truly knows Jesse except for maybe Lo. How could they? He doesn't let anyone in. Least of all me. But somehow, I manage to see him. Maybe it's because underneath all the bullshit, we're the same. Two lost, closed-off kids with trust issues, pretending to have their shit together.

We lock eyes for long seconds, much too long to be considered safe when driving. Finally, he peels his gaze from me. He's quiet for the rest of the ride home, but he's thinking so hard I can practically hear his thoughts. Just as he pulls into the driveway, his phone flashes with an incoming call. He quickly silences it, flipping it facedown onto his jean-covered thigh.

"I'll be there in a few," he tells me, and I take that as my not-so-subtle hint to go inside.

"Thanks for the ride," I mutter, grabbing my backpack before hopping out and shutting the car door none too gently. These secrets of his are driving me insane.

Once inside, I kick off my boots before plodding up the wooden stairs that feel cold underneath my tights-covered feet. I toss my backpack onto my bed and unzip the front pocket, feeling around for my phone. Unsurprisingly, there are multiple texts from my mom.

Hi, honey. Miss you!

Have you had a chance to go through your dad's things?

Sending peace, love, and light. Xoxoxo.

I roll my eyes, huffing out a laugh at that last one. *She*

was one hundred percent high when she sent that. And what part of "I'm not ready" does she not understand? Just the thought of sorting through my dad's things has me on the verge of a panic attack. I can't explain it.

Tossing my phone onto my bed, I grab my headphones, then blindly reach for a CD out of my case. I'm a mood listener—have a mix CD for every occasion—but right now, I just need something loud. Anything will do. I pop it in, snapping the lid shut before fitting the headphones around my neck.

The faint sound of Rise Against hits my ears as my curiosity has me moving toward the window that overlooks the front yard. Pulling back the curtain, I spot Jess standing outside his car, phone to his ear. He starts to pace the driveway, gesticulating wildly. I part the curtain a little more to get a better look, cocking my head to the side, transfixed with his every move. Suddenly, he stops his pacing, his bicep flexing as he drags his free hand through his hair. He angles his body toward the window and lifts his chin, then he's looking directly at me—or at least, it seems that way.

I release the curtain like it burned me, jumping out of sight. Probably not the smoothest course of action. I shake my head, internally chastising myself for my spastic behavior. I hate that I turn into such a *girl* when it comes to him.

I hear his car door slam shut once more, and I'm not at all surprised at the fact that he's leaving. Again.

Shoving my disappointment deep down into that box I place all unpleasant thoughts, I unbutton my jean shorts, pushing them down my legs, along with my tights. I swap them out for a comfy pair of track shorts that, ironically enough, have never seen a track a day in their life. Plucking my laptop from my bed, I lie on my stomach, pulling up the design I've been working on for the show Friday. I fit my headphones over my ears and slide the volume dial all the way up. Maybe if it's loud enough, it will drown out all thoughts of my dad and Jess.

CHAPTER TWENTY-ONE

Jess

I F MY STEERING WHEEL WERE A NECK, IT WOULD HAVE snapped under the pressure of my clenched hands by now. I can't bring myself to drive away this time. Every time I think I've successfully separated myself from my past, and I feel like I'm moving forward, something happens to pull me right back under. This time, it came in the form of a phone call from the devil herself. It seems the more I pull away, the more she latches on.

Not today, Satan.

Between that and my run-in with Henry earlier, I'm feeling more than a little on edge. I reach under the passenger seat, feeling for the bottle of Jack that I know is there, wanting to feel that familiar burn that's guaranteed to chase away all the guilt and self-loathing. At least for a few hours. Instead, I find the bundle of Dum-Dums Allie left behind. Still bent over, my eyes shift to her window again, seeking her out, but I don't see her this time. I throw the suckers onto the seat, then reach back down, feeling around again until my fingers meet cold glass.

The half-empty bottle feels cold and heavy in my hand. I unscrew the cap, then tip it back, letting the liquid burn my throat. I wipe my mouth with the back of my hand, reveling in the burn. But it's not enough. I go back for a second swig, hesitating once the bottle is at my lips. Screwing the cap back on, I toss the bottle into the back somewhere, setting my sights on the suckers.

Why the fuck am I out here drinking my problems away, when the perfect distraction is waiting right upstairs? Being with Allie, touching her, hearing the sweet fucking sounds that come from her mouth, is better than any altered state of mind. Even when she's not letting me touch her, being around her has a way of making everything else blur out of focus. She gives me something to look forward to.

Suckers in hand, I step out of the car and prowl toward the front door and up the stairs, taking them two at a time. I open the bedroom door to find her on her stomach, fingers tapping away on the keyboard of her laptop, oblivious of my arrival thanks to her headphones. Her legs are bent at the knees, her feet crossed at the ankles, bouncing to the beat of the music. She's wearing these tiny as fuck, dick-me-down shorts that do nothing to hide the swell of her perfect heart-shaped ass.

My cock jumps in my pants as I take in the sight. I'm across the room and straddling the back of her thighs in an instant. Allie jerks in surprise, whipping her headphones off as she tries to rotate her body beneath me.

"Jesus, Jess!" she screams, still squirming to get free. I drop the suckers onto the mattress next to us before bringing my hands to cup her ass cheeks. "I thought you left."

"Changed my mind. You're fucking perfect," I say with a squeeze. Allie rolls her eyes, but when I run my thumb along the seam of her pussy through the light gray shorts, she gives up the charade, sinking into the mattress. Now that she lets me touch her like this, I can't seem to stop. Her cheek presses against the sheet, her eyes falling shut as I continue to rub her. She arches her ass up, giving me better access, and holy shit, my dick is about to burst through my zipper.

"Hold still," I tell her, reaching into my pocket to grab my phone.

"What are you doing?" she asks, looking at me over her shoulder.

I snap a picture just before her eyes widen with realization. She reaches back to slap the phone out of my hand, and this time, when she tries to roll over, I let her. I catch both of her wrists in my hands, pinning them to the mattress as I fit my hips between her splayed thighs.

Gray eyes wild and cheeks flushed, she bucks beneath me, but the only thing she accomplishes is rubbing against my dick. I raise an eyebrow, looking down at where we meet.

Allie growls, frustrated, but I know that she's just as turned on as I am. I bring her wrists together, holding them with one hand so I can use my free hand to shove her laptop up the bed and out of the way before grabbing the suckers.

"You forgot these," I say before bringing the bundle to my mouth, biting one free. I let the rest fall before tearing the wrapper off with my teeth. Allie's breathing quickens, her eyes fixed on the hot pink sucker. "Open."

To my surprise, she does. I dip it into her mouth, and pillowy lips wrap around it, sucking. I groan, pushing my hips into her heat, and her dimples deepen when she realizes what she's doing to me.

"You think that's funny?" I ask.

Still smiling, she nods, her eyes sparkling with mischief as she rolls her hips into me.

I pop the sucker into my mouth before shoving up her white work shirt over her tits. Her nipples are hard as fuck through the see-through material of her black bra. Hooking a finger underneath the fabric, I tug it down to reveal her completely. I take the sucker from my mouth, swirling it around her nipple, then give the same treatment to the other side.

Pulling back, I gaze down at her. Her hands still above her head, nipples shining from the sucker. I'd take another picture right now if it wasn't for the fact that I don't want to do anything to fuck up where this is going. I lean down, swiping my tongue across her sticky, strawberry-flavored nipple. Allie moans, arching into my mouth. Freeing her wrists, I trail my hand down her arm and palm her perfect tit, tasting that one, too. After licking her clean, I move down her body, kissing her stomach along the way before stopping between her trembling thighs.

When I see the wet spot showing through her light gray shorts, I almost lose it. "Fuck, Allison." She doesn't know what she does to me, but I'm about to show her. I push her knees apart before tugging her shorts and underwear to the side. "Such a pretty little pussy. Let's make it even sweeter."

Allie gasps as I circle her clit with the sucker, and when I drag it lower to dip inside her, she clenches around it. I work it in and out, only giving slow, shallow thrusts.

"Jesse," she whispers. I lean forward, unable to resist any longer. When my tongue meets her clit, her knees snap shut, trapping my head between her thighs.

"My two favorite flavors," I mumble into her warm, wet pussy. "Allison and strawberry."

"That feels so good," she says, her fingers threading through my hair, pulling me closer.

I push the sucker in deeper until the pink disappears inside her, then I lap at her clit. My tongue and the sucker work in tandem, licking and sucking and fucking until Allie's panting and squirming with the need to come.

"I need to feel you again," I say, coming up for air. She nods frantically—thank fuck—and I sit back, holding the sucker in my mouth, and reach behind my head to pull my shirt off at the same time Allie gets rid of both her shirt and bra.

I move over her, my hands braced on either side of her head. Allie surprises me when she pulls the sucker from my mouth before bringing it to her own. When her tongue flicks out to swirl around it, I snatch it back from her, chucking it somewhere behind me before smashing my lips to hers. She wraps her legs around my waist, pulling me into her heat as she sucks my tongue into her mouth.

I smooth my hands down her sides, pulling away from her mouth as I crook my fingers into the waistband of her shorts. She lifts her hips, wordlessly giving me permission to play our new favorite game, and I don't waste any time sliding them down her slender legs. Unbuttoning my pants, I stand up to kick them off, my cock bobbing free. Her eyes zero in on my dick and she swallows hard.

I position myself over her again, her knees cradling my hips. I slide upward, feeling her coating my dick, slick and warm. "I need to be inside you," I say, voice strained. "Just a little bit."

Allie nods, and I press the head of my cock into her opening. I give her shallow thrusts, trying like hell not to push all the way inside her tight heat.

"You feel so fucking good," I tell her. Her feet are planted flat against the mattress, legs spread, but then she angles her hips, taking me a little deeper. Deeper than I've ever been with her. We both freeze, my dick notched against her opening.

"I want you," she says, her hand curling around the back of my neck. "I want to feel it all the way this time."

Not needing to be told twice, I reach for the drawer of the nightstand, feeling around for one of the foil packets I know is there. Sitting back on my knees, I rip it open before rolling it down my shaft, and then I'm back in position, my cock poised at her entrance.

I shift forward, pushing in farther, but Allie tenses, scooting up the mattress.

"Wait," she whispers, her fingers squeezing my biceps.

I pause, looking down at her. "What's wrong?" I search her wide eyes for clues.

"I haven't exactly done this before." Her cheeks turn pink with the admission.

What the fuck?

"Come again?"

"I'm a virgin."

CHAPTER TWENTY-TWO

Allie

"I'M A VIRGIN," I ADMIT. JESS CLENCHES HIS JAW, dropping his forehead to mine. My heart is thundering in my chest, but my need for him in this moment overpowers any fear I may have had about having sex for the first time.

"Say something," I plead.

"Why me?" he grits out.

"Why not you?" I counter.

"This isn't a good idea," he says, his voice strained.

"The best things never are," I say, repeating his words from the other night, trying to keep my voice from shaking. When he doesn't speak, I shift my hips, urging him on. Jesse's fists tighten against the mattress, and he swallows hard, his throat bobbing with the motion.

"Are you sure?" he asks, his hazel eyes blazing with indecision.

I gaze up at him, trying to convey sincerity with my eyes. "Please. I want this."

With those words, he pushes forward, finally giving in. The initial thrust steals my breath, my fingernails digging into the warm flesh of his arms.

"Breathe, Allison," Jesse coaxes, sweeping my hair out of my face with his thumb. "You have to relax."

I nod, taking a shaky breath. After giving me a minute to adjust, he moves again, wedging himself farther inside me with a strangled groan. I feel full—*too full*—and I stay stock-still, afraid to move a muscle.

Oh my God. Jesse Shepherd is inside *of me.*

"Colorblind" by Counting Crows wafts from my forgotten headphones somewhere above my head, as Jess leans down, brushing his lips against mine with a kiss more tender than I thought him to be capable of. Our noses are an inch apart and I can feel his breath on my lips, his eyes locking onto mine as he starts to move inside me. Releasing my death grip on his biceps, I slide my fingers into his hair, pulling him down to kiss me again. Jess snakes a hand between us, using two fingers to stroke me, and the tension slowly melts from my body, replaced with the need to *move.*

"More," I whisper into his lips, my hips shifting into his touch. He pulls out before slowly filling me again, and this time, the sting of pain is laced with pleasure.

"I've thought a lot about what it would be like to finally feel you from the inside," he says, pumping into me. "Nothing could have prepared me for the real thing. Fucking nothing."

His words wrap around me like a warm blanket while simultaneously igniting a fire in me. I lock my legs around his waist, pulling him deeper, circling my hips. Never breaking our connection, Jess sits back on his heels, one hand holding my thigh in place while the other continues its ministrations on my clit. His eyes burn with lust, fixated on where we meet, watching himself slide in and out.

"So goddamn tight," he groans. My hips lift from the mattress in an effort to get closer. Jesse's eyebrows tug together, forming a hard crease between them, his cheeks ruddy with exertion.

"I think I'm close," I say, bewildered at the fact. I always heard the first time was miserable.

"I can feel you squeezing me," Jess rasps, both hands circling the fold in my hips, controlling my movements. His pelvis grinds into me with each thrust, driving me closer to the edge. My vision grows hazy around the edges, every nerve ending buzzing, and when Jesse leans down to scrape his teeth across my nipple, I explode. My back bows off the bed as a strangled cry slips free. Jess fucks me through my orgasm, his movements becoming jerkier and frantic. With one last snap of his hips, he groans before collapsing on top of me.

We're both silent as the reality of what we just did washes over us. I feel raw and exposed and unexpectedly emotional. Jess peels himself from me, his sweat-slicked skin sticking to mine, before pulling out. There's the faintest streak of blood on the condom, and another on my inner thigh, but it's far from the massacre I feared.

Jesse's eyes zero in on the blood, his nostrils flaring, before he lowers himself until his face is between my thighs once more. I try to shut my legs, embarrassed, but he pries them open before placing open-mouthed kisses along my inner thighs, apparently unbothered with the blood. When his tongue meets my overly sensitive center, I flinch away, still too raw. But he holds me in place, giving a few soft strokes with the flat of his tongue, as if soothing away the sting.

Wordlessly, he stands, peeling the condom from his still-hard length, then strolls over to the bathroom to toss it into the trash can. His hair is damp with sweat and his muscles seem more pronounced, and I can't help but stare as he makes his way back to the bed, absently scratching his stomach.

I cannot believe I just lost my virginity. To that.

He bends over, grabbing a pack of cigarettes and a lighter from his discarded jeans. He strides toward the window, and I hear the flick of his lighter a second before he's sliding the window open. Bracing one hand on the frame, he leans in to rest his forehead on the back of his hand. He takes a drag, the smoke curling through the air in front of him.

I wrap a throw blanket around my shoulders, then I pad toward him, coming to a stop a few inches from his back.

"Did I hurt you?" he finally asks, his gruff voice breaking the silence. The streetlights illuminate his profile as he turns his head to the side, waiting for my reply.

"A little," I answer honestly.

"Do you regret it?" he asks, still not meeting my eyes.

"No."

He turns his head to look out the window once more, and a sinking feeling hits my gut.

"But you do," I accuse, frowning. I see him tense, but he doesn't deny it. My veins turn to ice as I take a step backwards, but he spins around, his hand clamping down on my wrist, holding me in place. I glance up at him, waiting for him to speak. He swallows hard, watching me intently, but he says nothing.

"Let me go."

He releases my wrist, and I turn for the bathroom, needing to put some distance between us. I lock both doors, then let the blanket fall to the floor, inspecting my reflection that appears as ragged as I feel. My hair is a tangled mess, my skin splotchy, my lips swollen. Morbid curiosity has my hand reaching down to feel between my legs. I feel raw. Exposed. Both physically and emotionally.

Turning for the shower, I flip the faucet. As I wait for the water to warm up, I tell myself that I'm fine. It's just sex. It had to be someone. I'm glad it's out of the way. It's fine. *I'm fine.*

Once the bathroom is good and steamy, I step into the shower, letting the hot water pour over me.

"Allison," Jesse thunders, pounding on the door, causing me to jolt. "Open the fucking door."

I don't answer, and the pounding stops for a minute before I hear it coming from the other side. "Goddammit, Allie."

If I was going to cry, now, with the water to conceal my tears, would be the time. But they don't fall. Just when I think he's given up, I hear a loud noise followed by the sound of wood splintering. The shower curtain is yanked open, revealing Jess, his eyes hard, chest rising and falling quickly.

"What the hell is wrong with you?" I ask, crossing my arms over my chest in a futile attempt at modesty considering I just gave him my virginity.

Ignoring my question, he steps into the shower, his hands reaching out to cup my face, forcing me to look into his eyes.

"I don't regret you," he says vehemently. My nose starts to sting with the promise of tears, my chin wobbling. I try to turn away from his grasp, but he holds me in place. "It's you who should regret me."

I frown, confused. "Why?"

"Because I'll fuck this up."

"What are you talking about?" I shake my head, not understanding where he's going with his. The shower beats down on my back, the water sliding from my hair onto his hands that still cup my face, running down his forearms. He rubs his thumb across my bottom lip, his eyes zeroing in on my mouth.

"I should walk away now, before it's too late."

"Or you could just…stay." I swallow hard, searching his eyes for any clue as to what's going on inside that head of his. I know it's only a matter of time before he leaves again. Then Lo and Dare will be back soon, and we'll have to go back to stolen moments when no one is looking. Our time together is fleeting, and I want to hold onto whatever this is for a little while longer.

"Or I could stay."

CHAPTER TWENTY-THREE

Allie

"**D**O YOU REMEMBER THE DAY WE MET?" I ASK, gathering my hair into a high ponytail before sinking into the hot tub. Jess smirks at me from the opposite side, eyes raking over my body. After he hulked out on the bathroom door the other night, he took us back to bed as if nothing happened. I was too sore for another round so soon, so he settled for licking me until I came with my thighs plastered to either side of his face.

I haven't had school and I've only worked a couple of shifts this week, and surprisingly enough, Jess hasn't pulled a vanishing act. We've spent the last few days together talking, laughing, *fucking*. Being with him like this is bittersweet. I feel like I'm on top of the world when we're in our own little bubble, but what happens when that bubble bursts? I can tell he's still on edge. I see his demeanor change every time his phone rings—though he hasn't answered it. Something is plaguing his thoughts. I just don't know what.

"Mhm," he says, tugging me closer by my legs until I'm straddling him. "When I told Sierra that you were my girlfriend."

"That wasn't the first time," I say, batting his hand away

when he peels the black triangle of my bikini top away from my chest.

"Yes it was," he argues, his voice adamant.

"Nope." I smile, shaking my head. "My dad taught guitar at the high school."

Jess settles back, hands grasping my waist, waiting for me to continue.

"I used to hang out under the bleachers to pass the time whenever he had to work." I think back to the first time I saw Jess, sweaty and panting at lacrosse practice as he jogged off the field to grab his water bottle. Halston caught me staring and told me everything she knew about him, which wasn't much. He had just moved there and was the shiny new toy every girl wanted to play with. I played it off, like he wasn't the hottest boy I'd ever seen, and eventually, she changed the subject. It wasn't until a few weeks later that we actually met.

"I lost track of time one day, and I knew my dad would be looking for me. I shot out from under the bleachers like a bat out of hell and ran right into you."

Jess frowns. "I would have remembered you."

"Well, you didn't." I laugh. "I dropped my journal at the same time you dropped your book. An old, worn paperback copy of *The Outsiders*." That wasn't the last time I'd seen him with it either.

"I vaguely remember this," he says, his thumbs rubbing my hips.

"You bent down to pick them up and then handed my journal to me."

"Always the gentleman." He smirks, obviously pleased with himself.

I snort out a laugh. "You clearly don't remember what you said to me next."

"Nope."

"You said, and I quote, 'Call me when you get your braces off.'"

Jess throws his head back, barking out a laugh. I float away from him, splashing water at his face.

"I'm glad you're so amused with yourself," I say, but I can't keep the smile from my lips. Seeing Jesse Shepherd happy is a beautiful fucking sight.

"No wonder you hated me when I saw you at Blackbear," he muses. "While we're confessing things," he says, gliding toward me, bracing his hands on the edge of the hot tub behind me, caging me in. "I didn't really care about what Sierra thought. I just wanted to talk to you."

I chew on my lip, circling my hands around the back of his neck as I lock my legs around his waist. "Oh yeah?"

He nods. "And look at us now."

I feel how hard he is through his swim shorts, and I raise a brow. "There's not enough chlorine in the world for me to have sex with you in here." It's bad enough that I'm in here without a hazmat suit with all the action this Jacuzzi gets.

Jess chuckles, nuzzling into my neck. "I can't help it. Your skin is soft and you fucking smell like butterscotch."

Smiling, I turn my head to give him better access. "I thought butterscotch reminded you of old ladies."

"Not anymore," he says, lifting me by my thighs as he stands. I tighten my hold on his neck, squealing as he walks us out of the hot tub.

"Where are we going?"

"You said no to the hot tub. I'll just have to fuck you on the next closest surface." He bends over, still holding me close, and digs a condom out of his discarded jeans.

"You just walk around with condoms in your pockets?" I tease, then I bring my tongue to lick the thick column of his neck, peppering kisses in between.

"I do now."

He lowers me to one of the padded wicker chaises on the far side of the patio. I look over toward the gate. It's dark outside, but anyone walking by would have a clear view of us thanks to the lights in the yard. Jess smirks, reading my mind as he teases the tie on the side of my bathing suit bottoms.

"Scared, Allie?"

I slip out from underneath him, then push on his chest until he's lying back on the chaise. He scrapes his teeth along his bottom lip, watching intently as I bring one knee to the edge of the chair. Reaching behind my neck, I tug on the string, letting my top fall open, my nipples tightening as the cool night air hits my overheated skin.

Jesse lunges for me, hooking an arm around my waist, causing an unexpected laugh to spill out of me. "I'll take that as a no."

"Jess!"

Lo's voice jolts me from sleep. I jerk away from Jess' warm body, heart pounding, and hold the blanket to my naked chest. We fell asleep out here last night after he pulled me onto his lap and told me to ride him.

I look down at his sleeping form, shaking his shoulder. "Jesse!" I hiss, hopping off the chair to find my bathing suit. I spot the pieces peeking out from under Jesse's shirt, and I snatch them up, getting dressed in record time.

What the hell are Lo and Dare doing back so early? I mentally calculate the days, having lost track of time without school as a gauge. *Saturday.* That means Jess and I have been holed up for almost an entire week.

Adjusting my top, I nudge his ass with my foot. "Get up!"

He finally starts to stir, sitting up with a groan. I throw his shirt at his chest, followed by his jeans, but he's in no such hurry, lazily scrubbing a hand down his face as he yawns. I glance back toward the patio door, knowing we're about two seconds away from getting caught red-handed. Jesse moves as slow as goddamn molasses, shoving his legs into his jeans before pulling them up—not bothering to button them—and I have to pry my eyes away from the sight.

"There you are," Lo says from behind me, right as I notice the used condom from last night on the ground. I cover it with my foot, bringing a hand up to shield my eyes from the sun as I turn around to face her.

"Hey," I say, forcing a smile, kicking the condom underneath the chair as casually as possible—making a mental note to come back to dispose of it later. "You guys are back early. How was it?"

"It was all right," she says with a shrug. "Ate some good food. Hung out at the pool. *Got married.*"

Jesse's head whips up at that last part, and Lo laughs, holding out her hand, showing off a dainty gold band with a single diamond.

"Oh my God." I laugh. "Congratulations!" I give Lo a big hug and she squeezes me back, smiling like a lunatic. I hug Dare next who gives me more of a shoulder pat, but even he looks thrilled. Well, for him, anyway.

"Jess?" Lo questions, a nervous lilt to her voice.

He gives a tight smile, standing to give Dare that handshake slash hug thing guys do, and then he's moving toward Lo, hugging her around her shoulders as her arms circle his waist. "I'm happy for you," he says—his tone sincere but somehow sad—before placing a kiss to the top of her head.

He pulls away, sliding a hand through his disheveled hair. "I gotta take a piss."

Dare and Lo exchange looks as he turns for the door.

The bubble has popped.

The awkward meter rises to an all-time high as I stand here in my bathing suit, not having the first clue what to say.

"I'll talk to him after he has a chance to digest the news," Lo says.

"Congratulations," I say again. "I'm going to put some clothes on."

And by *put some clothes on*, I mean find Jess.

CHAPTER TWENTY-FOUR

Jess

MY SISTER GOT MARRIED. *MY SISTER GOT MARRIED without me there.* I meant it when I said I was happy for her, but I won't say it feels good to know she didn't want me involved. It's just another reminder that you can't ever go back to the way things were. Lo's married and going back to school. Dare's got his shop. Allie's got her music. Everyone's reaching their goals and dreams, and I'm over here just…drifting with no real direction. No real purpose.

"You okay?" Allie's soft voice asks from the doorway of the bathroom. Hands braced on the edge of the sink, I meet her eyes in the reflection of the mirror. She's thrown a baggy T-shirt over her swimming suit, hair still up in a lopsided ponytail, but she looks fucking beautiful.

"Fine," I clip out, hating that I sound like an asshole when Allie didn't do a damn thing to deserve it.

She pushes off the doorframe, making her way toward me. Her arms wrap around my middle, palms flattening against my stomach, cheek pressing against my back. I squeeze my eyes shut, allowing her touch to calm the storm inside me.

I shouldn't have taken her virginity, but when she

offered it up on a fucking silver platter, I was too goddamn weak to walk away. This whole week, I ignored my obligations and allowed myself to pretend with Allie. I allowed myself to pretend my life wasn't a shit show, and I allowed myself to feel what it might be like to *really* be with her.

But now, the voicemails are piling up. Spring Break is over. Dare and Lo are home, and Allie's made it more than clear she doesn't want to be seen with a fuck-up like me in public.

"I have to go out of town," I say, feeling her tense behind me. "Have some stuff to take care of."

"Are you ever going to tell me where you go?" she asks, letting go of me. I spin around, lifting her up before setting her on the counter, standing between her knees.

"It's not for you to worry about." I rub the outsides of her thighs, unable to stop touching her.

She scowls at me, her lips twisting, making her dimple more prominent on the right side. "When will you be back?"

"Couple days." I shrug.

She pushes off the counter, her pussy rubbing against my cock as she slides down my body before stepping away. I groan and her lips tip up in a slow smile, knowing exactly what she's doing to me. She's trying to make it hard to leave, and it's working. "Guess I'll see you then."

Brat.

CHAPTER TWENTY-FIVE

Allie

"**A**RE YOU NERVOUS?" GARRETT ASKS, TAKING A stack of flyers from me. I've spent the whole week getting everything in order for tomorrow night, and now, all that's left to do is spread the word and hope like hell everything runs smoothly. Garrett's going to tell his crowd, Halston's going to tell the dorms and her friends who like to party, and I plan to spam every surface of Kerrigan. I've already hit Blackbear and Bad Intentions and put it out on social media. Between the three of us, I think we've covered all the bases.

"Nope."

"Liar," Halston accuses, as I pin one of the hot pink flyers to a bulletin board. "Seriously, nothing is going on this weekend. You should be worrying about being over capacity, if anything."

I snort. "Doubtful." The flyer boasts of dollar drinks for the first hour, so it should appeal to everyone whether it's their typical scene or not, but I'm not expecting anything crazy.

"She's right," Garrett says. "Chill. If you build it, they will come."

Halston and I exchange confused looks.

"Come on," Garrett prompts, clearly disappointed that we don't get the reference. "*Field of Dreams*? 1989. Kevin Costner. Guy turns his cornfield into a baseball field for dead ballplayers?"

"Sounds riveting," Halston deadpans.

"Sorry." I laugh with a shrug.

"You guys suck." He waves the stack of flyers at me. "I'm going to go hand these out to people who've seen movies made before the year 2010."

"Thanks for your help!" I call after his retreating back.

"Whatever happened with him?" Halston asks, hooking an arm around my shoulders as we walk toward her dorm.

"Nothing happened," I say, rolling my eyes. "I told you. We're friends. What's going on with you and Sully? Still giving him the cold shoulder?"

She drops her head back with a groan. "He's driving me insane, but yes. I'm still ignoring his existence."

"You're pretty upset for someone who claims to be cool with casual relationships," I say. She hasn't let him off the hook since that night Sierra was on him in the hot tub—not that I'm saying she *should*—but the more she avoids him, the harder he tries. We both know it's only a matter of time before she caves.

She scowls at me. "Okay, let's talk about how you fucked Jes—"

I cover her mouth with my hand. "We're both idiots. Point taken." As soon as I saw Halston when she got back Sunday night, she knew I'd slept with him. One look is all it took. Don't ask me how. I told her how we spent the whole week together, before he bailed. Again.

"Still nothing?" she asks. I shake my head. Six days.

That's how long it's been since I've heard from Jess. I hate that he can leave me so easily, but I hate it even more that I actually miss him when he's gone. It makes me feel weak. Dependent. Two things I never want to be.

"It's time to pull out the big guns."

"Such as?"

"Show him what he's missing."

When I still don't pick up her meaning, she rolls her eyes, stopping in her tracks to face me. "Send him a nude!" She reaches out to pop the top two buttons of my ribbed V-neck shirt with black, red, and white stripes. "You have great tits. Start there."

I smack her hand away, bringing the stack of flyers up to cover my chest. "You're an insane person."

"It's why you love me."

Lying in bed, I stare at my phone, debating on whether or not to take Halston's advice from earlier. At first, I didn't even consider it, but now that I'm in bed feeling all kinds of frustrated—sexually, and otherwise—it doesn't sound like such a terrible idea.

Fuck it.

Standing, I pull my shirt up, stopping when the ruffled hem just covers my nipples. I hold my phone below me, angling it so you can only see my bare stomach and my chest that stretches the fabric of my shirt. I might be stupid enough to send risqué pictures, but I'm not stupid enough to show my face.

I hit *send* before I can second-guess my decision. My fingers tap against my phone, anxiously waiting for his response. When I see the three little bubbles pop up, telling me he's typing, my stomach flips.

But then they disappear.

I wait a few more seconds, and when they don't pop back up, I toss my phone onto the bed. *Well, that was anticlimactic.* Deciding to call it a night, I head for the shower, feeling more than a little bitter.

It isn't until the water turns cold that I finally pry myself from the shower, wrapping my towel around me. When I open the door, I freeze, not expecting to find Jesse sitting at the foot of my bed, elbows braced on his knees, head hanging low. When he hears me, his head snaps up, his eyes filling with heat as they roam my body. I swallow hard under his perusal.

When he doesn't speak, I decide to be the one to close the distance between us. His eyes flare, almost imperceptibly, before he schools his expression. His jaw is set hard, his hands rolling into fists as I come to a stop between his spread knees. I reach down to brush a wayward lock of hair from his eyes, and he squeezes them shut, as if he's being physically tortured by my touch.

I take the opportunity to study his features, running my fingertips along his dark eyebrows, the crease between them, and the faint freckles across his nose. He inhales deeply but doesn't stop me. When I get to his lips, he snatches my wrist, his gaze burning into me. He releases me, never breaking eye contact as his hand moves toward the knot in my towel. He hesitates, waiting for me to shut it down, but I can't bring myself to do anything other than stand here, willing him to undo my towel. And that's exactly what he does. The white towel flutters to our feet, my bare ones and Jesse's boot-covered ones.

"I got your picture," he says, breaking the silence between us. My wet hair drips beads of water onto my chest and he leans forward to catch a drop that rolls down my sternum with his tongue. When his tongue hits my skin, every nerve ending tingles, my skin prickling with goosebumps. "Was someone missing me?" He circles my nipple with the tip of his finger, light as a feather.

"You're such an asshole," I snap, hitching a leg over his, my knee resting on the mattress.

"But you want me anyway." He makes quick work of unbuttoning his jeans, shoving them just low enough to pull himself out, already thick and hard. I bring my other leg up, straddling his lap, not wanting to prolong this for another second. Jess' hands find my hips as I lower myself onto him, sliding down his length.

"Fuck," he rasps, sounding pained, and my head falls back at the sensation.

"Six days is too long to go without this," I breathe, holding onto his shoulders for support.

"I've created a monster," he says, his voice taunting as he flexes his hips upward. "Tell me you missed me."

"No."

"Your pussy did," he says, tugging my earlobe between his teeth. "Missed me so much it's crying for me."

I feel myself clench around him and he groans, squeezing my ass, and before I know what's happening, he's flipped us around so I'm on my hands and knees. I look over my shoulder to see him fetch a condom from the drawer and roll it on, tossing the wrapper onto the floor.

At least one of us is thinking clearly.

Jess pushes between my shoulder blades until my chest is flat against the mattress, angles my hips upward, then slides into me from behind. I lurch forward with a gasp, not expecting how intense it would be like this.

"Get back here," he says, yanking my hips until my ass is flush against his pelvis. He holds me in place as he fucks me, my hands fisting the sheets, eyes squeezed shut.

"It's so deep," I mumble into the mattress.

He covers my body with his, his hands covering the backs of my own. "Not deep enough."

I feel his lips on the back of my neck, his sweat-slicked skin sticking to mine as he pumps his hips into me. I feel myself tightening around him as he slides in and out, over and over.

"Fuck, I need to come," Jesse says as he snakes a hand underneath me, rubbing my clit as he picks up the pace.

Oh my God. Just like that, I'm contracting around him, unable to stop from grinding into his hand, my clit pulsing under his fingertips. Once I slow my movements, Jesse sits up, fucking my boneless body until I feel him jerking inside me.

He pulls out of me, and I hear him dispose of the condom before he crawls back into bed behind my spent body, both of us lying across the bed horizontally, too tired and sated to right ourselves. His arm curls around me, cupping my breast, his chin resting above my head, and it only feels like seconds before I succumb to sleep.

CHAPTER TWENTY-SIX

Allie

J ESSE STAYED IN MY ROOM LAST NIGHT, EVEN THOUGH Dare and Lo were home. We're getting sloppy. Careless. But something has shifted, and I think we both feel it.

"That thing happening tonight?" Jess asks, bringing me out of my thoughts. I look over at his profile, one hand on the steering wheel, the other hand pushing through his hair. He insisted on driving me to school this morning, which is a first.

"Yep," I say, surprised he remembered the show.

Jess pulls into the parking lot, cutting the engine before getting out. He rounds the hood of the truck and then he's at my door, opening it for me.

"What are you doing?" I ask warily.

"Walking you to class."

I stay in my seat, momentarily stunned that he's not just dropping me off, and Jesse reaches across my lap to unbuckle my seatbelt. I raise an eyebrow at him.

"What's with the boyfriend act?"

"I'm walking you to class, not asking you to go steady. Chill."

I hop down, swinging my bag over my shoulder as I

make my way toward campus, binder in hand. Jess falls into step next to me, throwing his arm around my shoulder, bringing me in close.

What has gotten into him?

Once we get close to the courtyard where students are milling around, we get a couple of curious looks and double takes, but Jesse either doesn't notice it or doesn't acknowledge it. Straightening my posture, I hold my binder at my chest, Jesse's bruised knuckles hanging over my shoulder.

"Shepherd!" a gruff voice calls out.

Jess stops short at the sound of his name. When we turn around, it's to see a middle-aged man in a white polo with a red Wildcats logo.

"Heard you were back," the man says, smiling like he's genuinely happy to see him. "Staying out of trouble?"

"Never," Jess says as he's pulled in for a hug, the man clapping his back.

"Maybe I can help with that."

Jess looks at him inquisitively, his thick eyebrows pulling together.

"I have to get to class," I interrupt, hitching a thumb over my shoulder.

"Shit, this is Allie," Jesse says belatedly. "Allie, this is Coach Standifer. He's the reason I'm not in jail right now."

Coach Standifer holds his hand out to shake mine.

Something warms inside me as I witness their interaction. This is the first time I've seen Jess seem completely at ease with anyone. I can tell he respects him.

"Well, then I'll let you two catch up."

"One sec," Jesse says, holding up a finger. He pulls me off to the side, catching me off guard as he grasps my chin, angling my face toward him, then kisses me hard, sliding his tongue into my mouth. It feels like my stomach is being attacked by a swarm of angry butterflies and I press up onto my toes, sliding my free hand up his chest.

A forced cough from Coach Standifer has me pulling away abruptly, cheeks burning.

"I have some stuff to do today, but I'll see you tonight," Jesse says, his voice quiet and deep.

"Okay." I nod. "Nice meeting you," I say to Coach Standifer with an awkward wave before turning to walk away.

CHAPTER TWENTY-SEVEN

Allie

"Relax," Dylan says for the eight-hundredth time, his hands squeezing my shoulders in an effort to loosen me up. "The hard part's over."

"Seriously," Halston agrees. "Look around. You killed it."

I suck in a lungful of air, taking it all in. The place is packed, way more than it was the first night I came, and way more than I could've hoped for. The only thing that could make it better is if my dad were here.

"It's go time," I say. "You guys ready?"

Dylan nods before joining the rest of the band on stage as the DJ wraps up the last song. Halston wraps her arms around me, giving an excited squeal as he takes the stage.

Swinging his guitar over his shoulder, Dylan curls one hand around the mic stand. "We're The Liars."

Halston and I exchange looks when he doesn't elaborate, silence falling over the crowd.

"Not much of an intro, but okay," I say, clapping. Halston quickly follows suit until the audience joins in. The music starts, then everyone resumes their dancing, awkward introduction be damned.

They play perfectly. Dylan looks like he's born to be on stage, looking every bit of the quintessential tortured rock star.

"You have got to be kidding me," Halston all but growls a few songs in. I follow her gaze, landing on Sully, of all people. And right behind him?

Jesse.

He spots me at the same time, my insides warming at the sight of him. His eyebrows pinch together, looking me up and down with heat in his gaze, and that look alone was worth letting Halston doll me up.

After an hour of back and forth, we settled on a short red skater dress with tiny white flowers. It's low-cut, showing more cleavage than I'm used to, flaring out just below my butt. I drew the line at heels, much to Halston's dismay, settling on my black Docs instead.

Jesse pushes through the crowd, stalking toward me. My stomach flips as he gets closer, and when he's within arm's reach, he curls a hand around the back of my head, leaning down to kiss me without a single fuck given as to who sees. I stumble back, caught off guard, but he holds me in place as his tongue slips into my mouth, dancing with mine. My hands fly to his waist, holding on as he kisses me slow and hard, as if we're not in a crowded venue.

"Why are you here?" Halston's voice breaks through the trance, and I pull away, breathless.

"It's a free country, last time I checked," is Sully's smart-ass response.

I shake my head at their bickering as Jesse moves behind me, his front to my back. "You look beautiful," he says, bending down close to my ear. "I want to fuck you in this dress later."

A thrill rolls through me at his words, but when I glance up toward the stage, I see Dylan scowling at us, concern painting his features. I try to send him a reassuring smile, but his expression remains the same. Jesse's hand comes around me, his palm flattening on my stomach as his lips meet my neck.

"We're going to play a cover for you all. Hope you don't mind," Dylan announces. Caleb and Hunter exchange confused looks. I frown, not remembering a cover on his setlist.

When I hear the into for "Jessie's Girl," my jaw falls open.

What the fuck is he doing?

He tosses me a wink, and then starts to sing about wanting someone else's girl. I feel the moment Jesse catches on, his body stiffening behind me at the sound of his name coming from Dylan's mouth.

"Something you want to tell me, Allie girl?" Jess asks, his voice accusatory.

"I don't know what he's doing," I say, turning around to look him in the eye.

Jesse doesn't look convinced, his eyes set hard on the stage behind me. I tug his wrist, pulling him away from the crowd into the hall near the bathrooms.

"Just friends, huh?" he asks bitterly.

"We *are*," I insist. "He's just trying to get under your skin." *And I have no idea why.*

"Did you fuck him?"

I jerk back as if he slapped me. "Are you fucking kidding me?" I bark. "Yes, I turned around and had sex with someone else during the three seconds you were gone." Sarcasm drips from every word.

"A guy doesn't act like *that*," he says, pointing a finger toward the stage, "unless he's fucked you or he *wants to*. Which is it?"

"Neither. But you're one to talk. You've slept with half the town, and besides that," I say, my voice growing in volume, "we said we were just having fun."

He brings his palms to the wall on either side of my head, caging me in. "You want to know what the difference is, Allie? I'm honest about it—thanks for throwing it in my face, by the way—and we also said no lying. Those were the rules."

I open my mouth to argue, but he cuts me off.

"And we both know this isn't just *fun* anymore."

My mouth snaps shut, not expecting that. But he's right. This thing between us somehow became *more*, whether we like it or not.

"It was one kiss," I say, and Jess tries to take a step back, but I curl my fist into his T-shirt, holding him in place. "It was *before* I met you. We were both drunk after my dad's funeral and neither of us was thinking straight."

"Do you want him?"

"Not like that. Not like I want you."

"You make me fucking crazy."

"Feeling's mutual."

"Brat."

"Asshole."

Still fisting his shirt, I press up onto my toes and bring my lips to his. Jess groans, kissing me hard, but I cut it short, pulling back abruptly. "Now tell me you're sorry."

"Excuse me?"

"Tell me you're sorry for acting like I've ever been with anyone but you."

His eyes soften at my words. "This shit is new to me."

Internally, I scoff, a witty retort on the tip of my tongue. But his unexpected sincerity gives me pause. On one hand, I love the fact that he's giving me something real. On the other hand, I can't lie down and be his doormat whenever he pulls the bad-guy-sad-eyes routine.

"It's a pretty foreign concept for me, too, but you don't see me going all caveman on your ass."

Jesse smirks, leaning down to squeeze my ass through the thin material of my dress. "I wouldn't hate it if you did."

I laugh, rolling my eyes. "Come on." I tug on his hand, pulling him back toward the crowd. The Liars are playing their last song, and I don't want to miss it.

When we find Halston and Sully, Halston's laser-focused on the stage, dancing to the beat, ignoring Sully's presence while he broods behind her, arms folded across his chest.

I laugh, shaking my head. Seems the theme of the night is *dysfunctional*.

The last song ends abruptly, the vocals and lead guitar cutting out. My eyes whip over to see Dylan standing there like he's seen a ghost. He shrugs his guitar off and jumps down from the stage, prowling toward something. Or *someone*.

"Thanks for coming out," I hear Hunter's voice boom over the speaker. "We're The Liars. Follow us on the Gram for more shows. Now let's get fucked up!"

The audience breaks out into cheers, then the DJ starts playing "Sweet but Psycho". Everyone goes back to dancing and drinking, Dylan's little scene all but forgotten.

I watch as he shoulders through the crowd to a girl I've never seen in my life. Her eyes widen when she notices him, and I see her mouth *Dylan* right before he drops a shoulder, lifting her up fireman style. She slaps and kicks, but he doesn't so much as flinch as he carries her toward the exit.

What the fuck?

"Hang on," I tell Jess and Halston, then I'm making my way over to the front of the stage. Hunter spots me, coming to squat down close enough to hear me.

"What the hell was that?" I ask. Hunter shakes his head, lifting his palms with a shrug. "*Who* was that?"

"You know Romeo and Juliet?"

I nod. "Obviously."

"*That* would be Dylan's equivalent of Juliet."

My mouth falls open. I couldn't be more shocked if he slapped me in the face. Dylan has never mentioned a girl. I was always under the impression that he left the Eastern Shore to get away from his family, but now I'm wondering if this girl isn't an integral piece of the puzzle.

It's almost closing time, and The Lamppost is still jam-packed with people showing no signs of slowing down. I yawn, in some strange state of sleepy happiness, while Jess, Sully, and Halston have a heated debate over something I stopped listening to a long time ago. Other than Dylan bailing mid-song, the night went off without a hitch, and everything feels…*right*. For once.

I spot Victor by the bar and he waves me over. Anxious to see what he thinks about tonight, I tell Jess I'll be right back before slipping away.

"You did it, kid. I'm impressed," Victor says with a smile.

I can't help but beam at him, giddy with how tonight turned out. "Thanks for giving me a shot."

"Of course. Can I pull you away for a celebratory drink?"

My eyebrows jump to my hairline. I look back toward my friends, hesitating.

"It'll be quick. Can't exactly have you drinking out here since you're underage and everyone knows it. It'll give us a quiet place to talk about what's next for you."

Right. "Okay. One drink."

I follow him away through the mob of people, down the hall, and into a back room. He closes the door behind us, and a sense of unease settles over me, even though rationally, I know it makes sense. We can't exactly have a conversation over the noise of the club.

The room consists of a desk, a black leather couch, and not much else.

"Have a seat," he says, motioning toward the couch.

I glance back at the door, seeing people walking back and forth through the square window, deeming it safe before I sit on the cold leather, smoothing my dress down my thighs. He ambles toward the desk where a bottle of champagne in a bucket of ice and two glasses are waiting. Grabbing a white washcloth, he wipes off the bottle, then turns toward me.

"How do you feel about this becoming a permanent thing?" he asks, and when he pops the cork, I flinch, feeling both on edge and thrilled at the prospect of doing this on a regular basis.

"Really?" I ask as he hands me a glass. I take a tiny sip, the bubbly liquid warming my throat on the way down.

"Why not?" He gives a shrug, turning back for the

desk. "You managed to triple what I made the first night. It's a no-brainer." He takes a seat behind the desk, pulling several things out of the drawer. I can't tell for sure, but I think one of them is an envelope. He opens it up, then he's waving a stack of cash at me. "Your cut," he explains, holding it out for me.

My eyes bulge out of my skull. I wasn't expecting to walk away with money. Standing, I make my way toward him and he hands me the fat stack. "Thank you," I say, trying to casually flip through it. I don't want to count it in front of him, but there has to be at least a thousand bucks here.

When I peel my eyes from the money, I see him bending over a piece of glass, a rolled-up dollar bill to his nose as he sniffs, sliding it along two rows of white powder.

"You earned it," he says, wiping the excess powder from under his nose. "You want a line?"

"I'm good," I say, forcing a casual tone. As I take a step back, his hand darts out, sliding up the back of my thigh and dipping under my dress to squeeze my ass.

I slap his hand away, jumping back. Shock has rendered me speechless, and all I can do is stand there as my brain desperately tries to make sense of what the fuck just happened. He was friends with my dad. He's probably fifteen years my senior. Never in a million years did I see this coming.

"Don't be like that," he says, rolling his chair backwards before standing. The urge to bolt hits me just as the door flies open, smacking the wall so hard the handle leaves a hole in the wall. I jump as Jesse and Sully prowl through the room, two sets of eyes furious, two jaws set hard.

Oh, fuck.

Victor is visibly nervous, moving in front of the desk in an effort to hide the coke. "This is a private meet—"

He doesn't get to finish his sentence before Jess balls the collar of his shirt in one hand and cocks his other fist back, hitting him square in the face. Victor falls back onto his desk, holding his nose as blood leaks through his fingers. Jess drags him across the desk, knocking everything off in the process, before throwing him on the floor. Victor lands on top of shattered glass with a grunt, trying to kick at Jess as he approaches.

"Did he hurt you?" Sully asks, grabbing my shoulders and forcing me to look at him. I shake my head in answer.

"You offer my girl drugs?" Jess shouts, bringing my attention back to where he stands over Victor, who's still laid out. "Then you think you can *touch her*?"

"Jess, let's go," I say, moving toward him. Sully stops me by picking me up and planting me by the door like it's nothing.

"Stay here. I'll get him."

Sully goes to pull Jesse off, grabbing one of his arms, but Jesse's not finished yet. "Come on, man. You're scaring her."

That stops him, feral eyes looking over his shoulder to meet mine. I'm not fucking scared. I'm angry. Angry that Victor pulled this shit, angry with myself for freezing and not doing anything, and angry that Jess had to come to my rescue.

Jesse turns back around as Victor pulls his phone out of his pocket. Jess squats down to grab his collar in both hands, lifting his shoulders off the floor. "I'd think twice about that," he says, giving a pointed look at Victor's phone. "You have a club full of drunk underage kids, an office full of illegal substances, and a sexual assault case just waiting to happen." Jess' voice is low and menacing in a way I've never heard before. "And if you ever so much as look at her again, I'll fucking kill you." He throws him back down before standing, leaving Victor in a pile of dollar bills and broken glass.

"I think it's safe to say you blew your shot, Allison," Victor says, bracing one hand on the floor to pick himself up. Jess jerks toward him, but Sully beats him to it, kicking him in the balls. Victor falls back to the floor, curling in on himself as Sully squats down, gathering the dollar bills into a pile.

"By the way, I'll be keeping this," he says, tapping Victor on the forehead with the wad of cash. "Hope you don't mind."

CHAPTER TWENTY-EIGHT

Allie

I PRACTICALLY RAN OUT OF THAT BACK ROOM, AND Halston knew something was wrong the second she saw my face. She grabbed my hand, pulling me out of the building, and didn't stop until we got to her car. I explained what went down on the way, and then I had to talk her out of turning back around to kick Victor's ass. I needed to put as much distance between me and Victor as possible.

Which brings us to now, sitting on the couch in Lo's living room at two A.M.

"Has he ever tried anything like that before?" Halston asks, cracking open a water bottle.

"Never," I say, shaking my head. I've played back every little interaction with him in my mind, trying to find clues I might have missed. Then I blamed myself for not having better instincts. But that line of thinking is bullshit. I made a bad decision. I shouldn't have gone into that room with him, but it wasn't an invitation to feel me up.

I jump when the front door flies open, my eyes instantly locking onto Jesse's.

"Why the fuck did you leave without me?" he shouts, walking over to the couch with Sully close behind.

"I had to get out of there," I say lamely. "And you shouldn't have done that."

"Are you kidding me? What was I supposed to do, Allie? Stand there and watch? I told you that guy was smarmy. I knew the minute he led you away that he was going to pull some shit like that."

I look over to Halston. "Can you give Sully a ride home?"

Her lips twist, and I know she wants to say no, but she won't deny me. "No talking allowed," she says, pointing a finger at him, earning a smirk in response.

"This belongs to you," Sully says to me, dropping the cash onto the coffee table before he moves for the door.

"I don't want that asshole's money. I'll give it to the band."

I stand to hug Halston, promising to call her tomorrow, then it's just Jess and me.

Wordlessly, I lead him out the back door and through the gate that leads to the lake. The cool night air licks against my skin, but it's a welcomed sensation after spending all night in a hot, sweaty venue. The moon peeks through the clouds, casting eerie shadows from the pine trees across the sand. It's so quiet out here. Peaceful.

"Are you seriously mad at me?" he asks, looking over at me as we walk along the shoreline.

I sigh, running my hand through my hair. "No, I'm not mad at you. I'm mad at *him*. I was really excited about that job, and he ruined it by being a perv." I turn toward him, my hands reaching up to cup his face. "But you can't just go around punching people in the face every time they piss you off."

"Why not?"

"Because you could get hurt. Or *arrested*."

"If you think I'm ever going to stand by and watch someone hurt my—*you*—you don't know me at all."

I frown, and he swipes his thumb over my bottom lip.

"What's that for?"

"You called me your girl." He said it earlier, but I was too preoccupied to react. Conflicted doesn't even begin to cover how I feel.

"Is there a problem with that?" His voice is hard, but it's laced with vulnerability.

"Jess—" I start, but then he's lifting me by the backs of my thighs. My ankles lock around his waist, my arms shooting up to hold onto his shoulders as he walks us over to a giant rock that sits halfway in the water. He sets me down on the smooth surface, his hands gripping the outsides of my thighs.

"You want this. I can fucking feel it. Why are you so goddamn scared?"

I huff out a sad laugh. "You don't even tell me where you go when you disappear. You have this whole other life I know nothing about."

"I don't want to talk about that life when I'm with you. I don't want that shit touching you."

"It's not enough," I say, hating myself for saying the words.

"I'm trying to be good for you," he says, his palms sliding up my outer thighs, underneath my dress. "I'm trying to get out. I just need time."

Get out. Get out of what?

My heart goes haywire in my chest.

"I promise you that when I leave here, I'm not with anyone else. It's nothing like that. You just have to trust me."

225

Jess leans in, kissing the corner of my mouth, and I close my eyes, parting my lips in invitation. "Be with me, Allie," he whispers into my mouth before slipping his tongue inside.

It was supposed to be fun. But I'm in too deep to turn back now.

CHAPTER TWENTY-NINE

Allie

THE NEXT FEW WEEKS PASS, AND EVEN THOUGH EVERYTHING has changed, *nothing* has changed. Lo walked in on us sleeping together the following morning and didn't seem the least bit surprised about it. She told us both to be careful before throwing a box of condoms at us, and that was that.

Jess is still cagey as hell. On edge. He comes and goes like a ghost in the night, and I can tell this double life is starting to wear on him. It's wearing on me, too. I can't focus in class. My mind goes crazy with possible scenarios. I've imagined everything from him selling drugs to having a secret love child.

My mom's been calling a lot, with the anniversary of my dad right around the corner. She's still after me to get those divorce documents. When I finally asked her why it was so important, she dropped the bomb on me. She was getting married to the new guy—whose name I don't even remember—and she's on a bit of a time crunch. *Because she's pregnant.*

I had to laugh. If I didn't, I'd cry.

My phone rings as I'm walking across the courtyard at Kerrigan, coffee in hand. I dig it from my back pocket to see *Grandma* flashing across the screen. I stop short, knowing why she's calling.

"Hello?"

"Hey, sweetie. I just wanted to let you know the Carsons are out of the house."

"That's great," I say, with enthusiasm I don't feel.

"The cleaning company won't be there for a few days, but if you need a place to stay before that, it's yours."

I take a seat at one of the benches, setting my coffee on the ground. "Thanks, Grandma."

"Of course." She pauses. "How are you holding up?"

I swallow against the lump in my throat. "I'm fine," I lie. "What about you?"

"Hanging in there. It's hard to believe it's been a year."

I flick a tear away. "I know. Hey, Grandma, I've gotta get to work," I say, cutting the conversation short. I don't have to work, but I also don't want to talk about this right now. "Can I call you later?"

"Take your time. I'm sending something in the mail for your birthday, so be on the lookout."

"Sounds good. Love you."

Once we hang up, I pull my headphones out of my backpack and hit *play* before pulling them over my ears. Moving out was always a part of the plan. I can't stay there forever. I just didn't expect it to feel like this.

"Why *The Outsiders*?" I ask, my cheek resting on Jesse's bare chest.

"What?" he grumbles, sounding half-asleep. When he picked me up from school earlier, I didn't mention the phone call from my grandma. I'm not ready to leave just yet.

"*The Outsiders*. What do you like so much about it?"

Jess stretches, then his hand comes down onto my bare back, tracing his fingertips across my skin until goosebumps form in their wake. "When I was a kid, my mom would lock me in my room whenever Lo wasn't around to keep me out of her hair."

I feel my stomach twist at his words. He says it so casually, like it's the most common thing in the world.

"One time, I was in there for over a day. Lo stayed at her friend's house, and I'm pretty sure my mom forgot about me. I didn't have a TV or anything, and I'd sung every song I knew to pass the time. My stomach was growling, and the sun was going down, so I started cleaning up the room, looking for something to eat."

I press a kiss to his chest, my eyes burning with unshed tears.

"I didn't find anything to eat, but I did find that book. I think Lo must've brought it home from school or something," he muses. "Anyway, I read the whole thing in one sitting, which I thought was impressive as hell back then. Lo unlocked the door the next morning, and she never left me alone again after that."

"I hate your mom," I whisper.

"Me, too." Jess yawns. "I read it all the time after that. You know that poem in there? 'Nothing Gold Can Stay'?"

I nod. I've never read the book, but I'm familiar with the poem.

"Nothing perfect and beautiful can last forever. It resonated with me, even as a kid. After being disappointed so many times, you're bound to lose hope in everything."

We're both quiet for a while, lost in our own thoughts, until eventually, his breathing starts to even out, turning into soft snores.

CHAPTER THIRTY

Allie

"**A**LLIE!"

I turn at the sound of my name to see Dylan standing there, hands in his front pockets, looking contrite. I haven't talked to him since the night at The Lamppost, and I'm still mad at him for provoking Jess. Hunter and Caleb came into Blackbear yesterday, and I gave him the twelve-hundred bucks Victor gave me, telling him to divide it amongst themselves. When they asked why I didn't want it, I gave them a very watered-down version of what happened. And by the look on Dylan's face, they filled him in on it.

I keep walking toward the parking lot at school, but he jogs over, falling into step next to me. "Albert, come on. Are you okay?"

"I'm fine."

"You needed me—"

I pause, facing him. "What I *need* is for you to explain," I say, cutting him off. "Why did you provoke Jess like that? That was a fucked-up thing to do."

"I know." He chews on his lip ring.

I shake my head, exasperated. "That's it? Do you, like, have feelings for me or something?" The words sound so stupid out loud, but that's the only thing that makes sense.

"No. Yes. *No*," he says, running a hand through his hair. "Fuck, I don't know. I thought I did. But I think I was just fucked up over someone else and didn't want to admit it."

"That makes zero sense," I say, bewildered.

"Trust me. I know. The song thing was just me being a dick, but for the record, I still don't think he's good enough for you."

I tighten my grip on my backpack straps, turning to walk away, but Dylan grabs my arm, stopping me.

"But he protected you when I couldn't. So, I guess he's not a complete piece of shit."

"I'm not going to stand here and listen to you talk about someone I lo—" I snap my mouth shut, clenching my teeth together before I can finish that sentence. I didn't mean to say it. I didn't even mean to think it, but the thought kept repeating in my head as Dylan spoke about him.

"I have to go." I turn back around, stopping short when I see Jesse standing a few feet away, eyes trained on Dylan. His jaw is set hard, arms folded over his chest, but he's too far to have heard anything.

"What's he doing here?" He nods his chin toward Dylan when I get within hearing distance.

"He came to apologize." *Sort of.*

Jess continues to stare daggers at Dylan, and I'm afraid he's going to cause a scene on campus, but he surprises me by grabbing my hand, and leading me to his truck.

An incessant buzzing breaks through my consciousness and I slap a hand out to wake Jess, coming up empty.

Hearing the shower running, I groan, sitting up to silence his phone. *What is he doing up so early?* The buzzing stops just as my fingers make contact. I start to pull away, but I hesitate when a message appears, my hand hovering over the screen.

1616 E. Shea Blvd. Same time as last week.

I frown at the screen as dread unfurls in my stomach. This is it. This is the piece to the puzzle I've been waiting for. I chew on my thumbnail, feeling conflicted. I didn't mean to pry, but now that I've seen it, I can't pretend I haven't.

I hear the water cut off and I quickly grab my phone from the nightstand next to his and snap a picture of the address. A freshly showered Jess walks out just as I stuff my phone between my thighs. He stops short when he sees that I'm awake, towel tied low around his waist, wet hair slicked back away from his face with a single rogue strand falling into his eyes. My fingers itch to reach out and touch it.

Wordlessly, he moves toward me, sliding his hand through my hair, gripping it at the nape of my neck. I peer up at him, smoothing my palms up his stomach, feeling his muscles tense under my touch.

"I have to leave," he says, his voice gruff.

My hands fall away from his stomach. "Shocker."

"I'll be back before you even wake up tomorrow." He leans down to kiss me, but I turn my cheek, denying him. "Don't be a brat," he says before pulling my earlobe between his teeth. His lips trail down my neck, sucking on the sensitive skin. Goosebumps break out along my arms and I squeeze my thighs together to ease the ache.

The buzzing sounds again, and he pulls away, glancing down at his screen, his features tight.

I'm going to find out what he's hiding tonight.

CHAPTER THIRTY-ONE

Allie

"**W**HAT'S HE DOING HERE?" I SNAP AT Halston.

"He overheard our conversation," she says bitterly, shoving past me. "He threatened to tell Jess unless we let him come with us."

"Yeah, I'm a real asshole for trying to keep you two safe as you drive to a random ass address in the middle of the night," Sullivan deadpans.

"Wait, are you two a thing again?"

"No." Halston scoffs at the same time Sullivan says, "Yep."

My eyebrows shoot up. "Glad we cleared that up."

"You ready to go?" Halston asks. I wring my hands in front of me, suddenly second-guessing my plan. It's a little crazy to stalk the guy you're seeing to an unknown location, but bringing two people along—one of which is his best friend? That's full-blown bat shit.

"This is a bad idea."

"Do not even start that shit with me, Allison Parrish. We are going to that address, and you're going to get your answers."

I shake my head, still torn. This is something my

insane mother would do. *Love makes you crazy, baby.* No. I shake my mother's voice out of my head. This isn't love.

"This probably goes against guy code or some shit, but I agree with Hals."

I don't know if I'm more taken aback by the fact that he's siding with her, or the fact that he just called her *Hals*.

"I think he might be in trouble."

"What?" I shoot accusatory eyes at Halston who shrugs, conveying with her eyes that this is news to her, too. It's one thing to suspect, but to have someone else validate your suspicions makes it all too real.

"Relax. I don't know anything for sure. But you don't know what you're walking into. Shep's already going to kick my ass. He'd kill me if I let you two go alone."

"Guess we'll find out in about two hours," I say, showing them my phone screen with the directions and estimated travel time.

Approximately two hours and thirty-seven minutes later, we find ourselves in the parking lot of a sketchy, unmarked building. My stomach churns with nerves, and I think I might actually throw up right here and now.

"You ready for this, baby girl?" Halston asks, grabbing ahold of my hand. I suck in a breath, steeling myself for whatever we're about to walk into.

"Yep." My boots crunch against the loose gravel in the parking lot as we make our way toward the front of the building. At least, I think it's the front. There's nothing but a sliding steel door with three small rectangular windows.

The closer we get, the more nervous I get. My hands

feel clammy, and my pulse pounds in my ears. I can hear something rumbling inside, something *loud*, but I can't put my finger on it. Cheering, maybe?

Sullivan takes the lead, pressing his forehead into one of the glass windows. "Can't see shit. They're blacked out."

Unease licks up my spine as he pulls up the metal door. My jaw drops when I take in the scene in front of me. The sound is unmistakable now. A mob of people is gathered around something in the middle as "The Way You Like It" by Adema blares from the speakers, competing to be heard over the crowd's jeering.

"What the hell is this place?" Halston shouts, scanning our surroundings.

"Fuck if I know," Sullivan says. "But I'm gonna go out on a limb here and say it's not legal."

"Quick, shut the door and blend in." I have a feeling people aren't supposed to just waltz into a place like this.

Sully grabs ahold of the handle, sliding it back down before we make our way toward the edge of the crowd.

"Stay close," Sully says, reaching for mine and Halston's hands. Halston quirks a brow at him, hesitating, but she relents, giving him her manicured hand. With me in the lead, we start to push through the crowd. I'm thankful I'm wearing my trusty Docs, because this mob of people rivals some mosh pits. The tangy scent of blood and smoke hangs in the air, and slowly, it all starts to click into place. The black eyes. The bruises. The secretive phone calls.

Just before we break through to the front, I see a flash of a guy in blue shorts slamming to the hard ground. There's no ring. No pad on the floor. This guy's not even wearing gloves.

"So that's the big secret? Jess hangs out at some wannabe fight club?"

"No," I say, unsure if she can even hear me. "He's the one they're betting on." Letting go of Sullivan's hand, I barrel my way through until I'm front and center.

"Allie!" Halston shouts, but I don't listen.

My stomach drops as I take in the sight of Jess dripping with sweat, in nothing but jeans and boots, fists blocking his face as he and another guy circle each other like sharks in a tank. Jesse's hair falls over his forehead as he gives his opponent a taunting wink, motioning for him to come closer.

The crowd grows rowdy, jostling me, and I chance a look behind me to find Halston and Sullivan even farther away.

"Allie!" Sullivan's voice thunders, his big body shoulder-checking people as he tries to clear a safe path for Halston. I whip back around just in time to see Jesse's head snap toward the sound of my name. His eyes lock onto mine as shock morphs into anger.

Blue Shorts takes the opportunity to strike while Jesse's distracted, landing a punch to the jaw. Jesse jerks to the side with the force of the hit and I flinch as if I took the blow myself.

"Jesse!" My voice is a guttural, desperate thing as I watch in horror as he hits the ground, his head bouncing off the concrete. My hands fly to my mouth, and I'm momentarily frozen to my spot. Blue Shorts lifts his arms, strutting around the invisible perimeter, gloating as the crowd roars.

Snapping out of it, I rush forward, but Jesse holds a palm up, stopping me in my tracks. Sullivan's suddenly at my back, his arm hooking around my waist before pulling me away.

Jesse stands, dragging his forearm across his bloody mouth. He looks absolutely fucking feral.

"Get her out of here," he demands, pointing a finger at me. Sullivan's suddenly at my back, his arm hooking around my waist, holding me in place. I grind my jaw, my irritation with his command warring with my concern for him. Sully walks us backwards, the crowd swallowing us whole. Halston grabs onto my hand once we get within arm's reach, following us out.

I can't see Jess anymore from back here. I stand on my tiptoes, trying to spot him through gaps in the crowd, but all I can see are random flashes of flesh and the blue of his opponent's shorts.

Suddenly, the noise rises to a deafening level. The mob of people parts down the middle as Jesse prowls toward us, and I see Blue Shorts laid out on the ground behind him, unmoving. He doesn't stop until he's standing in front of me, his hand wrapping around my wrist as he pulls me away. I try snatching my wrist from his grasp, but he tightens his grip, tugging me toward a back door, Halston and Sullivan hot on our heels.

He releases his hold on me, shoving the door to the back parking lot open. We're only a couple of hours from home, but the air feels thick and warm here. Jesse turns to face me, running a bloodied hand through his hair.

"What the fuck are you doing here?"

"Getting answers."

He huffs out a laugh, throwing his arms open wide. "Well, you got 'em."

"Hardly." I still don't know why. It doesn't make any

sense that he'd keep this from me. So he fights for money. Big deal. It's better than where my mind went.

I hear the heavy door behind me opening again, and I whip my head around to see a group of smiling people spill out into the parking lot. A guy in a wife beater and black jeans ambles toward us, slapping a stack of cash into Jesse's open palm.

"You had me worried there for a second," he says, before turning to me. "Who's this pretty little thing?" His eyes rake over my body. I cross my arms over my chest, sending him the dirtiest look I can muster.

Jesse's eyes meet mine, void of any emotion. "No one important."

Okay, ouch.

I try to keep the hurt from showing on my face. Halston hooks an arm around my shoulders, and I feel Sullivan move in closer behind me, probably anticipating a fight.

"Mhm," the guy says, sounding unconvinced. Jess clenches his jaw, averting his eyes. I get the impression that this guy has some kind of power over him. He doesn't bite his tongue for anyone.

"Let's go," Jess says, moving past him, and we follow suit.

"Hey, Jess!" he calls out after us. Jesse turns to look over his shoulder, frowning, and I follow his gaze to find the man in the wife beater smirking at him. "I'll be in touch."

CHAPTER THIRTY-TWO

Jess

I GLANCE OVER AT ALLIE IN THE PASSENGER SEAT. SHE hasn't said a word since I all but dragged her to my truck and told her to get in. The last thing I expected was for her to show up here. My two worlds collided tonight, and she doesn't belong anywhere near this side of me.

When I saw her standing there, looking like a goddamn lamb in a lion's den, I lost it. I'm not a particularly skilled fighter. I don't win every time. I don't train like most of the guys I go up against. Lacrosse kept me in top shape, but what makes me good is that I can take a fucking beating, and still manage to get back up. I've spent my whole life fighting.

It started as a way to make money for school. My scholarship didn't pay for much, and I wasn't going to hit up Lo and Dare for help. I figured it was better than the alternative—also known as selling drugs. I planned on making a good enough chunk of cash to live on for the year, then walking away. But then, Crystal showed up, blowing my plans to shit in true Shepherd fashion.

I pull into the parking lot of the sketchy apartment complex, cutting the engine. Allie frowns, confusion painting her pretty features as she takes in our surroundings.

Wordlessly, I hop out of the truck, and she follows me. I make my way toward the steps where a guy with a 40 wrapped in a paper sack sits, nodding at us as we pass. Once we're upstairs, I dig my key out of my pocket and unlock the door. I don't like coming here. I've only been here a handful of times, and only when I absolutely have to, but I need Allie to see the real me.

Allie hesitates by the door, arms folded across her chest. I don't blame her. This place is a fucking sty. The kitchen and living room are combined, with nothing more than a bathroom and a small bedroom connected to a short hallway. The couch has cigarette burns and dark stains in its dingy fabric, along with the blue carpet. The roach-infested kitchen consists of old linoleum and grimy as fuck appliances that are older than I am.

"Say something," I urge, and she closes the door behind her.

"Where are we?"

I give her a bitter smile. "Home."

She shakes her head in disbelief. "I don't understand."

As if on cue, Crystal appears in the hall, her blonde hair a tangled, matted mess, wearing only a raggedy ass tank top and underwear.

"I thought I heard someone," she says, a dazed smile on her face. She walks over to where I sit on the couch, leaning down to hug me. I don't move to hug her back. I don't do anything but stare at Allie, unmoving.

"If I'd known I was having company, I'd have straightened up a little," she says, noticing Allie's presence.

I snort. As if all this place needs is *straightening up*. Allie's big gray eyes plead with me to fill her in. She looks all wrong standing in this shit hole.

"Crystal, this is Allie. Allie…meet my mom."

The scared, apprehensive look leaves Allie's eyes, and in its place is a mixture of anger and contempt.

"Nice to meet—" Crystal starts, walking toward Allie, but Allie stops her with a glare.

"Not interested in exchanging pleasantries. Thanks," she snaps before turning her attention back to me. "Jess, can you just tell me what's going on?"

"Who the fuck do you think you are?" Crystal slurs, moving toward Allie. I jump up off the couch, intercepting Crystal before she can touch a hair on Allie's head.

"Go to your room."

"You're going to let her disrespect your mother like that?"

"Go!"

Crystal jerks back at my tone, sending one last nasty look toward Allie before walking away with her tail between her legs. I pull out my phone, tapping out a quick text to Sullivan. Once I hear the door slam shut, I turn my attention back to Allie.

"This is my life, Allie." I spread my arms wide, gesturing to the space we're in. "This is who I am."

"This isn't you," she says vehemently.

I should've never let Crystal back into my life. She cried to me about Lo abandoning her like she was a child, which is a joke considering she's the one who abandoned us when we were actual children. She cried about being homeless. Cried that she had no one and nothing left. She fucking cried about everything. Like an idiot, I took pity on her. Got her this glamorous apartment and agreed to pay her rent if she left Lo alone. Lo had finally broken free. She deserved it.

I thought I could handle it. But you know that kids'

book? *If You Give a Mouse a Cookie*? That's Crystal. You give her an inch and she takes a hundred fuckin' miles. She tried demanding more money, and when I threatened to walk away, she went to Julian, the guy who runs the fighting ring. She borrowed money. A lot of fucking money. And Julian was all too happy to give it to her if it meant he could use it as leverage to keep me fighting.

So, there I was, all geared up to walk away and play it straight, but instead, I got stuck paying her debt. Guys like Julian don't fuck around. *Not* fighting meant signing her death warrant.

I was a fucking fool to think Crystal would've ever let me live a normal life. I was an even bigger fool to think I could be good enough for Allie.

"I'm not good." I've tried. No matter what I do—no matter how hard I try—the end result is the same.

"Jess," Allie says, her eyes starting to fill with tears. "I'm not judging you. How could you think I'd judge you after everything?"

"I'm not good *for you*," I say, "and if you stay with me, I'll only ruin you, too."

"How can you say that? Don't I get a say?"

"Stop!"

She flinches at my tone, and I hate that I'm responsible for the hurt on her face.

"I'm not going to change who I am, Allie," I say, my voice resigned. *I can't.*

"Who asked you to?" Her lip trembles and a tear rolls down her cheek. A knock on the door makes her jump, and a second later, Halston and Sullivan are stepping inside. I texted Sully the address and told him to take Allie back to River's Edge.

Halston tries to pull Allie in for a hug, but she shakes her head, stopping her.

"I won't beg you to be with me," Allie says through clenched teeth. "If I walk out that door, we're done."

Three sets of accusing eyes are trained on me. Sully looks disappointed. Halston looks livid. And Allie looks… broken.

"Go home, Allison."

CHAPTER THIRTY-THREE

Allie

THE NEXT FEW DAYS ARE A BLUR. I WALK AROUND IN a daze, alternating between wanting to cry and wanting to hit something. How does someone go from, *"Be with me, Allie,"* to breaking it off in a matter of days? I haven't heard from Jess since he told me to leave. Honestly, I'm glad he hasn't come back. Sleeping in his bed, surrounded by his scent, his belongings, his *family* is bad enough. Staying under the same roof is not an option.

When Halston and I got back to Lo's house, she knew something was up. My eyes were bloodshot, and my heart was broken. She asked where Jess was and I was conflicted, not knowing how much I should divulge, but Halston had no such qualms about telling her every detail from where we found him to where he was staying.

Halston stayed with me that night and has been glued to my side since, as if she's waiting for me to lose my shit. Even Dylan seems worried, watching me like a ticking timebomb that's seconds from exploding. But I'm fine. This was just fun. We always knew this thing had an expiration date.

File that under *lies I tell myself.*

CHAPTER THIRTY-FOUR

Jess

A KNOCK ON THE DOOR HAS CRYSTAL PEELING her ass off the couch to open it. The second she turns the knob, the door flies open, revealing Lo, who's clearly on a rampage if the look on her face is anything to go by. *Thanks a lot, Allie.*

"You," she says, pointing her finger in Crystal's face. "I should have known you were at the root of all of this."

"It's nice to see you too, Logan." Crystal says, making her way back over to the couch, plopping down beside me before reaching for the pack of cigarettes on the coffee table and lighting one up.

Lo huffs out a bitter laugh, eyeing the both of us. "Two peas in a fuckin' pod."

I grit my jaw, leaning back into the couch as I take a swig from the bottle of Jack in my hand.

"So, what? This is what you threw your future away for? So you could sit around and get drunk with Crystal?" Lo paces the floor in front of us. "Well, shit, Jess! We didn't even have to leave Oakland for that. And you," she says, directing her attention back to Crystal, "I know you're not exactly known for your virtue, but do you not have an iota of maternal instincts? Are you so pathetic and selfish that you're willing to ruin your son's life for your own gain?"

"He loves his mother," Crystal yells, standing. "Nothing wrong with that. Unlike your ungrateful ass."

"Shut the fuck up, Crystal. I feel responsible for you, but I don't love you. There's a difference."

"Why didn't you tell me?" Lo asks, hurt flashing in her eyes.

I shrug. "You paid your dues."

Her expression softens, and she tilts her head to the side. "It's not too late, Jess. Come home. Right now. Let's get in the car and go. Whatever it is, we can fix this."

Lo's eyes bore into me, pleading. I take another swig, averting my eyes. I want to. I want to go beg Allie to take me back and forget everything I said. But I've fucked everything up so badly, I can't see a way out.

"You're a fighter, Jess. You always have been. It's all you've ever known. But right now? You're fighting for the wrong fucking thing. Fight for *you*. Hell, fight for Allie. But don't waste another second fighting for her," she says, gesturing toward Crystal, her voice resigned. "You don't owe her a goddamn thing."

When I don't respond, she takes that as her answer and walks out the door.

"Always has had a flair for the dramatic," Crystal remarks, blowing out a plume of smoke between us. "Let her go." She pats my knee. "She's not like us, Jesse."

"I'm nothing like you," I spit.

Crystal lets out a cackle that morphs into a cough. "Look around you, baby. You're exactly like me."

Fuck. She's right. I've done nothing but drown myself in booze and wallow in my misery since I've been here.

Suddenly, I feel like the walls are closing in on me. My throat feels tight and beads of sweat form at my hairline.

This wasn't supposed to be my life. Lo's right. I don't know if anything is fixable, but I do know that I don't want this.

CHAPTER THIRTY-FIVE

Allie

Two weeks later

T ODAY IS MY NINETEENTH BIRTHDAY. IT'S ALSO THE first anniversary of the worst day of my life.

I tried to go about my day as if it were any other, but I couldn't bring myself to go to school. I couldn't bring myself to face Halston and Dylan—who have already flooded me with calls and messages. Even my mom tried to call me. And I couldn't face Lo, who knows nothing of the significance of today, but knows Jess and I aren't together. I threw my phone facedown onto the floor, grabbed my headphones, turned them all the way up, and started walking.

I didn't know where I was going. I don't know how long I wandered before I found myself standing in front of the cemetery gates. Suddenly, the guilt was overwhelming. My dad was in there, rotting in the ground all alone, and I haven't visited him once.

I swallowed hard, pushing through the gates, and made my way to his headstone. I didn't speak. I didn't cry. I just sat, cross-legged on top of his grave. I listened to my CD on a loop for hours, picking grass and watching other people come and go as they greeted their loved ones, before I uncrossed my stiff, numb legs and started walking once more.

Up next on the pity party tour was the vacation rental. I stood in front of my grandparents' closed garage, mustering up the strength to open the goddamn thing. Slowly, I brought my fingers up to the keypad, sliding the cover up before punching in the code. The door lurched before starting to rise, inch by inch.

The first thing I saw was the brand-new black car with the red ribbon still attached to the hood. The graduation present he never got to give me. I shook my head, eyes burning with tears, already regretting the decision. I thought it would be cathartic. *I thought wrong.* When I turned to leave, I spotted a box in the corner with my name written on it in my dad's handwriting and scooped it up before hightailing it out of there.

By the time I get back to Lo's, I'm kicking myself for leaving my phone behind. My feet are sore, body aching, and I'm glad to find the house empty because the emotional exhaustion from today is setting in. I feel raw and flayed. Like someone split me open, and all the ugly shit I keep locked up inside spilled out for everyone to see. Grieving. Abandoned. Heartbroken. *Alone.* In my mind's eye, I see myself bending down to pick them up one by one, stuffing them back inside me. But every time I get one thing locked up, another breaks free.

Pushing the door open, I walk back into my room, sitting on the floor next to where I left my phone. I stare at the box for long seconds before the need to hold something of his wins out.

I pluck a picture I've never seen before of my dad sitting on the floor with an acoustic guitar. I'm next to him with wispy hair much lighter than it is now as I attempt to hold my toy guitar just like him. I flip it over to find *ME AND MY GIRL—2003* written in my dad's signature handwriting. All caps and sloppy strokes. Tears blur my vision as Jimmy Eat World's "Hear You Me" plays on my headphones.

I sift through the rest of the contents of the box. With each photo and old birthday card I find, my throat gets tighter, my hot tears falling faster. The dam breaks, my grief hitting me like a Mack truck. It feels as if it was just yesterday that I stood over his casket, saying goodbye, instead of a year ago, making it hard to breathe.

In a moment of weakness, I pick up my phone, tapping out a text to Jesse. I shouldn't text him. He left me. But I miss him so much in this moment that it physically hurts. My thumb hovers over screen before I finally hit *send.*

I need you.

I stare at my screen, willing him to respond. When it's clear he's not going to, I clutch a picture of my dad to my chest and lie down on my side, head throbbing and heart breaking. Tucking my knees into my chest, I close my eyes and let the tears fall freely, until there aren't any left. When my eyelids feel like they weigh a thousand pounds, I give in to sleep, not bothering to get off the floor.

Warm lips press against my temple, stirring me from sleep. "Baby," Jess whispers, and the empathy in his voice—and the comfort I feel from it—has unshed tears welling up again already. I don't know what time it is. It seems like I've only been asleep for minutes, but the stiffness I feel from lying on the floor tells me it's been at least a couple of hours.

"I'm sorry," he says, kissing me again, this time on my cheek. "I'm sorry I wasn't here." He peppers kisses to my neck, my face, my lips, whispering his apologies in between. Jess scoops me up, carrying me to bed. He sets me on the edge of the mattress and peels my boots and clothes off, leaving me in nothing but my underwear. He follows suit, stripping down to his boxers, and then lies down, pulling me into him, my head resting on his chest, his thumb tracing patterns on my lower back.

"I'm so fucking sorry." His free hand pushes the hair from my face, some of the strands stuck to my cheek, glued there by dried-up tears. When I cover his hand with mine, giving it a squeeze, I feel his swollen knuckles under my fingertips at the same time Jess flinches slightly.

"Are you hurt?" I ask. I can't see, so I reach for the lamp on the side table, but he stops me, holding me in place.

"I'm fine," he assures me. "Go to sleep, Allie. We'll talk in the morning."

But I don't listen, snaking my hand between his legs, gripping his length. I'm desperate to feel him. Desperate to connect.

"Baby, stop. We don't have to do this tonight," he groans, but I feel him harden beneath the thin fabric of his boxers. I pull him out through the opening as he rolls onto his back, both hands raised, still unsure, as he looks down at my hand working him.

Needing to feel him one last time, I push my underwear down my legs and kick them to the floor before I climb over him, positioning him at my entrance. When I sink down onto him, we both groan, my head falling forward, hands braced against his chest, his fingers flying to clutch my hips. I slide up and down his length, his forearms flexing as he helps my movement. I ride him hard and slow, needing to get closer, but I can tell he's still holding back. I don't want to be treated like glass. Like I'm fragile. Emotional. Even if right now, I'm both of those things.

Bending forward, I kiss him, tasting the familiar tang of blood on his lips. He growls when I tug on his bottom lip with my teeth and then he has me pinned to the mattress, thrusting into me before I can blink.

Yes. This is what I need.

Clasping my wrists in his hands, he holds them above my head as he flexes into me. My knees cradle his hips as I take everything he gives me.

"Nothing is better than this. Fucking nothing," Jess rasps before leaning down to swipe his tongue across my nipple. I arch into him, jerking one hand free, needing to touch him. I run my fingers through his hair while meeting him thrust for thrust. We may not be the best communicators, but our bodies are intrinsically linked, inherently compatible.

His free hand slides down my body before hooking around my thigh, holding it in place as he pushes deeper. His movements are slow but firm, his sweat-slicked stomach sliding against mine. I take in every scent, every sound, every feeling, and commit it to memory, knowing that I'll call on this night every time I miss him. And it'll have to be enough.

"Fuck, I can't last much longer," he admits, his voice rough. I wrap both legs around him as he snakes a hand between us, using the flat of his fingers to rub me, bringing me to the brink along with him.

"Jess," I breathe, tumbling over the edge. He gives one more pump before letting go, then he plants a kiss on my collarbone before collapsing onto me, his harsh breathing fanning across my chest.

"I'm sorry I wasn't here, but I'm not going anywhere now. I won't leave you again. I won't lose this," he promises as I trace the damp skin of his back until goosebumps form beneath my fingertips. I swallow the lump in my throat, and I'm thankful the dark room allows my tears to fall unnoticed. Because the truth is, I'm the one leaving this time. And it has everything to do with the fact that I can't need him the way I do. I broke the rules. I got attached. I need to be the one to cut it off.

CHAPTER THIRTY-SIX

Jess

I WAKE UP, MUSCLES ACHING, BUT RELIEVED TO BE BACK with Allie. After Lo left, I put down the bottle and started to form a plan. I took enough fights over the last two weeks to pay off Crystal's debt and two months' rent. After that, she's on her own. For good this time. My phone died last night, and when I turned it on after my last fight, it instantly lit up with a call from an unfamiliar number.

"Hello?"

"Where are you?" a dude's voice shouts from my truck speaker.

"Who the fuck is this?" I scowl at my phone, taking another look at the number.

"It's Dylan."

My heart kicks in my chest as dread seeps in. The fact that he's calling me means he went out of his way to track my number down, and my first thought is something's happened to Allie.

"Is she okay?" I bite out.

"Do you know what today is?" he asks cryptically, instead of answering the goddamn question.

"No."

I hear him scoff on the other line, my patience wearing thin.

"Allie's dad died a year ago today. Which means it's also her birthday."

"Fuck!" I bring a fist down onto the steering wheel. I was on my way to Crystal's to grab the rest of my shit, already planning to head back to River's Edge, but I jerk the wheel, flipping a bitch in the middle of the highway.

"She didn't show up for class, and no one has seen her."

"I'm on my way."

Once I hung up the phone, I saw the text from Allie. Three words that cemented the fact that I'm the world's biggest piece of shit. *I need you.* I turned a two-hour trip into an hour twenty-five, tops. I knew getting her back wasn't going to be easy after the way I ended things at Crystal's apartment, but I also knew I had to be there for her. I didn't know where to start, so I went to Dare's first, not expecting to find her curled up on the bedroom floor.

Eyes still closed, I stretch my arm out, reaching for Allie, but all I find are cold sheets in her place. Opening my eyes, I see that the light is off in the bathroom through the open door. I stumble out of bed, heading for the hall. "Allie?" I call out. I yawn, scratching my stomach as I walk downstairs. When I find the kitchen and living room empty, my gut twists with dread. *Where the fuck did she go?*

I jog back up the stairs, taking them two at a time, and pull open the closet door to confirm my suspicion. Her suitcase is gone. I turn for the dresser, yanking out the drawers and flinging them to the floor, even though I already know they're all empty.

"Fuck!" I yell, bracing my hands against the top of the dresser before kicking the shit out of it.

"Jess!" I hear Lo yell right before she barrels into the

room in a T-shirt and baggy boxers, looking half-asleep. "You're back? What the hell?"

"She's gone. She's fucking gone."

Lo's expression morphs from angry to sympathetic in record time. "What happened?"

"I don't know. I thought—" I shake my head, playing last night's events over in my head. I should have fucking known she wasn't going to forgive me that fast. I just thought she wanted a distraction from her grief. Turns out, she was really saying goodbye. I knew something was off. It felt different, and not just because I didn't use a condom.

I spot my discarded jeans on the floor next to the bed and go to dig my phone out of the pocket when a blue sticky note on the nightstand catches my attention.

Nothing gold can stay.

I peel the note off the nightstand, feeling like I've been kicked in the stomach. "Fuck that." Reaching for my jeans, I find my phone and hit *call*. It rings through to voice-mail—no fucking surprise there—but I call right back again.

Pulling on my wrinkled ass jeans and T-shirt, I head back downstairs, but Lo blocks my path at the bottom of the steps.

"Stop and think, Jess."

"You don't know what the fuck you're talking about. *Move.*" Anyone else would step aside, but Lo stands her ground, knowing I'd never harm a hair on her head.

"Running after her like this isn't going to fix anything."

"I have to try. I can't—I've never—" I stutter, unable to find the right words, frustrated that I sound like a lovesick pussy. "I fucking love her, Lo."

She gives me a sad smile. "I know you do." She moves aside. "So don't fuck it up by scaring her off when she's already halfway out the door."

I've looked for Allie everywhere. I went to Blackbear. I showed up at Manzanita, questioning a very pissed-off Halston, and even called Dylan. When I finally find her, she's walking out of one of her classes at Kerrigan. She doesn't see me yet. She has her headphones on, eyes aimed at her Doc Martens. Her face is free of makeup, her hair down and straight, and she's wearing a hoodie that swallows up her tiny form, almost reaching her bare knees. When she looks up, her eyes find mine. She stops short a couple of feet away from me, and my heart clenches in my chest seeing the pain written on her face.

"Allie."

I move toward her, but she holds up a hand, shaking her head.

"I'm here now."

"But you weren't," she says so quietly I can barely hear the words.

"I'm so fucking sorry. I pushed you away because I thought I was protecting you."

"From what?" She scoffs.

"From *me!*" I take another step toward her. "I thought I could do it. I thought I could let you go. You went from being my distraction to my downfall, and I didn't know what the fuck to do with that. But when I woke up and you were gone, I've never felt anything like that in my life. I didn't expect to love you, Allie."

Her chin trembles as the first tear falls.

"And it turns out, I'm too selfish to save you from myself."

"You *left* me!" she shouts. Her glassy eyes dart around. Suddenly aware of our surroundings, she lowers her voice. "Everyone leaves."

Her words slice right through me. Her dad died. Her mom moved away. And I wasn't there when she needed me the most. Why would she trust me, when all I've ever done is leave?

"I can't do this," she says, moving past me. I want to chase after her. Every instinct in me is screaming to fight for her. But maybe this time I need a different approach.

CHAPTER THIRTY-SEVEN

TRAY IN HAND, I MAKE MY WAY OVER TO MY TABLE, dropping plates off for my customers. "Let me know if I can get you anything else," I say, offering a placid smile. When I turn back around, I see Jess sitting in my section.

I straighten my shoulders, walking past him like it's not killing me to see him. Like I'm not dying to touch him again. I make a beeline for the bathroom, quickly shutting the door behind me and pressing my back against it. I take a deep breath, trying to calm my racing heart.

The door opens behind me and I gasp, stumbling backward into a familiar chest.

Jesse's arms come around me, shutting the door behind us, and for a moment, I allow myself to sink into him. His nose is in my hair, his lips grazing my neck.

"I know I fucked up, but I'm not going anywhere this time, Allie Girl."

I squeeze my eyes shut, my nose starting to tingle with the promise of tears. *God, get it together, Allie.*

He presses a kiss against the back of my neck, and I shrug him off me, spinning around to face him.

"You're wasting your time."

He scrapes his teeth across his bottom lip, cocky expression firmly in place. "We'll see about that."

All week long, Jesse's been lurking around Blackbear, making it impossible for me to think of anything but him. I've been mentally wishing he'd just leave me alone, but when he didn't show during my shift today, I found myself feeling disappointed. I miss him. *God, do I miss him.*

I pull into my driveway, throwing the car in park before cutting the engine off. My grandma told me where the keys were once I moved in, and I finally decided to drive my graduation present. I don't have much of a choice now that I'm living alone. I need to get to work each day and then school once summer's over.

I climb out, shutting the door behind me.

"Nice ride."

My head snaps up, seeing Jesse standing by my front door with a box in his hand.

"How do you know where I live?"

"Halston's Team Jesse now."

I roll my eyes. *Traitor.* "What's with the box?"

"I missed your birthday." He smirks.

I walk past him, opening the front door. He follows me inside, eyeing the place curiously. It's a modest cabin-style home. Two bedrooms, two bathrooms. It's not much, but it's perfect for me. Jess sets the box on the kitchen counter, then takes a seat at one of the barstools.

"You shouldn't be here," I say, but my voice lacks conviction. It's hard to stay strong when all I want to do is be the way we were before it all went to shit.

"But I am." He smirks again. "Aren't you going to open your present?"

"If I do, will you leave?"

He shrugs. "If you want me to."

I blow out a breath, pulling the lid off the box. The inside is full of Dum-Dums, all butterscotch except for one strawberry. My face heats at the memory of Jess and the way he used the sucker on me, and with one look at his face, I can tell he's thinking the same thing.

"Keep looking."

I dig around the box, pulling out a stack of CD cases. I hold them up, my eyes questioning his.

"Open them."

I open the first case and inside it reads, *Songs I'd like to fuck you to*. On the inside sleeve, the tracks are listed. Everything from "Lollipop" by Lil Wayne to "Closer" by Nine Inch Nails. I laugh, closing the plastic case. "Very funny."

"Keep going," he says, but his expression isn't playful like I'd expect.

"Okay…" I open the next one. *Songs I've actually fucked you to*. "Colorblind" by Counting Crows is listed, and I pause, peering up at him. "You remember that?"

He nods.

One by one, I open the rest. *Songs that remind me of you. Songs for when you're sad. Songs for when I fuck up. Songs for when you miss your dad.*

"Jess," I whisper around the lump in my throat.

"Thought you might want some new listening material," he says.

Moving toward him, I throw my arms around his neck, hugging him tight. This is the most ridiculous, thoughtful thing anyone's ever done for me. I take in his scent. His warmth. He feels like home.

"Does this mean you forgive me?"

I pull back, sniffing. "I forgive you, Jess…"

"I feel a *but* coming on."

"But what's changed?" I search his eyes.

"I'm here, Allie."

"For how long?"

"Look in the bottom of the box," he says, flicking his chin toward it.

I feel around, plucking an envelope from the bottom. I open it up, reading the letter with the Wildcats logo. My eyes snap to his.

"Does this mean what I think it means?"

He nods. "I'm staying for good. Coach Standifer's starting MCLA lacrosse at Kerrigan next year. It's not as prestigious as the NCAA, but I get to be part of a team again." He tugs me closer by my belt loops. "And I get to go to school with you."

"I'm scared," I admit, feeling stupid and vulnerable for saying the words out loud.

"I need you, Allie. I'm not fucking leaving you again. I'm starting school here. I took a job at Henry's auto shop. I walked away from fighting." He runs a hand through his hair, blowing out a breath. "Nothing mattered to me before you. I self-sabotaged every good thing in my life before you came along. Part of me thinks I got kicked off the team on purpose, because it was easier to play that role, as fucked up as that sounds. But you make me want to be someone who deserves someone like you."

He wipes a tear from my cheek.

"I love you."

His eyes flare, zeroing in on my lips. "Say it again."

"I fucking love you." I feel my lips pull into a smile, and then he's standing from the stool and lifting me in his arms, my ankles crossing behind his back.

"I love you, too."

Legs still wrapped around his waist, I pull my shirt off over my head. "Then show me."

EPILOGUE

Allie

Six months later

MY DAD ALWAYS SAID THAT BOTH THE BEST AND worst things in life are unexpected. They're the moments that change your life indefinitely, and even if you see them coming, you're never prepared for the impact. It's what you do in the aftermath that matters. It's how you deal with the crisis—or good fortune—that defines you.

Closing my journal, I look up, seeking Jesse out as I sit on the same bleachers I watched him from a few years ago. Only this time, I'm not hiding underneath them. Since lacrosse is new at Kerrigan and there's little funding, they've been using the high school's field for practice and fall ball. It has me feeling more than a little sentimental being here, where my dad used to teach, with the boy who healed my broken heart.

The last six months have been a whirlwind. Technically, we don't live together, but he sleeps in my bed every single night, so I don't know who we think we're fooling. He works with Henry now, and though it's been a slow process, I can see the change in Jesse. He's healing, too, and being around Henry has a lot to do with it.

Crystal showed up in River's Edge in a desperate attempt to reel Jess back in. She started spitting some bullshit about him being worthless, and I didn't think. I just swung. I've never punched anyone in my life, but she was talking about the boy I love, threatening to undo everything we've worked for. I don't know who was more shocked. I turned, wide-eyed, to Lo and Jess with my hand over my mouth, apologizing profusely. To my surprise, Lo laughed like a hyena. Jess sent Crystal packing before telling me I couldn't just go around punching people whenever they pissed me off—repeating the same words I told him about Victor—but he couldn't keep the smile from his face when he said it.

As for my mom, she moved back to California with her new husband. I've got a little brother coming any day now, and she said she wanted to be close enough to see me on a regular basis. I'm cautiously optimistic.

A whistle blows, pulling me from my thoughts. Jesse jogs toward me, pulling his lacrosse helmet off before pushing his damp hair off his forehead.

"Hey, Allie Girl," he says, leaning down for a kiss.

"Gross, you're all sweaty!"

"You like it." He moves in, rubbing his face all over me, kissing my collarbone, and I laugh, pushing him away.

"Get a room!" Sully shouts, pulling his helmet up. He joined the lacrosse team, too. Don't ask me what's going on with Halston and him. They don't even know.

Jesse throws up a middle finger behind him, bringing his lips to mine. I wrap my arms around his neck, slipping my tongue into his mouth, uncaring of our audience.

He pulls away, eyes shining with lust. "Get in the truck."

"I'll meet you there," I say, pointing to my journal. He nods before jogging over to grab his stuff, and I open my journal once more.

Dad was right. The best things in life are always unexpected, and loving Jesse Shepherd is definitely the best thing in life.

Jess

Nothing gold can stay.

Nothing perfect and beautiful can last forever.

Nothing except Allison Parrish.

ACKNOWLEDGMENTS

First and foremost, to the readers, whether you're just discovering me or have been there since the beginning, thank you. I'm so grateful that you've taken a chance on me.

To my husband, who probably wished he could divorce me while I spent hours upon hours writing, thank you for being the fun parent and the most understanding, supportive person on the planet.

Leigh, thank you for listening to me bitch about this book and for always keeping it real. You're the Blair to my Serena. The Brooke to my Peyton. The Mary-Kate to my Ashley. But, like, in their New York Minute days. Not now.

Sarah Sentz! Thank you for busting your ass and cheering me on every step of the way. Your excitement for Jess and Allie, and your support means more than you'll ever know.

Sasha, you're a badass per usual. Thanks for being the sweetest.

Clarissa, you're selfless and supportive and one of the most genuine people I know. Thank you for everything.

Thank you to my amazing editor Paige Smith for working a miracle. I'm sorry if you need counseling after trying to whip this one into shape. Please don't break up with me. Letitia Hasser for never giving up until it's absolute perfection. You love me. Remember that for next time.

To the bloggers, thank you for busting your asses all day every day. I appreciate you. I probably won't ever have my shit together, and I'm so beyond thankful for everything you do to fit me into your busy schedules.<3

Lastly, my reader group—my sweet baby angels—I fucking love you. You're my happy place. Thank you for your endless support.

ABOUT THE AUTHOR

Charleigh Rose lives in Narnia with her husband and two young children. She's hopelessly devoted to unconventional love and pizza. When she isn't reading or mom-ing, she's writing moody, broody, swoony romance.

Stay in touch!

Website: authorcharleighrose.com

Facebook page: www.facebook.com/charleighroseprose

Facebook group: www.facebook.com/
groups/1120926904664447

Instagram: www.instagram.com/charleighrose

Newsletter: https://bit.ly/2hzVQy4

OTHER BOOKS BY
CHARLEIGH ROSE

Bad Habit

Bad Intentions

Yard Sale

Misbehaved

Rewrite the Star